# Fallin' for the Realest

## A Real Nigga Love Affair

Marshae

Fallin' for the Realest



Published by: Mz. Lady P Presents

# Acknowledgments

First and foremost, I would like to thank God for blessing me with wonderful gift of mines and my wonderful magnificent readers for patiently waiting on me to release my next reads. My fans are truly my inspiration that I need. Writing this book came with so many obstacles to overcome. Man! Man! Man! It was like running through hell wearing gasoline draws. There were many times that I wanted to breakdown and give the hell up but because of all of the support that I get from my friends, family, supporters, pen sisters/brother and publisher; I was able to get back up. For my fans that has been following me since The Wrong Way to Love era; y'all are really all the inspiration and motivation that I need in life. The reason why I kept getting up when life knocked me down. Although I don't personally know everyone just know that I love every last one of you. Y'all are the reason why I keep going the way I do.

My parents, Marcia Hatton and Ernest Jackson; I want to thank you two for believing in me even on the days when I didn't believe in me. Y'all was there to pick me back up and give me that extra boost of courage that I needed when I doubted myself.

My triple OG Charlotte Pearson. We go way back! LOL. I love you Nana. I honestly think if it wasn't because of you always threatening to chase me down the street with the metal bat hidden away in your closet [betchu didn't think I knew that didn't you ;)] if I didn't finish this book that I would've never gotten finished. You my dawg! I love you!

Corlynda Graham; I don't even know why I even deals with you. LBVS. You my so-called manager but never do anything but take all the credit on what I do. LOL. My huge amazing, crazy and mentally retarded ass family! I would love to thank all 24 of you borderline psychopaths. Y'all just don't know that I use y'all for inspiration when I develop my characters for my books. Everyday around y'all is never a dull moment. Y'all are too comical to be around. Every day is a challenge.

Jamina Saunders a.k.a MiMi; Aye! Where the drinks at?! It's time to turn up! Nigga, we made it! LMAO. She's my ghetto psychologist! She's cool as hell and just that person I need to balance my crazy ass out. She's my right hand while Shantesha Hill is my left. My best bishes for life! You is the one who I always run to when I need a listening but sometimes I have to be careful with the advice that you gives me. Some advice could help a playa out but the rest of it would put a mfa underneath the jail cell. Lmao. You are crazy as hell and have the nerve to call me crazy. I thank you for being that mental therapist that I need and for all of the advice that you give me. Whether if it's on relationships, politics whatever. I love you bookie!

Polee… My MCE [man crush everyday]. Have I ever told you lately how much I love you? ^//^ I have never met another person like you in all of the twenty-three years I have been living! You are just too cool and so down to Earth for me. Not only are you my best friend but also the good listening ear that I need whenever I' m stressed. I could be mad as hell but as soon as I hear your voice I'm back to my normal goofy and retarded self. Lol. You my homie on the real! You are my inspiration, my backbone, my muscle in these streets and my support system! You'll never know just how much your love and support means to me. I like you. A lot!

To my pen sisters and pen brother; Anita, Lem, Kiana, Shatocka, Kat Washington, Rosaldo a.k.a Chief, Keyandra, Michay and Terri. I know that whenever I feel like my back is up against the wall and I need somebody to give me that extra boost I could always count on one of y'all to give me your honest raw and uncut truth. I love y'all. You guys are the best! ((If y'all haven't read none of their work then I highly recommend that you do! I promise you won't be disappointed!))

And lastly to the World's Best Publisher that a girl like me could ever ask for Patrice Williams a.k.a Mz. Lady P. I want to thank you for believing me when others were against me and when I even doubted myself. I would also like to thank you for the patience that you had dealing with my ass. I know that I disappointed you but I promise that from this day forth that I would do my best to make you proud and to make Mz. Lady P Presents one of the best publishing companies to be with. I am so happy to be a part of this team! Mz. Lady P Presents stand up and represent!

To anybody else whose names that I didn't added. Please forgive me! It's just too many people that I love and appreciate to name all of y'all. My memory is not that great! Lol. Until the next book drops ;)

*Haters only hate on the things they can't have and the people they can't be. It's just a little thing called JEALOUSY. Continue to be my motivation for me to pull my pants down in public, bend over and tell all the haters in the world to kiss my ass!*

Add me on Facebook:

Authoress Marshae Hatton

Add my group: *Marshae's Reading Group* for sneak peaks, prizes, contests and giveaways.

Email me at: Marshaeh4@gmail.com

# Table of Contents

## Chapter One

**KELLY RENAE DAWSON**

"Can you slow ass bitches hurry the fuck up? Damn! I swear y'all take so fucking long getting dressed!" I yelled as I marched my five-foot-five-inches up the spiral stairway of the mini-mansion I shared with my two BBF's, best bitches forever, Aris and Mona. As I walked up the stairs, I took the time to admire my mansion. It's only been two years since it was first bought. My baby was gorgeous!

It had five bedrooms with three full bathrooms, polished wooden floors with marble steps and floor-to-ceiling windows. The gourmet kitchen had granite countertops with stainless steel appliances and a large center island, a built-in stove, and cherry wood cabinets. The master bathroom (which we all shared) had a Jacuzzi/Roman-style tub, an oversized shower, and a separate his and hers vanities with a powder and sitting area that Mona had installed over a month ago. Each bedroom was oversized and had its own private bathroom with marble vanity tops and huge tubs. Throughout the mansion, beautiful woodwork adorned the walls and doorframes, setting it all off.

The outside was as just as beautiful as the inside. Our house sat on over five acres of perfectly manicured lawn with roses bushes, fruit trees, palms and other decorative trees. We had a gated entrance and a huge paved circular driveway that was the home to our luxurious whips. To sum it all up, my home was the shit! I loved it. It was a gift to me from an old sponsor, if you know what I mean.

After reaching the top of the stairs, I marched my ass straight into Mona's room. As I neared her room, the sound of August Alsina's *Porn Star* started blaring through the speakers. As soon as I entered, a thick cloud of smoke hit me dead in my face. Not only were these bitches taking long as fuck to get dressed, but these bitches were smoking in my damn house! Without me!

"I know y'all are not smoking without me!" I yelled, standing it the doorway with my hands on my curvaceous hips.

"Oh, shit. My bad. Here."

Mona took one last pull from the blunt and held it towards me to take. I cocked my head to the side while giving her an 'are-you-serious' look.

She just gave me a goofy ass smile. Her ass was blowed! I just shook my head, walked up to her, and snatched the blunt from her. She giggled as I sat down at the edge of the bed and took a much-needed drag. I closed my eyes and let the smoke dance around in my lungs before exhaling, coughing hard as hell afterward. My lungs and throat were on fire!

"Shit! What the fuck is this?"

Aris came out the bathroom laughing, "You like that?"

"Hell yeah," I said, taking another hit, then passing it to her. She grabbed it and puffed from it too, exhaling the smoke through her nose as well. The only difference was she didn't choke.

"It's called Laughing Buddha," she smiled proudly. My eyes widened as I looked at her like she had two heads.

"And where did you get this from?"

She grinned, flashing those pretty ass dimples of hers. "If I tell you, I'll have to put a bullet in your ass for being nosey."

I sucked my teeth and rolled my eyes at her.

"Whatever."

I hated when she starts quoting Roman's slick ass who was Mona's older brother and Aris' ex. Everything that nigga did got under my skin. Don't get me wrong, I love him as I would love a brother, but that nigga is just too cocky for my ass. He goes walking around this muthafucka like he ain't got a care in the world. He plays too much for me.

Mona applied another coat of MAC lip gloss onto her pouty pink lips before smacking them one last time and standing up to join us.

"There she goes with those famous Roman quoting ass lines," she said, reading my mind.

Aris started laughing, flipping both of us the bird.

"Nah. I got this shit from this dude I let eat my pussy from time to time back in the day."

Me and Mona both screwed up our faces at the same time.

"Eww. TMI."

"Well shit, y'all should never have asked."

"Correction bitch," Mona held up her hand as if to say 'hold up.' "She asked you," she said, pointing over at me.

I rolled my eyes while getting off the bed. "Is y'all bitches ready now?"

They both glanced at one another over, silently complimenting each's other's outfit. Mona nodded her head.

"Yeah, we ready. AFTER we take some pictures for the Gram."

I was so through with these bitches! I had to laugh to stop myself from cursing their asses out. They do too much! But that's the reason why I love the both of their asses to death, and would kill for both of them. We all herded in front of the full-length mirror inside Mona's private bathroom and started snapping pictures in all types of poses.

Oh shit! I forgot to introduce myself! Damn, that's rude as fuck. Here I am babbling on and on, and we're not even on a first name basis. My fault.

My name is Kelly Re'Nae Dawson. But everybody calls me Kells. I'm twenty-four years old with no kids and currently single. I don't do the relationship thing. Too much drama and drama isn't what I need. Me and my girls aren't into all that drama shit. We like to chill, lay back and kick it without the exception of having to kick someone's ass, whether it be man or woman. Me and my bitches ain't into all that showing out and fighting shit, but best to believe we don't take shit from nobody! Muthafuckas will get cut quick, if not shot. We don't fuck around. Me and my girls are some bad females, and we let it be known every time we step out the muthafuckin' door. Everybody in Miami already knows that but tonight we are going to remind a few people just in case they forgot. We're going to shut the whole fucking club scene down!

I'm five-foot-five, a hundred and forty five pounds with skin of sweet caramel and hazel-green eyes. I have, a perfect oval-shaped face, slim nose with a nose ring, and some thick, sexy heart-shaped lips. I had naturally curly black hair that stopped in the middle of my back, but I always kept it done in expensive ass sew-ins. I don't like too many people touching my hair. So I do my own shit. No one has actually seen me with my hair down but my girls. My girls were beautiful, and so was I. I had the body that made the mouth water upon first glance. I had a shape of a coca cola bottle. Literally. I was slim-thick. Aayyee! Slim thick wit'cho cute ass! I had a pair of mouth-watering 40DD's, a thirty-two inch waist, and ass for days. Forty-five inches to be exact.

I was rocking the fuck out of this leopard print long-sleeved body jumpsuit that zipped up in the middle, showing off my twins. My babies were sitting up high, basking in their glory. The body suit I had on hugged all of my curves so damn well I was barely able to squeeze my ass into it. On my feet, I was rocking on a pair of Louboutin red bottom peep-toe booties with straps and a six-inch heel. I had my thirty-two-inch Brazilian weave pulled back in a messy bun, showing all my distinctive features.

Just like me, my girls were dressed to kill. Mona was the same height and weight as me with blemish-free cinnamon brown skin. She had almond shaped eyes that were the most captivating cognac color. Her eyebrows were perfectly arched, and she had some long ass eyelashes. Before I met Mona and Aris, I thought I was the baddest bitch walking around. Well, as you can see I have competition. Mona had high cheek bones, button nose, pouty pink lips and red hair that stopped in the middle of her back. Although she was all black, like myself, her smooth skin and defined features made her look exotic, as if she was mixed with something. And her body... Even though her breasts were a perky size B, her ass and hips made up for what she lacked up top. Her measurements were 36B, twenty-four in the waist and thirty-eight. She was rocking this all-white striped two-piece club dress that hugged her body like a second skin, and a pair of Prada strappy platform heels with a gold chain and six-inch heel. She had her hair in some large spiral curls that she'd had me put in.

Last but not least, was my down ass bitch, Aris. Out of all of us, she was the most exotic looking one. She was mixed with Cuban and Black. Aris was both short and thick, with a feisty attitude. She was five-foot-three, a hundred thirty-two pounds, with golden honey skin. Her skin looked like the sun had taken a break and come down to personally kiss her when she was coming out of her mother's womb. She had some pretty ass gray eyes. Her eyes resembled beautiful, flawless diamonds. She had a perfect V-shaped baby face, with a set of plump, kissable lips and a set of deep dimples in her cheeks. She had long black thick curly hair that stopped just above her plump ass. My girl had a body of a video vixen.

Many women were jealous of my bitch. Nicki Minaj ain't have shit on my girl. Her breasts were a perfect 32D's, she had a thirty-three-inch waist and forty-three inches in her ass and hips area. Tonight, she was wearing this sexy ass white plunge bra crop top that showed off her pierced belly button. A burnt orange bandage miniskirt that had her thick thighs on full display, and on her feet she had a pair of black leather BCBG knee high strappy lace-ups with a five-inch heel on the back. Her long hair was flat ironed bone straight, and her Chinese bangs outlined her beautiful face.

Now that you know how me and my bitches look, you know that I'm nowhere near overexaggerating. My bitches were BAD!

After taking a bunch of pictures and posting them on Instagram, we all got ready to leave. Grabbing a bottle of Peach Cîroc out of the freezer and the few pre-rolled blunts, we headed out the door all piling inside Kamron's cocaine white 2015 Denali Yukon XL truck with the butterscotch leather seats and thirty-four-inch rims. After setting up Pandora and listening to Future's *Rider* we were set. Mona popped open the bottle and Aris lit another L and put it into rotation. With that, we were gone.

# Chapter Two

**ARIS KA'MYA MILLER**

(Pronounced as Aries)

As soon as we pulled up at Bedrest, we noticed just how packed it was going to be. Of course, I should've known already, being that today was Friday and Fridays usually stayed packed to capacity. It was only midnight and the line was straight bending around the corner and down the street. The line was filled with all types of ratchets. Males and females. These hoes were out here looking like the lost colors of the rainbow. Bitches weave was in every color imaginable to the human brain and then some. Ratchets came in all sorts of sizes and forms. My mouth dropped as I looked at this BBW wearing nothing. Literally. She was wearing this fishnet body suit that clearly wasn't her size considering the quarter size holes and had black tape covering her nipples with a matching thong going inside her nasty looking ass. Her cheap weave looked like Stevie Wonder had fucked around and got a side job as a beautician. It was all lopsided and shit. She was standing there like shit was all gravy. Like this bitch didn't even care. I had to look away cause the liquor I consumed earlier was threating to come back up. I just sat there and shook my head.

Where the fuck did these hoes get the confidence from? Someone was clearly telling their asses lies. As the truck slowly crept around the corner and up to the door, I notice how every hoe had their eyes open wide eyeing the truck like it was a five-star steak with an all too familiar thirsty look was displayed so desperately. These hoes were trying to trap a thug.

"They must think that it's all paid nigga's riding in this truck. Look at the thirsty looks on their faces! Priceless!" Mona said laughing her ass off reading my mind.

"That's exactly what I was thinking!" I laughed giving her a high five.

Kells grinned pulling the truck into the valet parking and putting the truck into park.

"Well, we about to rain on these bitch's parade and give them the water they need. Dehydration isn't good for the body."

We all fell out laughing as a valet attendee opened Kells door first then mine and Mona's. He then handed Kells her ticket and took off. We stood there for a minute observing the disappointed looks over every female face in attendance.

"Damn, y'all need something to drink?" Kells asked sarcastically, faking concern.

Me and Mona fell out laughing. Kells never did get an answer. Instead, all we got was stares of hate and jealousy with a tad bit of envy. Right along with their stares, we got looks of lust from these bum ass niggas standing in line trying to floss fake ass threads. I recognized fake shit from a mile away. As we walked to the entrance, we got all kinds of catcalls. We just shook our heads and ignored them knowing damn well their asses didn't stand a chance with us. We were some bad bitches and bad bitches don't stand in line waiting so we just took our happy, high as hell asses straight inside the club.

Loud rap music thumped through the speakers as Future's *Jumpman* had everybody shouting along. People were literally elbow to elbow. But no matter how packed the club was as soon as we stepped in, muthafucka's start parting like the red sea did for Moses and his people. From the moment we exit the truck all the way until we're seated at our VIP booth, all eyes on us. Men howled like the dogs they were, and women continued to mean mug us. The three of us were getting cat calls left and right and by the time we sat down we had a handful of nothing but numbers. I just simply dropped them on the ground as soon as they were handed to me. Mona refused while Kells' hot pussy ass kept the ones she considers was good enough to get a nut from. When we were finally at our VIP booth, Kells was the first one to order. "Let me get a double shot of Patrón and two Cool-Blue Hawaiians."

The waitress quickly scribbled down the orders on her notepad as Kells shouted our order out. "Is that it?"

"Y'all want anything else?"

After me and Mona reassured her we didn't want anything else, the waitress nodded her head and left to go fulfill our order.

"Damn, I can't believe it's this packed up here!" I shouted over the blaring bass of the music. My voice was barely audible.

"Girl, tell me about it. I swear up and until now, someone had grabbed my ass about three times," Mona half-joked. She didn't know, but I saw more than just one nigga grab her ass. It couldn't be me. If it happened to Kells or me, we would've quickly checked their asses about that shit, but Mona let it slide and blamed it on them being drunk. Her ass was just too nice sometimes.

"See. If y'all asses had gotten ready when I told you to, y'all wouldn't be complaining. Now would you?"

I rolled my eyes and flipped both of my middles at her ass laughing. "Shut up, bitch."

Soon the waitress was back with our drinks that we ordered. We quickly got settled then started taking our drinks to the head until we had a bigger buzz than earlier. Kells kept the drinks coming until Nicki Minaj's *Anaconda* started blasting through the speakers. The crowd went wild, and everybody broke out into a twerk fest.

"Alright now. Let's see them asses clap. C'mon ladies shake what the good Lord blessed you with. It's twerking season," the DJ hollered in the microphone.

"My anaconda don't. My anaconda don't. My anaconda don't want none unless you got buns hun! Ooooohhhh! This is my shit," Kells screamed out as she grabbed both me and Mona's wrists and practically dragged us to the middle of the dance floor.

By the time the first chorus began to play me and my girls were shaking what our mommas gave us letting the music guide our hips into a hypnotizing rhythm. I was feeling the beat too much. And with both liquor and weed in my system I was showing my ass out on the dance floor. I began shaking my ass hard as if I was trying to outshine the whole club. I dropped it to the floor and bounced back up, grabbing my ankles and making my ass clap to the beat. Left cheek right cheek left cheek right cheek. I then started winding my hips in circular movements doing it just like how Shakira was doing it in her *Hips Don't Lie* video. Just like that, me and my girls took over the dance floor. A circle was formed around us and niggas began tricking out dollars.

That made us go even harder. The DJ kept playing back to back hits that had us wilding the fuck out. After Nicki he played, Ca$h Out's *She Twerking*, K. Stylis *Booty Me Down* and finished it off with Sage the Gemini *Red Nose*. By the time Red Nose was playing, I was tired as hell. I looked up and found my handsome ass brother, Kamron, hugging all up underneath Kells and Landon doing the Kid and Play dance move with Mona. I had no idea they were going to be there. In need of a drink, I turned around and began walking back to our spot in VIP. I only took two small steps before I felt someone gently grab me by my elbow and pulling me into his broad chest. Instantly my nostrils were filled with his Cool Water cologne. Damn he smelled good.

"Let me get a dance with you, Ma," he whispered in my ear sending chills down my spine and making my panties wet just at the sound of his deep baritone voice.

Slowly I lifted my eyes up and met the penetrating gaze of my admirer. I stood floored at this God like specimen before me. My clit started jumping all around in my panties. The good Lord knows he blessed him well in the looks department. He easily towered over my small frame, and from what I can tell he was six-four hard solid muscles with sexy, smooth chocolate Hershey's skin. He had almond-shaped brown eyes, a nicely trimmed full beard, thick eyebrows and the longest eyes lashes. And Oh God, those lips! Daddy was about to get out here on the dance floor. He had on a pair of red high top Prada sneakers, black Robin jeans and a fitted black t-shirt that hugged his muscular physique just the way I liked it. He wore a black and red fitted hat, two gold chains, and a diamond studded Rolex.

"Damn, girl. What's your name?" he asked in a thick southern accent, quickly bringing me back to reality. I cocked my head to the side, casting him a sideways glance.

"What's yours?" I asked instead.

"I asked you first."

"Well, I'm not answering until you answer first."

He grinned, flashing a pretty set of pearly white teeth. He chuckled as he grabbed the hem of my skirt and pulled me close while palming my ass. I was turned all the way on. He cocked his head to the side and had a look of amusement on his face. It didn't take a rocket scientist to find out that he was interested in my feisty ass. Hell, to be honest, I was interested to know what he was working with. After a long moment of silence with just us staring at each other, he finally spoke up.

"Q."

"Q," I repeated while nodding my head. "Let me ask you again in case you didn't hear me," I said boldly leaning into him, taking his bottom lip into my mouth, and lightly nibbling on it before letting it go.

"What's the name your mother gave you when you came into this world ass naked screaming like a little girl? Government name will do."

Q grinned, flashing me his irresistible smile.

"Since you're just dying to know, it's Quamir. Quamir Myles," he introduced himself. "You can call me Q, though. Happy now?"

I smiled, flashing him my dimples. "Quamir," I repeated in a seductive tone, liking the way his name just rolled off my tongue like silk, "I like."

"Now can I get your name?" he smiled.

I paused, wondering if I should give him my real name or not. After thinking for a while longer, I just shrugged my shoulders and said fuck it.

"Aris. Last name is not important."

"Aris," he said as if he liked the way my name sounded. I nodded my head up and down confirming it for him.

"Well, Miss Aris. Can I ask you a question?" he asked me smiling.

I shrugged my shoulders, "Shoot."

"Why the hell did you come out of the house with this little ass skirt on? And where is the rest of your shirt? Why the fuck is you out here showing the whole damn club what the fuck I got at home?" he asked with his face hardening in a tight, disapproving frown.

Just that quick, our little charade was over with and Q was back to being his over possessive boyfriend role. I rolled my eyes and sucked my teeth at him. Leave it up to Quamir's insecure ass to blow my damn high.

"Damn, Q, it's not that damn serious! It's just an outfit! My shirt is called a crop top, that's how it's made, and my skirt isn't even that short! You act like my breasts are spilling over the top and my ass is hanging out the bottom of my skirt. Damn."

"It might as well have been! Yo ass is too damn big to be wearing a skirt that stops just at the thighs."

"You know what… I'm not about to be doing this with you, Q. I came out tonight to have a good time, and I'll be damn if I let your attitude fuck up my night," I said, unwrapping my arms from around his neck and turning to walk away from him.

"Man, bring yo' ass back over here."

Q grabbed me by my elbow and pulled my back into his chest. "Every nigga in here is about to break they damn neck tryin' to look at your ass."

Instead of responding, I just rolled my eyes, turned around, and pressed my ass against him as the DJ slowed it down by putting on Sevyn Streeter's *It Won't Stop Remix* featuring Chris Brown. As the song played, my hips began moving to the beat. It took me a minute to get back in the mood because my high was blown, but somehow I managed. My hips winded and grinded into his pelvis. After a lot of twisting, I felt something big and thick poking against my ass cheeks. I just smiled and continued on. I bet you his ass wasn't mad anymore. After the song ended, he took me by the hand and led me off the dance floor and to VIP.

I was relieved when I saw the whole gang. Kamron had Kells sitting in his lap while gripping her thighs. I fell out laughing when I saw her move his hands and try to get up, only for him to pull her back down into his lap. She looked up at me with pleading eyes. I quickly turned my attention elsewhere and acted like I didn't notice her little sign for help. I don't know why she was always playing hard to get. Then I saw Mona and Landon sitting next to each other, chilling and talking it up having a good ole time.

"Wassup baby sis," Kamron greeted. Seeing how low his eyes were, I could tell that nigga was sitting on the moon. He was that high.

"What I tell yo' ass about calling me a baby? I'm grown, not a child."

"Girl, you still gon' be our baby sis no matter how old yo' ass gets. Besides, you the baby of the clique," Landon said, adding his two cents in.

"Ain't nobody asked you for your input, Landon Latrell Young," I spat with a fake attitude.

"Man, why you gotta put a nigga's whole government name out like that? Most muthafuckas only know me by my street name, and you just put my whole name out for the whole damn world to know."

"I don't care! Nigga, I'll say it again. I'll walk my short ass up to the DJ's booth and scream that shit into the microphone. What you gon' do?"

Landon said nothing and just mugged the shit out of me. He knew better than to try me because he knows that I'm good for following through on the words I speak.

"Man Kamron, could you move? Moooovvveee. Aris! Get your brother! He is fucking up my high man. Move, Kamron!" Kells screamed out sounding all dramatic, making everybody in the VIP bust out laughing. She could act and pretend that she doesn't like being all under Kamron if she wanted to. Everybody know her ass ain't doing shit but faking the funk. Kells is in love with Kamron's dirty draws she just loves playing hard to get.

"Fuck you calling Ari for? Aris ain't nobody, I'm the older brother the last time I checked. She can't save your ass."

"Don't drag me into y'all shit," I said laughing while taking a seat in Q's lap.

"You know just like we all know that if you really wanted to get up, you would have been moved out of his lap," Mona said laughing. "Bitch quit playing games with that man. You fooling with the right one. You better stop playing, before Kamron's retarded ass have your ass somewhere in a dark corner knocking shit all out of the frame for playing with him."

Kells flipped Mona off and everybody fell into a fit of laughter. I ignored the bickering between Kells and Kamron and focused my attention on Q. I heard enough of that shit at home.

# Chapter Three

**KAMRON CAREEM MILLER**

The whole crew was sitting and just chilling together in the VIP, enjoying each other's company. Mona and Landon were now slow dancing with each other, trying to flirt on the sly. I swear it's something up with those two, but they're quick to swear the relationship between them is innocent. Aris and my boy Q were still talking, laughing and joking around. I still had Kells in my lap, refusing to let her go. She couldn't get up to do shit. I could tell I was fucking up her night by her fish smelling ass attitude, but I didn't give a fuck. Her ass shouldn't have walked out the door with what the fuck she had on.

A nigga was pissed the fuck off when I saw her ass, but at the same time I was turned the fuck on. She had niggas drooling out of their mouths and grabbing their shits with the way her ass was bouncing when she walked. I would hate to body a nigga over her because I didn't play that shit when it comes to mine. Well, technically she's not my girl but shit, a nigga been trying to crack open that hard ass shell of hers for years.

Out of the twenty-seven years that I've been living on Earth, I was never the type of nigga that got turned down. Hell, with my six-foot-two frame, golden light-skin, boyish charm, and status as a young ruthless kingpin in the streets, I always got what I wanted, and I'm not just being cocky.

Even though Aris and I are biological siblings and had the same mother and father, I have a mixture of our Mom's and Dad's eyes while Aris' was blessed with our Pop's gray eyes. Aris' resembled those of diamonds, while I had a pair of grayish-blue eyes that made panties drop. I also had a deep dimple in my left cheek that all the ladies loved.

Tonight I was fly as shit. I was dressed in nothing but designer labels. I rocked some dark blue, baggy True Religion jeans, a white long-sleeved Ralph Lauren Polo shirt, an all-black Bellfield Baron Bomber jacket and some white, black and grey Air Jordan 13's. I kept my hair in a low, curly cut with tapered sides.

Hands down, I was that nigga. Pussy was thrown at me on a daily basis. All I had to do was make one phone call and I would have pussy waiting for me like a Little Caesar's pizza: Hot and Ready. The one thing in the world that I wanted I couldn't have. And I wanted Kells bad as hell and I let that shit be known every chance I got. I'd been chasing after her ass since baby sis introduced us to each other back when they were in the seventh grade and I was in the tenth. Her ass had been running circles around me for years. Kells was not only bad to the bone, but those eyes did something to a nigga. When I look into her eyes I don't see this hard thugged-out, out-spoken and carefree gangstress that she portrays herself to be. Instead, I see a little broken girl that got lost somewhere down the path of life that's in need of saving. And I'm willing to be that nigga to save her, if she would only open up. She be on that fuck-love-get-money type shit. And really, I was getting sick and tired of the shit. I hope she don't think a nigga going to keep chasing her ass. It's too much pussy in the world going around to be stuck on just chasing one. As my mind was in deep thought, Kells' ass was tryna be slick and get up.

"And where do you think you going?"

"Damn, nigga. Can I go to the bathroom?" she asked with an attitude.

I stared at her long and hard before loosening my grip from around her waist. "You got five minutes. And I mean exactly five minutes. So you better hurry up and bring that ass right back," I said.

She sucked her teeth and rolled her eyes at me for the umpteenth time that night. "Yeah nigga whatever," she mumbled under her breath, but just loud enough for me to hear her ass.

"I'm not playing with you, Kelly. Fucks with me if you want to and I'll be dragging yo' ass back here by yo' ankles," I said, serious as fuck.

I'm known in Miami as a nigga that doesn't just bark, but bites, too. I don't go around saying shit just to be saying it. My word is bond. Kells must've known that I would do exactly what I said, because she had her ass back in five minutes. The way her ass jiggled had a nigga stuck in a trance. I watched her ass jiggle as she made her way back over to me. Instead of sitting back in my lap she sat next to me, taking a swig of the Corona I'd been drinking. I just looked at her. I didn't want her sitting nowhere else but in my lap. I must've been staring a hole through her because she nervously started shifting in her seat.

"Why do you keep staring at me like that? I came back, didn't I?" she sassed.

"Come here," I calmly demanded, grabbing her by her waist and pulling her back into my lap.

"Damn, Kam. Why the fuck you all down my throat? I came out tonight to have fun. Not to be held hostage," she said, clearly agitated.

"And you can. Just with yo' man. You've been acting all funny and shit. Like you don't want to be with me."

"First of all," she began to say. "You're not my man and I'm not your woman and secon-"

"And we can change all that shit. Right here and right now. I can just say fuck all these other hoes and turn in my playa's card just for you, ma," I said seriously as shit, which I was. At that moment, all I wanted from Kells was for her to give us a chance. I'm willing physically and mentally to get rid of all these money hungry thots just for her ass. A nigga getting too damn old, all I want to do is settle down with one female and start working on expanding my family. And I would like it if that woman was Kelly Re'Nae Dawson. If only she could see how serious I was.

Kells just stared at me long and hard, debating whether or not to believe in me. Her pause was giving me hope, but not too much. I learned at an early age not to put all your eggs in one basket. After a brief pause, she just rolled her eyes and sucked her teeth. "Boy I'm not even going to go there with you," she said taking a drink of her Patrón.

I knew she was going to say that shit and really, I was getting tired of the same song playing. This shit was starting to get frustrating. Every rejection was like a knockout punch to my ego. Rejection didn't settle well with me. I was starting to get pissed off at this cat and mouse game she was always playing.

"Stand up, ma," I said calmly, helping her out of my lap. With her now standing in front of me, I grabbed her by her hips and repositioned her on my lap in a riding position. I cuffed her ass and gave it a hard squeeze while pulling her closer to me until our faces where only mere inches apart. I gently pressed my forehead into hers and just sat there inhaling her angelic scent with the faint smell of her Prada fragrance. My baby was smelling so damn good that my lil' soldier began to salute her ass. My dick was so hard that my lil' nigga was trying to break free from my True Religion jeans. I moved Kells around in my lap until she felt me knocking on her door to paradise, waiting to be let in.

"You see this shit, ma?" I whispered into her ear. "Only you got this kind of effect on me."

I then took her earlobe into my mouth and began sucking on it softly and gently. She moaned softly then tilted her head to the side, giving me better access.

"Mmmm...Kamron....what are you...doing to me," she moaned in my ear, barely getting her sentence out.

"I'm just tryna show you how serious I am about you, girl," I said, never stopping my game.

I went back into putting in more work, grabbing the back of her bun and yanking her head back, licking up and down her neck, back up to her earlobe and stuck my tongue inside it leaving a wet trail wherever my tongue danced. I felt Kells' body shake when I did that shit. I continued teasing her neck licking and sucking, leaving my mark on her ass for the next nigga to see.

Soon she started gyrating her hips into me, causing friction between us. That only made me go even harder. I didn't give a fuck about us being in a packed club and everybody watching. If muthafucka's wanted to be nosey and watch then shit, I was about to give they ass a show 'cause now a nigga was about to do more damage. Truth be told that shit had the both of us turned the fuck on. Soon we were both dry fucking each other in VIP. I was so into it that I didn't even see Veronica, one of my jump-offs, standing in front of me with her hands on her hips and a mean mug on her face.

"Really, Kamron! That's what the fuck we on now! That's how you going to do me?" she screamed out, bringing me and Kelly back down to reality.

"Out of all the shit I do for you and this is how you play me?!" she continued to scream, gathering unwanted attention from those around us.

I felt stuck like I'd been caught with my hands in the cookie jar or some shit. Why? I don't know, considering the fact this bitch ain't shit to me but a cum bucket that I used from time to time.

"I should kick you and this bitch's ass!" she spat while staring Kells down.

Ah shit. This ignorant bitch done fucked up now. Calling Kells out her name was the ultimate no-no. I've seen her crazy ass cut a few niggas up over that shit. Before I could even stop her, Kells was already up on her feet with her fists balled up at her side. When Kells moved, so did Mona and Aris. In the next heartbeat, they were standing next to Kells' side ready to bust a bitch's grape if they needed to. Veronica was about to get an ass whooping she didn't want.

"Bitch? Who the fuck is you calling a bitch?" Kells barked.

Veronica's neck snapped. "You, bitch! Who else am I fucking talking to!"

Kells stepped up in Veronica's face with a menacing scowl on her face. If looks could kill, Veronica's ass would be leaving this muthafucka in a body bag.

"Nah, boo. You can't be talking to me," she said, all calm and shit.

"You the only bitch in here that's all in my man's face!"

I cringed when she said that shit. Like who the fuck told this girl that I was her man? Bitches be confusing a fuck with a relationship. That's exactly why I was so ready to settle down. Kells starting laughing like this bitch had said the funniest shit ever.

"Bitch, yo' man?" she laughed mockingly. "Bitch, this is all me!" Kells pointed to me, catching me off-guard. After the shock wore down, a crooked grin graced my lips. I wanted to jump and buss out the Nae Nae so damn bad, but I kept my nonchalant attitude. I knew Kelly was only claiming a nigga now because she wanted to get a reaction out of Veronica, but hey I wasn't complaining. Just hearing her say that I belonged to her sounded good as a muthafucka.

I smiled as Veronica's face scrunched up into a deeper frown. "If he was your man then why he be calling me over damn near every night to suck his dick!"

Kells' hand went up to her chest as she took a dramatic gasp for effect.

"Oh, so just because he lets you suck his dick you feeling a little special now?" Kells laughed. "Bitch, get the fuck out of here with that shit! All yo' ass is, is a fucking bucket for my nigga to dump his shit in! Okay you fucked him a few times whoopity to the fucking do. Now Kelly is in this bitch and I'm very possessive over mine! So since he didn't give you your walking papers by now, I'm going to go 'head and give'em to you. Bitch, beat ya feet and get the fuck out of my face! You been dismissed!"

Kelly had just bossed up on a muthafucka. Within moments she was staking her claim and was challenging any muthafucka who had a problem with it. Veronica stood there dumbfounded with her mouth wide open. She looked back and forth between me and Kelly.

"You just going to let her talk to me like that? Really, Kam? You swore up and down you weren't into the relationship thing and I respected that. But then this bitch just comes out of nowhere and now you claiming each other?" she sounded hurt but I didn't care. Ain't nobody tell her ass to start catching feelings. Instead of answering, I just grabbed Kells by her hips and pulled her into my chest.

"You heard her, right? Let's not start with this dumb shit, Veronica. She's the only woman I want. My future wife. So let's get that through your thick head. Just like you respect me, you will respect her as well. I'm not going to keep telling yo' ass. So go 'head with that shit while I'm still being nice. Be stupid and keep calling her out of her name and I won't be responsible for the aftermath. Now, you've been dismissed."

I grabbed Kells and planted a wet and greedy kiss on her soft lips while sliding my tongue inside her mouth, showing just how much I loved her ass. This was my future wife right here! I had to laugh because my whole crew began clapping and cheering for us like we'd just won the best couple of the year reward.

"'Bout damn time! I was tired as fuck of this cat and mouse game y'all was playing," Aris grinned. Out of everyone there, she knew just how I felt about Kells and has always been rooting for us from the jump. She didn't like none of the girls that I used to talk to in the past but she was Team Kelly all the way.

"Who are you telling," Mona added.

Veronica just sat there shocked as hell and pissed off at the same time. Before anyone could see it, Veronica reached out and grabbed Kells by her hair, yanking her head back. She swung but missed. Big mistake on her end. Like a pro, Kells dipped and came back up and two-pieced her ass so damn quick that if you blinked you would've missed it. Veronica fell to the ground, her mouth and nose bleeding profusely. Kells was on her ass like white on rice. She pounced on that ass and began throwing blows from left to right. Hitting everything in plain view. Baby had those hands like Mayweather.

"I told yo ass...not to fuck with me...ignorant ass bitch... you just had to...test my gangsta," she breathed all out in one breath as her fists rained all over Veronica's body.

"Aaagggh! Please stop!" she screamed out as she tried to block the deadly blows Kells was putting on that ass. "Kamron, help me!" she cried, pissing Kelly off even more.

"Help you! No this bitch didn't just scream out for help?!" Kells screamed out pushing Veronica forcefully onto her ass and began stumping her into the ground. I watched on in bewilderment as her foot came down repeatedly across Veronica's stomach, ribs, and head.

I glanced up for a second and the whole fucking club was watching. I was in disbelief that no one tried to even make an attempt and stop Kelly's crazy ass from beating Veronica into a pulp. Q and Landon just sat back and watched on in amusement. Aris' and Mona's asses were smiling from ear-to-ear with their arms crossed at the chest.

I reached out and grabbed Kells by her wrist, damn near snapping it in half.

"That's enough!" I said through gritted teeth.

I was pissed! This shit was going too far. Veronica stopped all moving activity. I didn't know if shawty was alive or not and really I didn't care because I tried warning her stubborn ass about fucking with Kelly's demented ass.

Kells looked at me with a deranged look on her face. If looks could kill....

"So you trynna save this bitch?" she asked me with an attitude.

"That's enough Kelly," I repeated again in case she didn't hear me. "You gon' fuck around and catch a murder case."

Kells just looked at me for a moment then started shaking her head. "You know what Kamron, fuck you and that bitch! Since you care about her ass so fucking much, check her pulse for me and see if the bitch is breathing! And yo ass always wondering why I won't give you a chance. Because you always worrying about your hoes! I'm done with yo' ass!" Kells turned on her heels, grabbed her pocketbook and keys, and left.

I looked around at all the stares and ran my hands through my curls. This shit here was embarrassing. It was high school all over again. Muthafuckas were pointing their fingers and whispering under their breath like I didn't know what the fuck they were talking about. I let out a frustrated sigh and went chasing after Kells' ass. I hurried up and parted through the crowd, ignoring all these thirsty ass bitches trying throw themselves at me. By the time I made it outside, I saw Kells waiting for the Valet to bring my truck around. I quietly creeped up behind her as she glanced down at her cell phone going through her missed calls and messages. The valet pulled up, hopped out, and handed her the keys.

"I'll take those," I said snatching them from him before Kells could get her pretty little fingers around them. I reached in my back pocket and pulled out a couple Benjamins and gave them to the young patron. He eagerly accepted and went on with his business. I then turned around to Kells who was looking at me as if I had two heads instead of one.

"Well, get in," I said all nonchalantly, pissing her off more while opening the passenger side door.

She shook her head from side to side. "Nah, I'm cool on that, Kam. I got real nigga that's gonna come to pick me up now," she said checking her phone again.

Now it was my turn to be pissed off. Just her mentioning another nigga coming to pick her up was enough to get my blood to boil.

"Do not play with me, Kelly," I growled through gritted teeth. "Get yo' ass in the car now before I beat yo muthafuckin ass outside of this club!" I was dead ass and waiting for her to try my gangsta just so I could show her who the fuck I am, in case she forgot.

She must have seen how serious I was, seeing that her ass got in the truck with not much more resistance. Satisfied, I climbed inside the driver's seat, started the truck, and pulled off. The whole drive to her house was quiet. I kept one eye on the road and the other on her. Her phone went off for the fifth time since we'd been on the road. I watched her as she hit the ignore button and placed her phone back in her purse. Not even a minute later, her phone rang again. Whoever this thirsty ass nigga was, he was blowing her line up.

"What the fuck does he want?" she tried mumbling, but I still picked it up using my spidey senses.

I respectively turned the volume down on the system so she could answer her phone. She looked over at me and I looked back while steering with one hand.

"Go 'head and answer the shit. It seems like whoever it is needs to holla ASAP," I said heatedly. I was mad and she knew it.

Kells just sucked her teeth and rolled her eyes at me. "Whatever, Kam." After two more rings, she answered. "What?" she screamed.

I strained my ears to hear what he was saying on the other line. Hell, I didn't have to do much since he was loud enough to hear across town.

"Why you ignoring me? I know you see me calling blowing yo' phone the fuck up!" he yelled.

Kells sucked her teeth. "Because I was with my girls!" she yelled back, matching his tone.

"So! Them bitches more important to you than yo' man!" he barked.

Oh nah. This nigga was fucking up. There was no way I was going to sit there and let him disrespect my family like that. Them bitches he was referring to were my sisters. He got me fucked up. I was just about to say something but Kells beat me to it.

Kells removed the phone from her ear and looked at it like it was contagious or some shit, then lit into his ass.

"Hold the fuck up! Let's get some things straightened out. First of all, don't you ever in yo' irrelevant ass life disrespect my girls like that by calling them out their names. Strike one nigga. Make strike two and ya gon' have a bullet resting between your thoughts! Fucks with me if you want to!" she paused, "Second of all nigga, you ain't my man! You just a conversation and a fuck for when I need a nut. So come correct, nigga!" she checked his ass.

I couldn't hold back the smile that came across my face. That was that feisty shit that I loved about her ass. She was making my dick hard with that shit. She never hesitated to check a muthafucka when needed.

"Damn bae, chill. You know I didn't mean any of that shit. I'm sorry. You right, it was wrong of me calling your girls out of their names. I apologize. It's just that I miss yo' fine ass. You got a nigga pussy whipped," he admitted.

This ole soft ass nigga! I swear I can't stand niggas like him. They just get under my skin with their wishy washy attitude. How the fuck you gon' call somebody out on some shit but when a muthafucka bites back, he switching up and singing a whole different song. I wish Kells' ass would try talking to me like she's talking to dude on the phone. I wouldn't hesitate to tell her about herself then fuck the shit out of her right afterwards.

"I miss you too," I heard Kells say. I whipped my head so quick that I damn near drove off the side of the road. The smile I had on my face instantly turned upside down. Did I just hear correctly? Again, I was pissed.

"Word?" I could hear the nigga smiling through the phone at her confession. "So can I see you tonight?"

Kells hesitated before giving him her reply, but before the words even left her mouth I snatched her phone from her. "Hell nah, bruh! She busy fucking with a real nigga tonight. So find you another pussy to dive in. Matter of fact, lose my wife number!" I yelled, ending the call. I rolled the window down then tossed that bitch out.

Kells had her mouth wide open in shock, not believing what I just did. After the shock wore off, she got into my ass. "Why the fuck would you throw my phone out of the window, Kamron?" she screamed, knocking me upside my damn head. The truck swerved to the left, causing other cars to lay on their horns.

"Yo, if you ever put your fucking hands on me again it's going to be a serious fucking problem," I growled through clenched teeth.

"Why the fuck did you throw my phone out of the window like you paid for it? I can't believe you did that shit! I should knock yo' bright ass out for that shit, muthafucka," she spat mushing the side of my forehead.

Lil' Momma was really trying to test my gangsta tonight. I wasn't the type of nigga to put my hands on women and I did everything in my power to stop myself from yoking their asses up. But Kells was making the shit hard with that smart ass mouth of hers.

"Man, fuck that phone!" I roared with the vein in my forehead thumping. "That shit ain't nothing but an accessory that can be replaced. I don't give a fuck if I bought the phone or not. You must got me fucking confused with those lame ass soft pussies that you're used to bossin' up on. I'm sorry ma, but I'm not that kind of nigga. I'm a real muthafuckin' nigga but you already know that now don't you. Fuck I look like sitting up here and listenin' to my girl cake up on the phone with the next nigga? Sit yo ditzy ass down somewhere with that shit!"

"How many times do I have to tell you, Kamron? You are not my man!" Kelly yelled out, sounding frustrated.

I grinned crookedly, flashing her the cocky ass smirked that she loved but hate at the same time as well. "Yea, I'mma just let you continue to think that for right now. But you know just like I know that you are mine. But just in case yo' ass caught amnesia, let me remind you on who the fuck I am. I am a muthafuckin' Miller. My pops is the one and only Kaseem "Killer Mills" Miller. I was always taught, since I was a young nigga still sucking on my momma's titty, that whatever the fuck I want, to go out and make that shit happen. I been staked claim, but your ditzy confused ass wants to still be childish and play these little ass high school games. Cool, go ahead and play 'em. Play until yo' muthafuckin heart is content. Just know I'm a selfish, impatient ass nigga. Play too long and I'mma start unplugging and disconnecting shit."

Kelly folded her arms across her chest, sucked her teeth, and rolled her eyes at me. She knew better than to try to continue this argument. This was not a debate that she was going to win and she knew it.

"Oh, and another thing. Keep yo hands to your muthafuckin' self. You already hit me twice and I didn't do shit. But hit me again and watch what the fuck I'll do to your ass," I warned her through gritted teeth.

"Whatever nigga," she tried to mumble but I was still able to hear her.

I quickly cut my eyes at her, looking at her through tiny slits, before focusing them back onto the road. Kelly's ass was just going to have to learn the hard way that I was not the nigga to try to boss up on. For the rest of the ride, the car was silent besides the radio playing lowly in the cut. Kelly still had her attitude and made it known by huffing, puffing and sucking her teeth. She got one more time to suck them muthafuckas and I'm going to pull over onto the side of the road and give her something real long and thick to suck on.

Twenty minutes later, I was pulling up in the circular driveway and getting ready to put the car in park when all of a sudden Kelly punched the shit out of my ass then took off running into the house. I hurried and threw the truck in park, snatched the keys out of the ignition, and was right on her ass. As I approached the door, she tried to close it, but I put my foot in the way, stopping her from shutting the door all the way.

"Fucking move, Kamron!" she screamed, pushing the door.

"You think I'm playing with your ass?!" I barked at her, pushing against the door.

She put up a fight for a minute before saying fuck it and running up the stairs. I rushed into the mansion, slammed the door behind me, and took the stairs three at a time. When she made it to the top, I reached out, grabbed her ankle, and snatched her ass back making her ass fall on her stomach but catching herself with her hands. I climbed on top of her wrapping my hands around her throat but not adding any pressure.

"I told you about your damn hands, Kelly. Why the fuck do you have to be so damn hardheaded, huh?" Instead getting scared like a normal muthafucka would've, Kells just smiled then grabbed my dick through my jeans and gave it a seductive squeeze, catching me off-guard. Her was like this rough shit. Seeing her reaction caused my dick to do flips. I don't know when and where, but her ass gained the strength of ten men and flipped me over so that she was on top now.

She grabbed my hands and pinned them down above my head with hers.

"And as I said Kamron. What...the....fuck.... are you going to do?" she whispered in my ear, nibbling on my neck as her hand continued to rub my soldier to life.

"You like this shit, don't you?" I asked her, looking into those sexy eyes of hers.

She grinned mischievously and started grinding her womanhood against my dick. My shit was at full attention. Kells was placing small teasing kisses on the side of my neck and back up to my ear. She then took my ear in her warm mouth and started sucking on it. Not on no punk shit, but a groan actually escaped from my lips. She grinned with satisfaction as she made a wet trail with her tongue from my ear, to my neck, and down my stomach, where she lifted my shirt up and outlined my well defined abs with her tongue. She had me feeling too good but I was no punk ass nigga. She thought she was in control but I was going to punish that ass for all the games she had been playing and the shit she put a nigga through tonight. Before she went down any further, I grabbed her by her hair and roughly yanked her ass back up to me where I kissed her so deeply it took her breath away.

She moaned, opened her mouth, and slipped her tongue inside mine. Our tongues danced slowly and sensually but with the sexual greed that we had for each other. We both took turns trying to devour the other. With no effort, I picked Kells up, wrapped her thick legs around my waist, and carried her off to her room.

From there on, we were at each other like two dogs in heat. In record time, I had her ass out of that jumpsuit and had her pumps thrown across the floor. I laid her down on the bed, moved her thong to the side a little, and slid two fingers inside just to feel how tight and wet she was. Surprisingly, Kells' pussy was gripping my fingers. Satisfied, I pulled my fingers out, tasted them, then spread those lips apart and began kissing on them like the ones on her face.

"Mmmm...oohhh shit, daddy," she moaned, biting on her bottom lip and cuffing the back of my head.

Damn, she tasted so good. She tasted like she bathed in strawberries and cream.

"Mmmm...Ma, you taste so fucking good," I closed my eyes and really began to put in work, making my tongue flick across her clit in a fast pace, then slowing it down. Kells moaned and pushed my head further down, trying to drown me in the pussy.

"Ooohh. Baby, that shit feels so good... don't stop. Yea, just like that."

I continued eating her pussy as if it was the last meal I was going to eat before I died. I groaned, slurped, and slid two fingers inside of her tightness and worked them in and out.

I continued to wreak havoc on her sensitive skin. I pinched, rubbed, and then spanked her now sensitive clit, causing her hips to naturally rise and moved against my moving tongue and fingers. I swear she tasted so sweet. The way she was moaning and grinding on a nigga's face had my dick standing up and hard as a rock. I continued slurping, never skipping a beat, while giving her clit a spanking with my tongue. I looked up just in time to see her head go back and her eyes close tightly. Soon her legs started to shake, letting me know she was close to cumming. Determined to make her cum, I began sucking her clit even faster and harder.

"Ahh, Fuck! I finna cum!"

Slurp. Lick. Lick. Slurp. "Mmm. Give me that shit, Ma."

I moaned into her pussy, sending a wave of vibrations throughout her body, making her arched her back as she moaned loudly. Her hips bucked, muscles tightened and legs started shaking harder.

"Go 'head baby. Cum on Daddy's tongue," I mumbled into her pussy putting her ass in a state of shock. As if on command, her body shook violently like she was having a seizure as she came hard into my mouth. I felt her body stiff in my arms and I didn't stop and greedily licked and sucked up every drop of her sweetness.

Spent, she fell back into the bed, breathing heavily while trying to come down from one of the many orgasmic highs I was going to put her body through.

"I didn't know you squirt, baby. Pussy was sweet and messy at the same damn time," I commented with a laugh, while smacking her ass, watching with amazement as it jiggled. It should be illegal to have that much ass.

"Fuck you," she panted, still out of breath. I watched her watch me as I reached into the back of my True Religions and pulled out a Magnum XXL.

"Don't worry, because that's exactly what I'm going to do."

In a matter of seconds, I had the condom open, using my teeth and rolled it down my eleven-inch dick. Kells' eyes bulged out when she stole a quick glance at my shit. I was far from the little nigga she thought I was. My dick was long, thick and curvy, with veins protruding. I could only imagine what was going through her head just at the thought of the damage my dick was going to do to her insides.

"Kam. Wait a min-" she started saying before I cut that shit off.

"Don't 'Kam' me. I'mma show yo' ass just how much trouble that mouth of yours can get you into," I said, slapping my thick tool against her sensitive clit a couple times before sliding the head in.

The feeling of my tip pushing inside of her tight walls had the both of us sucking in a breath and her arching her back.

"Oh, shit," she moaned out.

Her pussy felt like it was being stretched open wider with every inch I was putting inside of her. I hissed, then cuffed her ass and lifted her bottom half off the bed as I pushed half of my length inside of her. I held it there as we both sat there enjoying the feel of one another. Like a surgical glove to a surgeon, Kells fit me perfectly. This moment only confirmed what my future looked like and Kelly was most definitely there holding a nigga down.

"Shit. Shit. Shit. Shit. Shit," she chanted over and over again as her nails dug into my back. I swear her tight ass pussy was cutting off my blood circulation.

"Ssss...Damn Kells. You been holding back on a nigga," I hissed into her ear while slowly stroking in and out of her tight hole. I grabbed one of her legs and put it on my shoulder and used the curve of my dick to find that spot that was soon going to have her shaking and cursing all at the same damn time.

"Oohhh....Fuck! KAMRON!" she screamed out.

With no effort at all, I had that spot. It was literally right there. And now that I found it, there was no way I was going to let go. I had both of her legs on my shoulders, pushed them up to her head, and got into a push-up position. I slid inside of her very slowly, filling her up with all of my inches, pulling out slowly and slamming back into her. Kelly gasped and rolled her eyes to the back of her head when I did that. I did it again, and this time I had her legs shaking. I teased her a couple more times, giving her pussy a chance to fully adjust to me, before I began drilling into her ass. I would go hard and fast with strokes so deep they had her ass on mute. Then I would slow it down and rotate my hips into a circle so that I was hitting all her spots, and finished it off with more jaw-dropping and mouth-gapping strokes.

"Ooohh Fuck. Fuck. Fuck. Fuck. Fuck. Ooooohhh Kamron, baby, my spot. You in too deep. Too deep! Oh, my fucking, GOD! You're too big for me," she screamed out in a mixture of both pleasure and pain as she placed her hands on my lower abs trying to slow down my thrusts. I smacked her hands away and pinned them down above her head, still giving her those death strokes she was going to get well acquainted with in the long run.

"Don't run now! Ain't no running. Take this dick girl!" I groaned through clenched teeth, keeping my movements going. It was hard as fuck tryna keep myself from busting early. So hard that I gritted my teeth and bit my inner cheek. I was giving her rough and powerful strokes that were meant to punish her spot mercilessly. Her legs shook and her hips bucked back again, trying to run from the D. I held her down in place so that there was no more running. I watched as her back arched, hands tightly clenching the sheets, and legs shaking out of control as she coated my shit with her sweet essence.

"What happened to all of that reckless shit that you were spitting earlier? Huhn?" I asked her, slamming into her.

"Oohhh shit!" she managed to moan out in between loud gasps for breath.

I slowly pulled out of her pussy, my dick was covered with her juices. She was so wet her fluids were dripping from the tip of the condom.

"Turn that ass around," I demanded, after slapping her hard on the ass, watching it jiggle. "Bend over and arch that back for me. I want to see that big ass booty bounce back on this dick."

Kelly was hesitant at first but nervously did what I said to do. Ass up and face kissing the sheets. Gripping her ass cheeks in my hands, I spread them open, and slowly entered her again making her gasp again.

"Fuck Kamron! Oh my God," she panted heavily and tensed up. Her pussy was so damn tight that she was pushing my shit out.

"Relax ma so that I can get deep in these guts."

I gave Kells' ass a couple firm slaps, making her cheeks turn red while slowly stroking in and out of her. I wanted her to loosen up for me so that I could hit that spot that she wanted me to hit. It took a while, but Kelly finally relaxed underneath me.

I pulled out, one hand I had on her hip. I used the other to lift her other leg up higher on the bed and to deepen the arch she had in her back. Slowly, I reentered her and went deep, making her groan out loud. In a slow steady rhythm, I moved in and out of her. Kells' body shook as she cooed softly.

"Rock on my dick, Kells," I groaned, slapping her big juicy ass again. I had to bite on my bottom lip to keep from screaming like a little girl.

Kelly turned her head so that she was looking back at me sliding in and out of her. Our eyes connected and she started moving back and forth, slowly getting into it. She started off slow and steady, tightening her muscles around my shit and cumming a couple of times before she began to toss that shit back, making her big juicy ass clap.

"Mmm… fuck Kelly!" I groaned out as I tossed my head back and bit my bottom lip in an attempt to keep me from nutting so quick.

Each time Kells eased all the way down onto my dick and squeezed her muscles, it throbbed. "Bounce that shit on this dick! Fuck, baby."

"Like this daddy?" she asked in a sweet innocent voice, filled with mischief.

How Kelly was throwing that shit back and meeting my every thrusts, you would've never guessed that it was the same person who was running from the dick just minutes ago. Her ass was fucking me like a porn star.

"Oh shit!" I grunted when she started throwing her ass back in a circle. My toes started balling up until they cracked and went numb. I felt the head swelling and my dick throbbing, signaling that a nigga was about to nut and real soon.

I gripped her hips and slammed all eleven inches of me deep inside of her, making her scream until her lungs went raw. I pinned Kelly down with my weight and repeatedly jabbed at her g-spot over and over again until her body started shaking and she collapsed. My ass went into hyper drive, pounding harder and faster.

"Oooohh. Fuuccckk! Grrrrrrrrrrrrr!" I roared as my shit throbbed and I shot my hot semen into the condom. That was one of the biggest nuts that I'd had in a long time. It didn't take long before my breathing started slowing down and I was drifting off to sleep. Fuck, Kelly had that Nyquil pussy and I was hooked.

# Chapter Four

**KELLY**

*THE NEXT MORNING…*

When I woke up this morning, Kamron was already gone, which wasn't anything new to me. I kind of expected for him to be gone, so why was I so disappointed to wake up in an empty bed? The question was one I already knew the answer to. I wanted Kamron, but I was not up to play many games with him.

Honestly, I've been in love with Kamron since the first day I laid eyes on his sexy fine yellow ass. I've been knowing Kamron damn near all of my life and always had this crush on him. Everyone in the crew already knows about my feelings for him, I'm just trying to keep it safe. I'd known for years how Kamron felt about me, I just never took him seriously. We've always flirted with each other through the years but last night was the first time we'd ever been intimate.

For as long as I can remember, we'd been playing this cat and mouse game. Shit with Kam has always been wishy washy. One minute we'd be sitting down discussing our future together, and the next minute this nigga had a new bitch sitting pretty on his arm. Kamron had too many hoes for my liking. He was a thot magnet. Everywhere he went, he was attracting a new thot from somewhere. He even brought out all of the old thots from retirement just to chase his ass. Women flocked to Kam like flies' flock to shit. Bitches would even travel across the country for his ass once he blessed them with the D. They act like this nigga was the best damn thing since sliced bread and after last night I now see why! Kamron got that dope fiend dick! Whew! He had a bitch's pussy doing all kinds of tricks last night, that's how good that shit was!

In order to protect myself from a heartbreak, I fucked with Kamron the long way. All there could ever be between us is casual sex and until I knew that Kamron was serious about us then that's all it'd ever be. Handing myself fully over to Kamron and loving him scared the fuck out of me. We're too much alike. Kamron had the ability to break my heart, rewrap it so that its new, then break it all over again.

No lie, if it wasn't for the fact that Kam was one of the biggest man whores ever known in our generation, then I would have been given in to him and let these bitches know that he was all mine. Either get with the program, or take a bullet to the dome. Either way, Kam was mine.

I got up this morning, climbing out of bed with limp noodles for legs. Soon as I stood up, I fell hard as fuck on my ass. I took a few minutes, sitting on the floor, before I got up for a second try. I then went into the bathroom to handle my morning hygiene and take a quick shower. I could still smell the faint scent of Kamron's cologne on me and that shit had me shaking. I washed myself from head to toe twice with my Enchanted Apple body wash, rinsed and climbed out of the tub. Grabbing my silk robe from off the hook on the back of the bathroom door, I slid it on and tied it loosely around my waist. Inside my bedroom, I went into the walk-in closet looking for something that I could just throw on. After standing in my closet for ten minutes, I finally decided on a black sport's bra from PINK and a matching pair of black leggings. After I finished getting dressed, I slipped my feet into my white and black shell-toed Adidas, tossed my thirty-inch Brazilian weave into a loose bun and went downstairs to see what I could eat.

When I entered the kitchen, Mona was sitting at the kitchen island fixing one of her morning fruit smoothies and Aris was standing at the stove finishing breakfast.

"What y'all bitches up to?" I asked, entering the kitchen, taking a green grape off of Mona's plate and eating it.

Aris and Mona flashed each other a big, wide silly grin before they both turned their gazes upon me. "You sounded like you was having fun last night," Mona said to me with this huge mischievous grin on her face. "Who's the lucky man to bring home?"

I grabbed a plate out of the kitchen cabinet and began staking it with homemade strawberry waffles, eggs, bacon, sausage, and sweet honey biscuits. Aris made hers and brought over Mona's, joining her at the kitchen island. They were both waiting on me to reply and I was taking my sweet time to think of a lie. Now, I don't normally lie to my girls, but if they knew that it was Kamron having me up there speaking in tongues they would surely laugh and tease my ass with I-Told-You-So's.

"Jason," I lied, thinking about the dude who called me last night when I was in the truck with Kam. Speaking of last night, I need to go out today and get a new phone since Kamron tossed my last one out of the window. Bright yellow bastard!

Aris' arched her eyebrow and tooted her lips to the side as if she knew I was lying. "Really? Little dick Jason?" she asked, making us fall over laughing. I was laughing so hard that the eggs I was chewing on went down the wrong tunnel and I started choking.

"Damn girl!" Mona exclaimed, slapping me hard on the back. Aris fell over laughing even harder with her goofy ass. After I stopped laughing, I grabbed my cup of lemon sweet tea and downed it in one gulp.

"I didn't know Jason was slangin' dick like that," Mona said, making me spit my tea out.

"Shid from the way Kells tell it, that nigga dick can't even make it past the ass cheeks."

I couldn't do shit but laugh at those two. As you can probably see, I leave nothing out when it comes to my girls. We don't hold any secrets so all of us know everything that there is to know.

"Yea, well I don't know what the fuck he did last night, but that nigga sure as in hell did something new. I think he went to go get a dick transplant or something."

"Hell nah! Not a dick transplant!" Aris and Mona screamed out at the same time, doubling over cracking up. They were laughing so hard that not only did they have tears coming out of their eyes, but they were coughing up a fit.

I just shook my head at these two silly broads and tried to hurry and finish up my breakfast before they start asking questions again.

"You know what's even funnier about little dick Jason getting a dick enhancement?" Aris asked Mona still laughing.

"What?" Mona giggled, taking a sip from her smoothie.

"This bitch said that it was Jason she was fucking last night but when I was coming in this morning Kam was sneaking out of her bedroom."

My eyes widened and I damn near choked on my tea when Aris said that.

Mona's hand shot up to her mouth as she gasped loudly, sounding all dramatic and shit. "Say it isn't so?" she asked playfully, looking back and forth between me and Ari.

"I don't know what she's talking about," I said, trying to sound confident with my words while rising up from my seat and placing my plate into the dishwasher.

"Bitch, you going to hell for lying on that boy like that!" Aris screamed out, her and Mona fell out laughing again. I swear these bitches were all kinds of retarded.

"You knew this bitch was lying when she said that that boy got a dick transplant," Mona breathed out breathlessly.

"So you fucked Kamron last night, huhn?" Aris asked me bluntly and with a smug grin.

I laughed and shook my head. "Bitch, I plead the fifth."

"Yea, she did!" Mona and E yelled out in unison, laughing again.

I just rolled my eyes and gave the both of them the finger, all with a smile on my face. I couldn't lie to these bitches to save my own life. They know me like they knew the back of their own hands. While Aris and Mona were getting their six-seven chuckles out the alarm chimed saying that the front door had opened and in walked Kamron, Landon, and Mona's ten-month old son Levi. Speaking of the muthafuckin' devil. I should kick Aris in her ass cause she done talked this nigga into existence. Bitch.

Landon walked up behind Mona with Levi fitting snugly in his strong arms. "What you eating?" he asked her peering over her shoulder and into her half-eaten plate.

"Food," she smartly replied.

"Hey, mama's baby," Mona cooed.

She was reaching out to grab Levi from Landon's arms when all of a sudden Aris swooped in and grabbed him first. "Let me see my baby. Hey, tete's dooda butt! Hey, tete baby," she cooed, blowing into the side of Levi's neck making him burst out laughing.

"Man, quit calling him that shit, Ari!" Landon yelled with his face contorted into a frown. "He a boy! That shit sound gayer than a muthafucka!"

Aris held Levi tighter in her arms, tooted her nose up at Landon, and mugged him up and down. "Nigga, whose daddy is you?" she asked him.

When Landon didn't respond to her question, she continued on with her rant. "Right! No one's!" she exclaimed, rolling her eyes and flipping her long black hair over her shoulders. "Gon' try to tell me what I can and cannot call my nephew. He got tete messed up! Ain't that right, dooda?"

Levi, not understanding what the hell we were talking about, grabbed Aris by her cheeks and burst out into a fit of giggles. Just hearing him giggle made everybody laugh.

I smiled and glanced up at Kamron who had yet said anything since he walked his ass through the front door. He was just staring me up and down with lust-filled eyes while biting down on his bottom lip. I swear that shit was so fucking sexy to me. I had to squeeze my legs together and close my eyes to stop the flashbacks from last night from taking over my thoughts. When I opened them, Kamron was staring up at me with a cocky ass grin on his face. Immediately, I contorted my face and frowned up at him.

"The fuck is you lookin' at lil' nigga?" I snapped.

Kamron smirked. "C'mon, ma. Now you know ain't shit little about me," he smartly replied back.

Mona and Aris started snickering and Landon looked back in forth between us with a look of confusion on his face.

"What they talkin' bout?" I heard him ask Aris and Mona.

I sucked my teeth and rolled my eyes at them. I felt my cheeks heat up as embarrassment filled me. Mona and Aris weren't helping the situation with them steady snickering.

"What the fuck ever." With an attitude, I leaned against the kitchen counter with my arms folded under my breasts and just stared at Kam with a dirty mug on my face. I swear I hated and loved this nigga at the same damn time.

"Here, take this shit before I give it to one of my other bitches," Kamron said, making me roll my eyes and pushing an AT&T bag into my hand. Rude muthafucka.

I snatched the bag from him and opened it, spilling all of the contents out onto the counter. Kamron had replaced my Galaxy Note 5 with a gold iPhone 6 Plus and a case to match. I wasn't a big fan of

Apple, so I made a note to go down to AT&T whenever I got the time and change out this iPhone 6 for another Samsung. I loved my Note 5.

"Don't worry about trying to get it activated or nothing. I already handled all of that shit and even took it upon myself to change your damn number. Only numbers that's in there are mine, Ari's, Mo's, and Landon's. Don't let me catch another nigga calling yo' shit or it's gonna be lights out for him and your ass, too."

"What happened to your last phone?" Aris asked me.

"That's the same thing I want to know," Mona added.

"Yo stupid ass brother tossed it out on the highway last night all because I answered it while being in the car with him," I said rolling my eyes at his dumb ass.

"You damn right I was going to toss that bitch! That shit was disrespectful as fuck. The fuck I look like listening to my bitch cake up with the next nigga and not do nothing?! Her ass lucky that's all the fuck I did and didn't go searching for this nigga," Kam said with an attitude as he means mugged me hard as fuck like I pissed in his cereal this morning or some shit.

"This retarded ass nigga told me to answer the damn phone!" I yelled out with frustration.

"And yo' dizzy ass should've known that shit was a set-up!" he yelled back, getting in my face.

Landon, Mona and Aris were dying on the floor laughing at the usual bickering between us. This shit wasn't new to none of us. Me and Kamron were too much alike and I think that's another reason why it would never work between us. We can't stand in the same room for ten minutes without arguing.

"You know what? I'm sick and tired of your muthafuckin' mouth. Yo' attitude is going to get you fucked up. Keep talkin' shit and I'm going to be that nigga that's going to shut yo' ass up for good."

"Whatever, Kamron! You ain't gon' do shit but choke on this nut that I'm about to give you if you don't shut the fuck up! And who in the fuck do you think you talkin' to like that? I ain't none of them other hoes that you're used to fucking around with. Nigga, I will give it to your ass raw and-eep!" A loud squeak left my mouth as Kamron snatched me by the wrist and tossed me over his shoulder.

"Blah… blah… blah… the end! You talking to a boss ass nigga! I've been trying to tell you that all of this disrespect is gonna get you into some shit that you ain't ready for. But no! You wanna be hardheaded and not listen. That's alright because I don't talk much. I'm all about my actions," Kam raised his hand and slapped me hard on the ass, turning around to walk out of the kitchen.

"Owww Kam! Please don't! I'm sorry! I'll shut up!" I cried out as I grabbed onto the kitchen's door frame.

"Nah, buddy! Don't try to switch shit up now! I'mma teach yo ass!" he said snatching my hand down.

"Please Kamron, don't! Aris! Mo! Don't just stand there, get this nigga off of me! Kamron noooooo!!! My pussy is still sore from last night! Don't! Stop! Biiitttccchhhhheeeeesssssss!"

Those bitches stayed in the kitchen fucking laughing while Kamron carried my ass all the way up those stairs and into my room, slamming the door and locking it. I felt like that lil' white bitch off of King Kong when that big ass ape kidnapped her ass and climbed up that tall ass building. Fuck! My damn mouth got me into some shit that I can't talk myself out of! Dammit!

# Chapter Five

**ARIS**

*"Mmmmm… oooohhh Kamron… Stop!"*

*"You want me to stop?"*

SMACK! SMACK! SMACK!

*"Nigga, you better not stop!"*

Mona and I stood outside of Kelly's door with our hands across our mouths dying. I couldn't breathe I was laughing so fucking hard! I mean I was laughing so hard that my ribs were hurting and my throat was raw. Mo was sliding down the hallway wall, her face red and wet from tears. Kelly's ass thought she was so slick and thought that we weren't hip to the muthafuckin' game. That lie she told us about fucking Jason last night still tickled me whenever I think of it. I knew it was a lie as soon as the words left her mouth, I just didn't say anything because the shit was so funny. I don't know why Kells continued to play with my brother's feelings like that. They been playing this crazy cat and mouse game since high school. She used the excuse of Kamron always having a bitch on his arm and them being exactly alike as why she won't get with him. She can tell that shit to someone who doesn't know her, but we know. Kelly Re'Nae Dawson wants my brother!

They were made for each other! Both of their mouths are reckless ass fuck, neither has a filter, both are hot headed and have enough screws missing combined to start their own mental psych. Kamron has been in love with Kells since the first time he laid eyes on her and so has Kells, quiet as kept. Kam is going to get tired of chasing her hard headed ass, and she's going to be left in the end looking stupid because she let the one get away.

"What are y'all perverts doing hanging out in the middle of the hallway outside of Kells' door?" Landon whispered, appearing basically out of thin air and scaring the hell out of me and Mo.

"Damn, nigga. Make some noise the next time, why don't you. I almost had a heart attack," Mona whispered harshly with her left hand clenching her chest.

"What the hell is y'all doing?" Landon asked us as if it wasn't obvious.

"We not doing nothing!" Me and Mona said at the same time in an innocent childlike voice.

"Ahhh shit Kamron baby, I'm cumming!" Kells screamed out.

I swear me and Mona's faces turned all the way red we were so embarrassed. Landon gave us a look like, 'really'. Hell, we couldn't do shit but laugh off our embarrassment.

"Man, y'all are some fucking perverts," Landon said shaking his head.

"C'mere. I need to talk to you for a sec," Landon said, grabbing Mona's hand and started pulling her down the hall towards her bedroom.

"Why? What's going on?" Mona asked him with confusion written all over her face.

"Just follow me," he whispered.

"And y'all say y'all are just friends. Yea right," I scoffed and giggled at them. "Your secret is safe with me. I won't tell nobody."

Mona spun on her heels and gave me the finger before she was ushered into her room by Landon. I took my precious time getting off of the floor and trucking my peeping Tom ass into my bedroom. As soon as I closed the bedroom door, I locked it and immediately began to strip from my outfit that I wore to the club last night.

I didn't make it in until damn near six o'clock this morning fucking around with Quamir's ass last night. We didn't leave the club until four this morning. I went back to his crib but we got into an argument because I was too damn tired to have sex with his ass. So I politely grabbed my shit and caught a cab home after saying 'fuck you with a dirty dick' to his ass. After coming home, I started on breakfast since I was having a hard time falling asleep.

The way my body was feeling, I was too tired to even climb in the tub and wash my dusty ass. Grabbing an oversized t-shirt and a pair of my brother's boxers that I jacked from him a while back, I slipped them on and climbed into my California King-sized sleigh bed, grabbed my four-foot-tall teddy bear, and tucked it in between my legs.

Just seeing everybody in their puppy love phase reminded me of my first love, Mona's older brother and Kamron's best friend, Roman Cayden Clarkson. Just thinking about him saddened me and made me wish things could return to how it was. Back to when I was all his and he was mine. As much as I love Quamir and appreciate him for putting the pieces of my heart back together; he will never make my heart stop beating and my stomach to flutter with butterflies the way Rome does. Even after all of these years, that man still has such a strong hold over me.

Rome… he has been my first of many things. Rome was the one who gave me my first real kiss when I was eleven and he was fourteen, and the man I gave my virginity to. He was the first person to ever hold my heart the way he did and was the first person to ever give me my first real heartbreak.

I'd known Roman my whole life because me, him, Mona, and Kam all grew up together. His pops, Tyreek "Ty" Morgan, and my dad grew up together with two other ruthless muthafuckas that flushed all of the East coast with that top grade fish scale.

Rome was my best friend before he became my man. Whenever I needed advice or just a shoulder to cry on, Rome was the person who I always ran to. Rome had always spit the raw hardcore truth. He didn't give a fuck if he hurt your feelings or not. He never held his tongue and always said whatever was on his mind. And I think that's why I fell for him the way I did. We always had a thing for each other, but because he was eighteen and I was fifteen we decided to just to remain best friends who occasionally messed around with each other from time to time and saw other people.

Of course everything was kept a secret from the family. If my dad ever found out about us, then he would surely have sent Rome to an early grave. He was very overprotective when it came to me. Hell, he was obsessed with protecting me even when I was still inside of my mother's womb. And when my mother died after giving birth to me, he took it beyond to the extreme. He made it his job to spoil me rotten and made sure that I wanted for nothing. I was and will always be his little spoiled princess.

Thinking about my dad had me feeling all sad on the inside. Because he is wanted in damn near every state imagined, my father had to flee to Columbia where he lives a peaceful life in a beautiful mansion with his new wife, Edith. Me and my brother would fly out there on his birthday and holidays to visit the old man. I am truly daddy's little girl.

Rome has a nonchalant, I don't give a fuck attitude that could turn me on and off at the same fucking time. He knew everything about me and my feelings for him, but when it came to himself he was so secretive with his shit. It wasn't until I was a Sophomore in high school and started dating this guy named Jacquese that Rome started letting his true feelings show around me. He hated Jacquese with a passion and did everything in his power to scare him off. It was a good thing that he didn't scare easily and stayed around for two years, which irked the shit out of Roman. It was comical seeing Roman wear his heart on his sleeve when it came to me. The day I turned eighteen was the day Rome snatched me from Jacquese, abruptly ending our relationship without my consent, and confessed his true feelings to me in front of our friends and both of our fathers. Surprisingly, my father took it well and was rooting for the two of us to be together. After that, life was exactly how I wanted it to be. Perfect.

Things were going so good for us. Me and my girls had just graduated from high school at the top of our class with honors and full scholarships to whatever college of our choice, and after being in the drug game for over thirty years, my father had finally retired and handed the empire that he built with his blood, sweat and tears over to my brother with Roman being his right hand and Landon his left.

I was very skeptical about Roman being involved in the drug game because of the attention it would bring. I've seen a lot of shit happen growing up. These streets don't love no muthafuckin' body. There are only two outcomes when you're involved in the game. You're either buried six feet under or in somebody's jail serving several life sentences. Eventually, I accepted the fact that Rome was going to do what Rome wanted to do. Besides the groupie bitches that came with the territory, our relationship was damn near perfect. But of course, there is no such thing as being all the way perfect. There will always be some type of flaws.

A year after of being together and being drama-free Rome and I had our first real fallout. Unfortunately, this fallout was the cause of our breakup and my broken heart.

Rome and I had gotten into over Jacquese's ass. Ironic, huhn? Well anyway, me, Kells and Mona had finally decided to get out of the house and have some girl time. With me being all up under Rome, Mona falling in love with her much older boyfriend that Rome had no idea about, and Kelly doing her own thing, we didn't have much time to hang out like we normally do. Of course our hot in the pants asses went to the club to show off what our Momma's blessed us with. I was trying to be grown and tear the muthafuckin' bar up. I'm talking about I was throwing shots back like they weren't shit. Between the weed and the drinks, a bitch was feeling too good. So when Jacquese walked his sexy ass up behind me and started grinding his dick all into my ass I didn't bother to stop him.

In fact, I was throwing this big ass booty back all over him giving him one last time to remember something that he would never have ever again. I danced with Jacquese for about three songs. When the third song was finished, I was done but before I was even able to pull away Rome, Kam and Lay where pushing their way through the club over towards the dance floor. Judging from the way Rome's face turned red and his fists steadily clenching at his sides, I knew that he saw what I was doing and was beyond pissed. Long ass story short… Rome laid Jacquese out and dragged my little ass out of that club like I was little ass child.

We argued the whole way home. Instead of going back to his crib where I'm usually at majority of the time, he took me back to the condo that me and the girls shared. Some hurtful words were exchanged and Rome put me out of his car, slammed the door, and speed out of the driveway. He didn't even make sure that I was safe in the house like he normally does. That whole night I tossed and turned. We had never argued like that and when we did, we normally made up before going to bed. I called Rome several times to apologize, but he was being a dick and kept sending me straight to voicemail each time.

Determined to get back into my man's good graces, I took a quick shower, tossed on my mink coat with nothing underneath it, and drove all the way to his house. My mind, nor my heart, were prepared for what I walked in on. Rome was laid out against the couch with his eyes closed and his head tossed back while his ex-hoe Ebony was straddling his waist riding his ass into the cushions. They were so engrossed in what they were doing that neither of them noticed me standing there with tears streaming down my face until I tried to quietly walk back out of the door and accidently bumped into something, alerting them.

The look on Rome's face was priceless. He tried to say something to justify his actions but I didn't want to hear none of that shit he was trying to say. I took off running like a bat out of hell going over the speed limit and breaking every traffic rule there was. It was amazing that I managed to make it home unscarred with blurry eyes. I quickly packed a bag and checked myself into a hotel for a couple days before Roman brought his cheating ass back home to stop me. I ended up staying cooped in a hotel for three weeks, crying my eyes out, and dead to the world.

My phone was ringing so damn much from calls and texts from the crew that I just turned it off and tossed it back into my purse. A month passed and I was finally strong enough to come out of the rock I had hidden myself under. When I came back home, not only was everybody pissed, worried and angry at me, but Rome was in jail for the possession of an unauthorized weapon serving a five to seven-year sentence.

***

*KNOCK! KNOCK! KNOCK! BANG! BANG! BANG!*

The sound of someone beating on my damn door like the they were twelve raiding this bitch woke me up from my peaceful ass slumber. I finally was able to fall asleep and now here comes this muthafucka banging on my door, waking me up. Groaning, I grabbed my pillow and pulled it over my head, trying to ignore the noise and fall back to sleep. But when the banging got even louder, I quickly jumped out of my bed, throwing the covers onto the floor, and snatched it open ready to cuss whoever the fuck on the other side out.

"What the fuck is wrong with you bitches?!" I yelled in Mona's and Kelly's face with steam coming from my ears.

Mona and Kelly cocked their heads to the side and looked at me like I done lost my goddamn mind. Mona looked at Kelly and Kelly returned the same who-the-fuck-does-this-bitch-think-she-talking-to look at her before turning her attention onto me.

"You was sleep?" Mona asked me.

I looked at this bitch like 'really'. "Nah, I just had my eyes close for a really long time and is grumpy for no reason at all," I said sarcastically.

"Anyway," Kells sang as she pushed past me and into my room with Mona following right behind her. Like I invited these two bitches in. I watched as the both of them took a seat on my bed like they belonged in here.

"Girl, it's time for you to get up now. It's going on three o'clock in the afternoon and we still need to go grocery shopping for tomorrow's BBQ and hit the mall before they close today."

"Man, you bitches could've went by yourselves! Y'all did not have to wake me up for that bullshit," I barked with an attitude as I climbed back into my bed and pulled the covers over my head.

"Un huhn, boo boo kitty," Kelly jumped off of the bed and quickly snatched the covers off of me. "Since when do we go anywhere without the other? Bitch if you don't get up and get dressed I'mma go take my ass downstairs, grab a bucket with some ice, and do the Ice Bucket Challenge in this muthafucka."

My head quickly snapped up and I looked at Kells with squinted eyes. "Bitch, you wouldn't dare."

Kells looked back and forth between me and Mona. Mona was bugging the fuck up at us. "This yellow bitch must be trying to take me as a joke," she mumbled as she stormed out of my room.

I knew when I heard her heels click clacking against the marble stairs that she was serious as hell. I hurried up and jumped out of my bed like that muthafucka had caught on fire and did a full throttle to the bathroom. Mona was lying back on my bed cracking up.

I was in the middle of washing up with my favorite vanilla and Piña Colada scented body wash when all of the sudden the shower curtain was snatched back and Kelly was pouring a bucket of ice cold water over my head and down my back.

"Aaaaahhhhhhhhhhh!!!!!! You dirty bitch!" I screamed out as I tried to curl up underneath the showerhead.

Both Kells and Mona were standing in the middle of my bathroom doubled over in laughter.

"I bet you the next time I say get up and do something yo' ass is going to get up and do it now isn't you?"

"I swear, on my momma's grave, I'm telling Kamron on you!" I screamed out at her, sounding like a big ass kid.

At the mention of my brother, Kelly sucked her teeth and rolled her eyes at me. "Honey boo! Kamron ain't gon do shit to me. Now hurry yo' ass up we got shit to do," she said, walking out of the bedroom with Mona on her heels.

Because of Kells' ass I had to cut the water on scorching hot just to stop shaking. I swear I'm going to get her ass back. That shit was so foul. After I washed up and rinsed off, I climbed out of the tub and quickly handled my hygiene. When I stepped back into my bedroom, Kelly was messing around in my perfume collection and Mona was tickling Levi and blowing on his stomach. The sight of my god baby brought the biggest smile onto my face. My baby was so handsome with his little cute bowlegged self! Levi had smooth mocha skin like his mother, a head full of soft curly hair, and two of the deepest, adorable dimples!

Mona had him dressed in a pair of True Religion cargo khaki pants, a plain white V-neck t-shirt, a jean jacket and a pair of white low top Adidas sneakers. Mo was dressed exactly like her son, except she had on some khaki shorts that hugged her ass and hips. Kells was dressed simple and cute in a white Givenchy shirt dress and a pair of nude gladiator thigh high heeled boots. Seeing that khaki, brown, and nude were the colors everybody was wearing, I went into my walk-in closet in search of something similar.

After tossing every article of clothing that I owned onto the floor, I finally found an outfit that was simple and cute to wear. I decided to wear my blue denim skin tight boyfriend distressed skinny jeans, a white, short-sleeved crop top, royal blue long-sleeved floral print shirt that stopped at my knees and a pair of brown knee-high stiletto boots. The 18k gold-plated rhinestone African diamond beaded necklace, bracelet, earrings, and ring set made the outfit pop. Since my hair was wet thanks to Kelly's ass it was back in its natural thick curly state. I didn't really want to mess with it so I just left it alone. After getting dressed, I applied eyeliner and mascara onto my eyes making them seem brighter, a light pink lipstick and sprayed myself down with my favorite Juicy Couture perfume.

Grabbing my Jackie O shades from my purse and making sure I had my phone and keys, I was ready to go. "Alright bitches, let's go and shut some shit down!"

I looked up and both Kelly and Mona where staring up at me. "What?" I asked.

"You must have been recently thinking about Rome. I haven't seen you wear that necklace set or wear that perfume in over five years," Mona said with a small smirk.

I rolled my eyes, hating the fact that these bitches know me so damn well. "No, I'm wearing this necklace set because it brings the outfit out and I thought I picked up my Chanel Chance perfume," I lied.

Mona and Kelly burst out laughing.

"Uh huhn, bitch, don't even try that one. Those are two different bottles and scents," Kelly added.

"Man, are you bitches ready? Damn! Y'all made me get out of bed just to make fun of me and shit," I yelled, clearly agitated.

"Let's go before I end up cussing this bitch out. Damn, when was the last time Q rang that bell? She so grumpy when she doesn't get any dick… I mean sleep," Kells giggled while walking out of the room.

Mona giggled as she strapped Levi into his car seat and grabbed his diaper bag. While everybody went to go pile up in my brother's truck, I stayed behind to set the alarm and lock the house up. After making sure all of the doors were locked and that I had everything I needed, I climbed into the passenger seat, buckled my seat belt, and was ready to go. Kelly started up the car and off to Dolphin Mall we went.

***

After being in the mall for damn near three hours, I was so ready to leave. My damn feet where hurting and I had an attitude that was out of this world. I was so ready to snap on any and everything. Since being here, Q had done nothing but blow up my phone with calls and texts asking for my whereabouts. It was becoming so consistent that I put his ass on the block list for the day. I don't know where he picked up his insecure ways, but he needed to drop that shit off, and quick. I'm not used to a man wanting to know my every single move, wanting to be all underneath me, and telling me what I can and cannot wear. That was so annoying to me. I mean yeah, when I was with Rome he did call and check up on me and gave his nod of approval on my outfits whenever I was with the girls, but not like how Q was doing it. Q was taking shit to the next level.

I hardly ever went anywhere if he wasn't there with me. He thought that every man I came across of wanted to get me into their bed. Well, that was the reason half of the time, but I'm not checking for anybody else and he knows that. I was so ready to go home and lay down in bed. I only had about five hours of sleep today and the bed has been calling my name.

I was happy as hell that Mona and Kells felt the same way that I did and were just about done shopping. Levi was getting a little cranky and was throwing a tantrum because Mona wouldn't let him out of the stroller. We were coming out of The Children's Place and were on our way out of the mall when I spotted Veronica and her little clique making their way over in our direction.

"Broke bitches approaching at one o'clock," Mona said.

Veronica started walking up to us grinning and shit like she just didn't get her ass stumped by Kelly last night. Besides her face being a little swollen, her face looked pretty much alright. The miracles that MAC can do. It was about three girls total and I stared at every last one of them in the face. The girl on the left side of Veronica was silent for the most part. She kind of looked familiar to me, but I couldn't quite put my finger on it. When my eyes redirected themselves to the girl on Veronica's right my mouth dropped open in shock. Ebony was standing on Veronica's right with a smug smile on her face as she looked me up and down.

My skin started crawling and my blood began to boil from just looking at this home wrecking bitch. I hated this bitch with a muthafuckin' passion. I'm not a violent person at all, so it was taking everything in me to keep myself from jumping this bitch and smacking that smug ass smile off of her face.

"Hey Aris. It's been a while. Almost five years since the last time we seen each other. When's the last time have you talked to my baby daddy? How is my baby daddy doing anyway? I heard that he's supposed to be getting out soon."

"Baby daddy?!" Me and Mona shrieked at the same time.

Ebony laughed. "Oh, you haven't heard? Me and Roman have a four-year-old son together. His junior, Roman Cayden Clarkson Jr," she smirked.

I swear it felt like my heart stopped beating and broke all over again at Ebony's revelation. I was supposed to the only one carrying Rome's babies, and to know that this bald-headed trick got one up over me not only pissed me off, but made me hate Rome's stupid ass even more. How could he?

"Bitch, that ain't my brother's baby," Mona spat heatedly. I could tell by the way her eyebrow dipped downwards and her fists clenched at her sides that she was ready to beat Ebony's ass.

"I can bet every last single dime that's in my bank account that he is."

Mona sucked her teeth and flicked her wrist at Ebony. "Don't bet off the little last bit of money yo' broke ass has left. That small chump change won't even put a dent in my pockets."

"You know just like me and my girls know that baby ain't Roman's. Trust me, if it was Roman would have been told me about him if he was one hundred percent sure. You's a hoe Ebony. That baby could belong to the postman as far as everybody know," Mona said confidently.

It was like she was directing her words towards me. Trying to assure me that Ebony's baby wasn't a part of Rome. I heard what she was getting at loud and clear, but the pain in my heart didn't soften up one bit.

"Well, well, well. We meet again," Veronica said while staring directly at Kelly.

"I see yo' ass ain't have enough last night. But that's alright because I have no problem with beating that ass again. Mo hold this," she said handling Mona her bags.

"Bitch, please. You caught me while I was under the influence of alcohol. If I wasn't so drunk last night then trust yo' ass would've gotten that ass whooped," Veronica spat heatedly with an eye roll.

"Oh, yea?" Kelly asked with a raised eyebrow. "Well since neither one of us is under the influence of alcohol and you feeling froggy, then stop the bullshit and bust a fucking move. You ain't got shit that I want to hear, so unless you ready to throw them thangs, then bitch I advise you to keep moving because this right here," she pointed back and forth between herself and Veronica, "ain't what you want. I normally don't fight because breaking a nail on irrelevant bitches isn't me, but since I left my gun out in the car, I'll make this one exception. So what is it gonna be?"

Again, Veronica sucked her teeth and rolled her eyes at Kelly. "Umm… bitch no. Who the fuck fights in a mall full of people. That shit is so ratchet and ghetto. I don't know what Kamron sees in you! Although you dress in high end fashion, that you probably sucked a couple of dicks for, you are still a loud mouth bitch from the ghetto! Ole ratchet ass."

I could tell from by the way Kelly's chest was caving in and out that she was pissed at Veronica calling her out like that.

"Well, isn't that the pot calling the kettle black. If I'm ratchet and from the ghetto, then bitch you are from the slums. You looked like the type who lived and probably still lives off of Section 8 and government assistance selling food stamps just to get like me," Kelly said laughing and judging by the way Veronica's face turned all the way red, Kelly hit right on the head.

"Whatever, bitch. I will catch your ass one day and when I do, you going to wish that you never opened your legs up to my man. Kamron is all mine and I will kill you first before I let you have him."

"Is that a threat?" Kelly asked, her hazel eyes turning dark.

Veronica smirked and shrugged her shoulders. "Take it how you wanna take it. C'mon girls. We got better shit to do than to argue with these fake uppity bitches," Veronica spun on her heels and began walking away with her clique right on her heels. Ebony smiled at me, then waved. "See you later, Aris. Oh and Kelly, don't think I forgot about that time you tripped me in the hallway back in high school. Bitch, the next time I see you that's yo' ass guaranteed," she threatens before scattering away.

"Did that bitch just threaten me?" Kelly asked rhetorically and in disbelief. Everybody that knows Kelly knows to never threaten her. When you do it's like waking up a deadly beast from deep inside of her.

Kelly began to take off running behind Veronica and her clique but couldn't since me and Mona were holding her back.

"BITCH!" Kelly screamed out heatedly, gathering attention from all of those around us.

I was just as pissed off as she was. I wanted to snatch Ebony's ass up so fucking bad and beat the breaks off of her, but didn't because of the neighborhood we were in. The police here don't mind putting muthafuckas in jail for disturbing the peace and domestic violence, and since today was Saturday that means a muthafucka won't get out until Monday.

"Man, that bitch lucky my nephew is with us today, otherwise I wouldn't have hesitated to bash that bitch's face into these marble floors," Kelly spat as she grabbed her bags from Mona.

Me and Mona kept quiet and followed Kelly out of the mall to the car, each lost in our own thoughts. Just seeing Ebony's ass and knowing that Rome was supposed to be getting out soon was enough to send my ass to the asylum. I was not ready or prepared to deal with Rome once he got out. I knew for a fact that he's going to be pissed because for four straight years I have been ignoring all of his calls, letters and visit request and that shit scared the fuck out of me. Rome is just like my brother in so many ways. Their tempers are out of this world. Nobody wanted to be around them when they went into one of their little episodes.

After leaving the mall, we made one last stop at the grocery store to get groceries for tomorrow's annual cookout and groceries for home. Every forth Sunday of the month, my brother would gather his close business associates and crew members and invite them over to our party house for a night of fun festivities. And guess who's in charge for cooking everything? You guessed right, me, Mona and Kells. Since it was so late and no one was in the mood to cook dinner, we stopped at our favorite pastimes TGI Friday's and ate there.

By the time we made it home, it was going on nine thirty. I was beyond exhausted and so were my girls. Nothing was said as we all retired back into our bedrooms. When I made it to my room, I hurried up and kicked my heels off, then took everything that I had in my hands and tossed that shit on the floor. My feet were killing me! I was already tired before we left and now my body was past exhausted. All I wanted to do was quickly take a shower and lay down. My bed was calling my name. After soaking my body for a little while in some hot water, I grabbed one of my terry cloth towels, wrapped it around my body, and walked into my bedroom.

I was in the middle of bending over and drying off the back of my legs when my bedroom door opened and Q walked his ass in. I rolled my eyes and sucked my teeth in irritation. I was still pissed at him from the argument we had last night and him blowing my phone up earlier.

"I've been calling yo' ass all day today. Why haven't you answered my calls?"

Again, I rolled my eyes at him. I love Quamir, but over the years we have been together he had become very clingy and insecure. If I went too long without calling or texting him, he would automatically assume that I'm out cheating on him and flip the fuck out. I don't understand his behavior at all, because I have never given him a reason to even entertain such a thought. I've been faithful to him the entire two years that we have been together.

I'm just about through with his clinginess. You know how you'll be so into someone, crushing on their ass hard as hell, but once time goes by and you get to know each other you looking back like what the fuck was I thinking? That's how I feel about mine and Q's situation. I don't know if I could really call our situation a relationship anymore. With Q all we do is stay at his house, fuck, eat, argue then fuck some more. Whenever we do go out it's when the crew throws a party or a little get together. I hardly ever go out with the girl's anymore unless he's there.

Don't get me wrong, when we first got together we had a blast. Q used to send me flowers every day with sweet little notes attached to them, take me out to the movies, out to eat, and cater to my every want or need. It seemed like once I finally caved in and gave him the nookie, whatever Aris wanted came to a screeching stop. We can't go anywhere now without Q trying to get into a confrontation with someone who is admiring me from a far. When I was with Rome, we did more than just sitting in the house and stare at the ceilings all day long. We actually went out and had dates and had fun while doing so. Even if it was going to the movies and out to eat, we had a blast. Rome… damn, there I go comparing them again. Shit. Ever since I thought about Roman earlier today, I can't get him off of my mind. Simple shit reminds me of him.

I ignored Q standing there in front of my bedroom door with his arms folded across his chest and looking so damn sexy. I had to bit on my body lip and squeeze my thighs together to stop myself from jumping his bones. Damn, that man was so damn sexy. Still ignoring him, I headed straight towards my dresser to find me something to put on. I was too tired to argue with Q. That's the only reason why he brought his ass here and I was tired. All the fuck I want to do is take my black ass to bed. I was in the dresser shuffling some clothes around when Q walked up behind me and wrapped his arms around my waist.

"You know I hate it when you ignore me," he mumbled into the side of my neck as he placed soft butterfly kisses on the side of my neck.

As if on his command, my body began to shake and an involuntary moan escaped my lips. I hate it when my body betrays me. I wasn't in the mood for sex but with Q kissing all of my spots on the side of my neck and massaging my breasts together in his large hands, I was more than ready to jump up and down on his pogo stick. I tilted my head to the side when Q started sucking on my spot behind my ear. I was so damn hot that I had a mini-pool in between my legs and was unconsciously backing my ass up against his hardened member.

Grabbing me by my hips, Q lifted me up and sat me on top of my dresser. Gently, he parted my legs and stepped in between them. Running his hands through my hair, he tangled his fingers up in it and roughly titled my head back. A surprised squeak left my lips as I waited impatiently for what was to come next.

"You know I hate when you ignore me, Aris. Why do you continue to play with me like that? You know my mind shifts into overdrive and I start thinking the worse when you ignore me," he mumbled in a soft hoarse voice as his wet tongue licked up and down my neck. My breathing started to speed up. I was damn near on the verge on panting. My whole body was lit.

"You fuckin' around on me, Aris?" he asked me his tone hardening a bit.

I was so caught up with the way his tongue was working against my neck and his hands gripping my thighs that I didn't quite catch his question or the attitude he suddenly caught until Q's teeth were sinking into my shoulder, making me yelp out.

"Ouch! Quamir, that hurts," I whined.

Q continued biting me for a few seconds longer before finally releasing my flesh from being hostage. "Answer my question, Aris."

"What was the question again?" I asked him feeling completely dumb because I didn't hear him the first time.

"You fuckin' around on me?" he asked again this time in a dark tone.

My eyebrows dipped downwards in confusion. "Of course not, Quamir! Why would you think that?"

Instead of answering me he just stared at me long and hard before he grabbed my waist, slid me towards the edge of the dresser, and pushed his dick inside of me with no hesitation. I didn't even have enough time to remember when the fuck did he unbuckle his belt and pull his dick out. My eyes widened and my mouth fell open in shock. No lie, I felt like he was ripping a bitch in half as he violently thrusted in and out of me, hitting spots that only Rome could hit. Dammit, Aris stop thinking about Rome's trifling dirty dick ass and comparing him to Q!

Moaning, I reached in between our bodies and pushed against Q's abs. I'd been with Quamir for almost two years and he has never gone that deep before. It'd been a long ass time since that unexplored territory had been touched. Every time the tip of his dick touched that spot, my body would shake and a jolt of both pain and pleasure would shoot up inside of me. That shit had me thinking I was a virgin again, taking dick for the first time.

"Uh huhn, move your hands and take this dick!" Q's voice boomed as he slapped my hand away, lifted my legs into the crests of his elbows and dug even deeper.

"Shit! Oh my Goodness! Aww… fuck!!" I screamed out as my muscles contracted around his shaft and a gush of clear liquid shot out of me, wetting up Q's t-shirt and jeans.

"Damn baby…" he groaned in the back of his throat as he slowed down just a little bit and watched me squirt in amazement. Again that was something that only Rome could do, make me squirt on his command. Picking me up, Q carried me over to the bed, flipped me onto my stomach and started fucking me like crazy. Any normal day, I would be able to take the dick and match his ass stroke for stroke, but for the first time ever, Q had me running and ready to climb up on these walls just to get away from his ass. A perfect mixture of pain and pleasure shot through my body with every thrust. I was so damn wet that my shit was sounding like that good mac and cheese being stirred.

"Fuck!" he shouted. "Girl, you got that pussy that would make a nigga commit murder and be happy to serve time. Shit," he groaned as he smacked me hard on the ass. So hard that I started screaming from the pain.

"Mmm baby, throw that ass back for daddy. Wet my dick up. Squirt for me one last time."

"I can't baby! Ooohhhh… I… can't… do it," I shouted out breathlessly.

"Yes you can."

SMACK.

My mouth fell open into a perfect "O" as my legs began to shake like I was trying to win a tipdrill dance off for Nelly. My toes curled up and my hands clawed the sheets so hard that the expensive threads began to tear. All it took was for Q to hit that spot again and everything that I was trying to hold in came gushing out of me.

"Oh my fucking Jesus Christ! Ohhh baby, I'm cumming! Aaahhhhhh!!" I screamed as I released all of my fluids all over him wetting up my sheets.

"That's what the fuck I'm talkin' 'bout!" he yelled, slapping his chest proudly.

I felt his dick swell up inside of me and wanted to buss out doing the Millie Wap. I have never been this happy. Q's thrusts became faster and more violent than before. I actually started crying because it was hurting so bad, but feeling so damn good. I ended up cumming one last time before Q growled and emptied his seeds deep inside of my womb. It wasn't until then that I realized that we didn't use any protection.

"What the fuck Quamir!" I screamed as I pushed him off of me.

"What?" He asked sounding stupid as fuck.

"Don't fucking sit up here and ask me that stupid shit. Why the fuck you didn't pull out?" I asked him angrily through clenched teeth. "You know I'm not on birth control so why the fuck wouldn't you pull out? That's the third time you did that shit!"

Quamir smacked his teeth and rolled his eyes at me. "Because I'm tired of using condoms with your ass. You my woman. Why the fuck do

I gotta keep wearing condoms?" He said to me with an attitude of his own as he flopped on the other side of the bed.

"Because nigga you know that I'm not ready for any kids right now. That's the whole reason why we're using condoms in the first fucking place!" I yelled at him only telling him half the truth. You see I love kids and one day would love to have my own but with just not with Quamir. The real reason why I don't want any kids with Q is because I'm getting real sick and tired of him right now and me having one of his babies would mean that I would be tied to his ass for life. I don't think I can do another eighteen years with his ass. These two years with him has already taken its toll on me.

"Since yo funky ass act like you have a problem with having my baby, then go get on some fucking birth control. I'm tired of pulling out and I'm done using condoms." He snapped at me and with that he pulled the covers over his head ending our disagreement.

I sat there and watched him in disbelief until he started snoring before I jumped up out of bed and went into the bathroom to clean up. After taking a quick wash up I went back into my bedroom grabbed all of the pillows off the bed and snatch the cover off of Quamir's ass taking everything into one of the guest bedrooms with me.

The other guest bedroom already had pillows and shit in there so I took the ones I had in my hands and tossed it in the closet. Yeah, I was on my Queen Petty shit. So the fuck what. Fuck Quamir Alexander Myles. Before laying down I made sure that the door was locked before getting comfortable underneath the covers. I fell into a deep comatose sleep that night with Rome on the brain dreaming about us when he didn't fuck Ebony's trifling ass and when we were still happy together.

# Chapter Six

**ROMAN CAYDEN CLARKSON**

I was in my cell pacing the floor as I impatiently waited for the damn CO to come back here and release my ass. I swear the government is quick as fuck to throw a young black man in jail, but when it's time to give them they walking papers, they want to take all fucking day. Fuck that! I ain't trying to be in here more than I already have to. After being locked in here and caged like an animal for four and a half years, a nigga was ready to walk outside and smell the fresh air.

Today was the day that I'd be walking out of this muthafucka with my freedom! This was the first and last time that I would ever be stepping back into this bitch. I was so ready to go that I didn't pack shit but the letters, pictures that my baby sis sent me over the years, and my commissary check. The government could kiss my ass if they thought I was just going to leave a ten-thousand-dollar commissary check here. My roomie could have all my shit. I didn't want to take home anything that reminded me of this muthafuckin' place.

My heart was beating loudly and my blood was rushing through my veins as the reality of me finally walking up out of this hellhole set in. The thought of finally getting out was bittersweet for a nigga like me.

It was sweet because I would finally be getting my ass far away from this son of a bitch, but bitter because I knew for a fact that Aris wouldn't be waiting for me with open arms the moment I walked out of these prison doors. Aris… damn, that's my baby right there and I hate it that I fucked up with her. I still couldn't believe she left a nigga hanging like that. To say that I was hurt behind Aris' actions would be putting it very lightly. I was pissed, confused, but most of all, I was hurt. I understand why she did what she did, but at the same time I thought that we were better than that. Before messing around on a more personal, intimate level, we were best friends before anything else and that shit hurts. I tried everything in my power to reach out to Aris and try to explain what happened. But she wasn't trying to hear nothing that I had to say.

I tried writing letters but each letter that I wrote was returned back to me unopened. I tried calling on three-way, but whenever she would hear my voice, she would quickly hang up the phone. I even went as far as convincing Kamron to trick her into coming to see me. Aris would believe that he was coming up here to see a friend, but once those doors opened and I stepped out she took off running. She was so pissed at Kam for tricking her that she stopped talking to him for a couple of months. And y'all know Kam was pissed at my ass as well. I tried everything that I could while being behind bars, but now that I was getting out, I was going to do everything in my power to get her to listen to me. Even if I had to knock her little ass out with some chloroform and kidnap her ass, just so that she could listen to what I had to say, I would do it.

That shit that happened with Ebony's ass was not what it seemed. And she would know if she would just sit the fuck down and listen to me. Speaking of Ebony, as soon as I see her I'm wrapping my hands around her throat and choking that hoe. Usually, I would never condone any man putting their hands on a female, but fuck that! That bitch Ebony set me up and trapped me with a baby. I still couldn't believe it. I was doing my first year up here when she told me that bullshit. I wanted to hop over the table and smack that little smirk on her face off when she opened her mouth and said it. Supposedly, I have a son with her evil, conniving ass. I was hotter than fish grease when she named her son after me.

Ebony is looser than a ran through prostitute in her late fifties, still trying to suck dick for a quick dollar. Her ass would fuck anything or anyone all in the name of the dollar. For all I know, that baby could be Uncle Sam's baby, but she swore up and down that he was mine. So far she hasn't brought the baby up here to see me yet. But she has sent me pictures of him. I can't tell if he's my son or not. He looks just like Ebony's ass. I know one thing is for certain and two things is for sure, I'm not claiming full responsibility of a child that I'm not sure is even mine until those blood results comes back. She better hope and pray that RJ is mine. If he is then I'm going to man up and take care of mine. But if he isn't… I swear I'm going to make that bitch disappear from the face of this Earth.

"Time to go, Clarkson! Come on. Grab your things and let's go. You're finally out of here," one of the correctional officers said as she unlocked the cell door and opened it for me.

"About fucking time," I snapped harshly. I was damn ready to get out of this muthafucka.

I looked at my celly, shook hands with him, and gave him a brotherly hug before leaving out. I looked up at thirsty ass Officer Givens smiling at me and flashing all thirty twos. You would've think from by how hard she was smiling that it was her being released and not me. I followed her out and to the room where they would be processing me and handing me the things that I came up in here with.

"Now that you're about to be a free man, why don't we get together and hang out sometimes," Givens whispered in my ear as she discreetly grabbed my mans through my Ralph Lauren Polo blue denim jeans and gave it a squeeze.

All I could do was chuckle and shake my head at her desperate ass. Ever since I stepped foot up in this bitch, her ass and a few other CO's had been trying to get me to bend they ass over and drop dick in them, but I wasn't going to. I didn't come up in here to slide into some pork pussy. All I wanted to do was finish my time and get the fuck up out of here.

"I'm sorry ma, but I'm not interested in you. I thought you would have been gotten the hint when you continued to try to throw the pussy at me and I wasn't catching. I don't want you or any ran through female that works in this bitch. Only bitch that's worthy of my dick is my wife who's, by the way, patiently waiting for Daddy to come home. I don't stick my dick in hoes. Now if it was me six years ago, then I wouldn't mind busting this nut all over your face and making your mammy lick it off, but as you can see I'm a change man," I spat harshly and with an arrogant smirk.

Givens' face turned all the way red and her breathing picked up. I guess she was mad since she was now pushing my ass. "Hurry up and move it Clarkson, before I take you back to your cell," she spat.

"Bitch you wish," I said laughing, further pissing her off. I stepped into the processing room and waited damn near three hours until they finally gave me my walking papers. The whole time I was waiting, Givens was glaring at me. I flipped her ass off, grabbed my commissary check, and stuffed it into the front of my pants pocket.

"I'm not worried! You will be back, Clarkson!" she spat at my departing back.

I chunked up the deuces at her ass. "Bitch, suck my dick and swallow these hollow tips!"

As soon as I stepped out of those prison gates, I inhaled a deep breath of fresh air and slowly exhaled it out. A nigga was finally free! I was so fucking happy that I bust out doing the crip walk and hitting the Dougie. Finally, I had my freedom!

I looked up in just enough time to see an all-black 2016 Porsche Cayenne truck pull up and stop in front of me. I stopped my ceremonial dance and mugged the car up and down. It pissed me off because I couldn't see who was sitting behind the tinted windows. I wasn't in for muthafuckas just pulling up on me and I didn't know who the fuck they are. In the hood that shit only meant one thing. Jail had made a nigga paranoid like a muthafucka. I had to always be on my guard in this bitch. There will always be a jealous fucka stalking you from the shadows, patiently waiting for you to slip up so that you can get fucked up. I'd made a lot of enemies behind these walls. Ain't no telling who this muthafucka was.

I was standing there mugging the car and studying it like it was an SAT test when all of a sudden the driver's side door rolled down, and Kamron climbed halfway out of it.

"Nigga, quit looking like you scared to move all because of a car stopping," he laughed.

The passenger side window rolled down. "I see jail done made my nigga soft! It's okay you can breathe, my nigga. It's just us," Landon added laughing.

I breathed a sigh of release. Thank God it was just these fools.

"My niggas!" I yelled out with my arms wide open. Kam threw the truck into park as Landon opened the passenger door and stepped out.

"What the fuck is up, my nigga?" Landon smiled as we slapped hands and gave each other dap. Kam got out of the car and followed suit, pulling me into a brotherly hug.

"I see this muthafucka went to jail and just buff up on a nigga, huhn? Looking like the super Incredible Hulk and shit," Kam joked, pushing me.

"This corny ass nigga," I said to Landon, laughing and punching Kam in the arm.

"Shid, I ain't had nothing but time in that muthafucka. Pumping iron is way better than just sitting there and staring at the same ugly muthafuckas all damn day long. I appreciate y'all niggas holding me down through my bid. Kam, I appreciate the outfit and the shoes. Lord, knows that the shit I went in with is past outdated."

Landon and Kam started laughing. "You know it's all good, bro. I know you would do the same thing for me if the shoe was on the other foot, so don't even trip off of it."

"Yea, yea, yea. Enough with the chit chatting. We can do that shit on the road. Let's get the fuck up out of here before they decide to arrest all of our asses," Landon laughed, me and Kam joined him soon after. That would make their day.

Kam climbed back into the driver's seat, Landon hopped in the back and I climbed into the passenger's seat. The interior was a soft butter cream with black lining. The seats were so fucking soft a nigga melted in them. As soon as I had on my seatbelt, Kam tossed the gears into drive and burnt rubber.

"So what you about to do now that you free, my nigga?" Landon asked me from the backseat.

"The same shit I was doing before they tossed my black ass in a cage like an animal. Get this money."

"I know that's wassup," Kamron said, nodding his head in agreement.

"But first, I'mma lay low for a few days. Catch up with Ebony's hoe ass and see this shit about my supposed son and then I'mma try to catch up with the wife and get her to listen to a nigga for once. It's been damn near five years and not once has her ass sent a letter to at least see if a nigga was still breathing."

"Yea, that was cold-blooded shit right there."

"But, can you even blame sis?" Landon quipped.

I sighed while rubbing my fingers through my curly hair. That's the same question I have been asking myself ever since I was tossed in the joint. I won't put all the blame on Aris for leaving a nigga to rot behind those bars just based off on what she walked in on and saw. But at the same time, I do blame her for being hardheaded and not listening to me. If she would've just listened, then all of this shit could have been avoided. I would still have my girl and shit still would've been the same before I left.

"I don't, but at the same time, a part of me does."

Instead of responding, Landon and Kam just nodded their heads up and down. A comfortable silence filled the car and I was left deep in my own thoughts. Besides me, Kam and Lay knows the whole truth about what the hell happened that night. I sat the both of them down and explained everything. At first it was hard as fuck to get them to listen to me, because they were trying to tear my head off my shoulders. Both Landon and Kamron was ready to box a nigga right there in the visiting room in front of all of the CO's. I can still remember the way their faces were tightened with anger as they mugged me up and down. I was snatched out of my thoughts at the smell of marijuana invading my senses. A nigga had been drug free for damn near five years now, but the crave instantly came back the moment I smelled that shit. That shit was so strong a nigga was getting a contact just from smelling it.

"Nigga, the fuck is that shit?" I asked, turning in my seat and looking back at Landon lifting out of his seats and patting his pockets for a lighter with a blunt hanging from the corner of his mouth. After finding one, he flickered it and put the red burning flame to the tip.

Landon fell out laughing as he took a hard pull from the weed and then started blowing smoke rings in the air.

"Girl Scout Cookies," he answered, leaning forward in his seat and passing the blunt off to me. I hurried up and grabbed the blunt out of his hand with no hesitation. Putting the tip to my mouth, I inhaled a hard puff, held it in my lungs for a few seconds, covered my nose with my hand then exhaled slowly through my nose. I was instantly thrown into a coughing fit. Me coughing had Landon and Kamron bugging the fuck up. Meanwhile my fucking lungs and throat were feeling like someone was brewing a fire in the pit of my shit.

"Shit! Nigga, this some good shit! Do you have some Thin Mints, my nigga?" I cracked, making them laugh harder. Landon was in the back choking on his own spit, and Kamron was laughing so hard the nigga started swerving from lane to lane. Thank God it wasn't that many cars out on the road, or all of us would've been on the twelve o'clock news.

I was in the middle of taking another pull from the L when Kam's rude ass tried to snap on me.

"Damn nigga, quit hogging all of the weed and let somebody else hit it."

I cocked my head to the side and through tiny slits, I looked at this yellow ass nigga like he had magically sprouted extra heads and shit from talking to me the way he did.

"Nigga was it you that just finished doing a four and a half year bid? Did your ass had to eat, sleep, shower, and shit around other niggas who nine times out of ten was staring at yo' fresh meat ass like you was the next five course meal until you had to beat they ass for not knowing that they had a problem with their eyes? Nah bruh, I don't think yo' name is Roman Cayden Clarkson. Nigga, I ain't had a nice home cooked meal, a hot, decent bath, pussy to slid up in, my own privacy, nor a nice, warm soft bed to sleep in four years' nigga, while yo' horse mouth ass had all of this to come home to! Damn, a nigga just got his walking papers, let me enjoy my freedom a little bit longer before I go back for going upside of your big watermelon head ass," I snapped back while mugging Kamron with a frown. Landon was in tears by the time I finished my little rant and Kamron was mad as a bitch, but I didn't give a fuck.

I took one last pull from the blunt before finally passing it over to Kamron's big cry baby ass. He snatched the blunt from me, mumbled something under his breath, and finally hit before putting the blunt into rotation.

We were on the road for a half an hour when I picked up another's muthafucka's cologne mixed with the scent of weed. Turning in my seat, I looked behind my seat at this ole black muthafucka who was just staring at me with a blank expression on his face. I had a surprised expression on mine. Nigga was so damn quiet that I wouldn't have ever noticed him sitting there if I didn't smell his cheap ass cologne.

"Yo, who the fuck is this nigga?" I asked. I was directing my question to Kam and Landon but kept my eyes on dude.

"Oh shit, my bad bruh. This is my homeboy from Dallas Quamir. Q this is Mona's brother Rome. Rome this is Q," Landon introduced us.

"Wassup, bruh. I heard a lot about you from Lay and Kam. It's nice to finally meet the fourth musketeer," Q greeted, sticking his hand out waiting for me to bump his fist.

*The forth?! This nigga got me fucked up.*

I looked up at this nigga's face, then back down to his hand, and stared at the muthafucka like it was contagious or some shit. After leaving him hanging for a little longer, I hit him with a simple head nod and turned around in my seat. I was being rude and petty as fuck, but I didn't care.

Q still had his fist out looking like a complete dumb ass for a few seconds longer before he retracted it. I could tell ole boy was pissed. So what? Fuck that nigga. He was they friend, not mine. I didn't know this nigga from a can of paint, therefore I wouldn't be fucking around with dude like that. I'm like Drake. No New Friends, Please.

I politely reclined my seat back as far as I could and kicked my feet up on the dashboard. It was a long ass ride back to the city and my ass was about to get comfortable. The King is back home, so it's time for these muthafuckas to bow the fuck down.

***

After being on the road for almost three hours, we finally made it back to the city. My city. Miami baby. Just being back home in my city had my blood rushing. It felt good as fuck to be home. For most of the time during the ride back, the car was quiet besides the music the radio playing low in the background. Every now and then, I would glance back at fuck boy sitting in the back seat staring at me with his face tighter than a bitch with Botox. Whenever our eyes would meet, I would grin arrogantly at him pissing him off even more. That nigga had smoke coming from his ears he was so fucking pissed off. Through the whole drive I didn't ask any questions, hell I thought we were on our way to the last address I had on the girls. That was until we turned down this street that only had one house on the street. Kam went down to the house sitting on the corner and pulled the truck into the driveway. I slowly climbed out of the truck and looked up at the mansion in awe. It was beautiful. The mansion sat on six acres of beautiful, well-manicured land with a jaw-dropping oceanfront view.

"Damn, this muthafucka is bad," I said, letting out a whistle.

"I know, but you should see my real house," Kamron said smirking and shit.

I cocked my head to the side and looked at Kamron. "This ain't you?"

Kamron and Landon chuckled. "Nah bruh. This is the party house. The crib muthafuckas come to where they want to get away from everybody and just want peace and quiet," Landon informed me.

I didn't say anything or ask any more questions as we walked up the paved driveway and into the house. As soon as I stepped into the foyer, my nose was insulted by the smell of somebody's good home cooking. I know that smell from anywhere. I couldn't help the grin that crossed my face. I turned around and looked back at Kamron and Landon and noticed them smiling at me with mischievous grins.

"Ma here?" I asked them.

Kamron just stood there and crossed his arms across his board chest. "Why don't you go in the kitchen and see."

That was all I needed to hear before I took off jogging towards the kitchen. As soon as I pushed open the kitchen's double doors I saw her. My beautiful mother, Carmen Clarkson, was standing in front of the stove with her back towards me, stirring a large pot of collard greens. Now, normally I'm not the sentimental or emotionally type of guy, but seeing my mother standing there after all these years was bringing tears to a nigga's eyes.

I hadn't seen my mother since I was eighteen years old. It seemed like my life completely changed once me and Kam turned eighteen. The year I turned eighteen was the year Kaseem and my pops reluctantly handed the family's empire over to us to run. That was also the year our dads had to leave the States and never come back. Back then mine and Kam's pops were wanted by every government agency in America. To avoid going to jail and serving several life sentences and possibly the death penalty, they packed up and moved to Columbia with my pop's friend/connect, the most ruthless nigga to ever do the game dirty and live to tell it, Airion Rivera Sr. Our dads thought it was best for us to stay behind in the States and try to live the life opposite of theirs. They knew the risk it could have been taking us along and wanted differently for us. As you can see, their dreams of wanting us to stay away from the game and becoming something different were just that… dreams.

Although we had money that could let us live luxurious for many generations to come, Kam and I still wanted to make our own shit. Hustling was just in our blood. We were born to do this shit. And since our fathers were against us hustling, me and Kam copped from the Jamaicans and put together our own little squad, selling the best marijuana around. We weren't seeing the same numbers like my dad was with cocaine, but we were still making a killing off of selling marijuana, pills, and syrup. I mean our weed was so muthafuckin' good that you had to get high to bring yo' last high down.

We flew under our dads' radar for about two years before they miraculously found out about our little hustle. It still bothers me to this day because I thought we were careful enough not to be seen much. Boy, me and Kam thought they were going to chew us up then spit us out to the sharks when they found out. But surprisingly, they decided to take us under their wings and help us make a name for ourselves.

I know y'all probably thinking that just because we were the sons of the greatest to ever do it that everything was just handed down to us. Well your assumption is wrong. Just because we were the sons of kingpins, we didn't get treated any differently than the rest. We literally had to start from the bottom and work our way up the scale. We went from standing on the corner putting in long hours through the night to owning our own little team and moving more keys, then finally taking over our dads' operation when they finally retired. We were our dads' protégés. Flipping and moving weight faster than anyone on the squad. A lot of muthafuckas didn't like it, but after making a few examples out of a few people, we got the loyalty and respect that we earned by ourselves and without our fathers' help. When my dad fled to Columbia, my mom went right along with him. And although our parents moved to another country, whenever we needed anything or were in any kind of trouble, Kaseem Miller and Tyreek Morgan wouldn't hesitate to sneak back into the States and make the streets bleed.

Quietly, I walked up behind my mother and wrapped my arms around her slim waist.

"Damn, girl you got it smelling good in here!" I said, disguising my voice.

I felt my mother's body tense up in my arms and heat radiating off of her body she was so mad. She politely turned the stove down and turned around ready to go the fuck off.

"Negro, I know you just can't possibly think that yo' balls are that big for you to come and wrap—," she cut her sentence short when she noticed that it was me standing there. "Aaaaahhhhhhh!" she screamed so loud that my ears were ringing. "My baby! Oh my God my baby!" she screamed out as she jumped in my arms and wrapped her arms around my neck, holding me tightly. "Thank you Lord, my baby is finally home!" By now she was in a full-blown cry.

I wrapped my arms around her waist and hugged her as if I was still that little boy growing up following my mother around like her second shadow. Her body was so soft and warm that I couldn't help but to relax in her presence. I felt like a little kid all over again.

"Ma, I love you and all and I missed you like something terrible, but damn could you please loosen up on a nigga? You cutting a nigga's oxygen off," I joked making her laugh.

She did what I asked and pulled away a little bit, but not before slapping me in the arm. "Boy watch yo' mouth around me."

"Damn, ma. That shit hurts," I whined with my bottom lip poked out.

*SMACK!*

"Boy do not play with me. You ain't too old to get an ass whopping," she warned me sternly.

I smiled and rubbed my arm where she'd hit me. For ma to be so damn little, her punches hurts like a bitch. I remember growing up how she would whoop my daddy's ass just for coming home late and not answering any of her calls or text messages. Those hands I do not want. I chose not to respond because nine times out of ten, a cuss word was bound to slide out. I can't help it, sometimes I got a foul ass mouth.

"Ma! What's the matter? I heard you screaming and… Oh my God, Roman!" Mona screamed as she ran and jumped in my arms, wrapping her arms around my neck and her legs around my waist, damn near knocking me off of my feet. I had to grip her waist and jump shifting her body in my arms before she fell on her ass. I heard whimpering, and I knew right then and there she was crying. I laughed and hugged my baby sis just as tightly as she was hugging me. I let her cry on my shoulder and get herself together a little longer before I slowly pulled away and looked down into her eyes.

"I know this ain't my baby sis standing up here looking grown as hell. Damn, where did the time go? I guess it's time to for me to go home and start dusting off my guns," I said, but was only half-joking with her.

"Boy whatever," Mona laughed and at the same time playfully rolled her eyes at me. She could laugh all she wanted to, but I was serious as fuck. Baby sis didn't look anything like she was looking now a few years ago. Time had really changed my baby.

"Oh my God, Roman! I thought you had three more years to do. What happened? How did you get out? When the hell did you get out? Why didn't you tell me?! You didn't pull an El Chapo, did you?" she asked me, firing each question off after the other her last question came off serious ass fuck. Everyone standing in the kitchen laughed at Mona's question about me escaping prison. Leave it up to her ass to think of some shit like that.

"First off, no I did not escape from jail. I got out early on good behavior. They released my black ass today and I didn't tell anyone because I wanted it to be a surprise. The only people who knew I was being released today are the same muthafuckas who picked my ass up," I explained and nodding my head towards Kam and Landon.

"Should've known," Mona mumbled, rolling her eyes at them. "They sneaky asses ran off too damn quick this morning, leaving us women to cook everything and Kells on the grill. I wanted to go," she said with a cute pout.

"Children of mine, you do know that I am still standing here right?" Ma asked with her hands on her wide hips.

"Sorry ma," Mona and I said at the same time. Momma hated it whenever anyone cussed around her. Even daddy. She wouldn't hesitate to pop somebody in the mouth for cussing, but let her do it and she would always use the excuse of her being grown. Like we still some little ass kids.

"Speaking of Kells, where in the hell did her and Aris take their asses off to?" Kamron asked Mona after opening the lid to Ma's greens and sneaking a taste. Momma caught his ass just in time to slap the fuck out of the back of his head.

"Damn ma," Kamron said, laughing and rubbing the spot momma hit him at.

"Kamron Careem Miller, I'm not going to keep repeating myself about your got dang on mouth! Cuss again and watch I wash yo' mouth with some dish detergent," she snapped.

"Damn. My bad ma, it just slipped out," Kamron said, laughing.

Momma's hand went back to slap him again but Kamron quickly dogged her attack running to the other side of the kitchen laughing.

"I'mma get yo' bright ass, watch," Momma threatened, playfully pointing her finger at Kamron.

"Ooohhhh," Kamron gasped, covering his mouth up with his hands and sounding like a big ass kid getting ready to snitch. "Momma cussed."

"So what, little nigga? I'm grown," Momma said flipping her hair over her shoulders and turning back to her food, making everybody laugh. See, what I told you.

"Honey, I'm home!" Kelly's loud mouthed ass yelled from the foyer.

"Then bring yo' ass in the kitchen!" Kamron yelled out.

Momma quickly cut her eyes over at him and Kamron flashed his boyish smile at her before apologizing again.

I heard two females giggling and the front door slamming shut, followed by the sound of heels clicking against the hard floors. No lie, a nigga's heartrate started speeding up knowing that the love of my life was about to walk into the kitchen with her loud mouthed ass friend. A few seconds passed and finally the kitchen doors opened with Kelly stepping inside first and Aris right after her. Both were laughing and oblivious to the fact that I was standing there.

I couldn't contain the smile that spread across my face as I looked her up and down. A nigga was smiling so damn hard my cheeks were hurting. Her skin seemed to have an everlasting glow to it and the smile on her face made me smile even harder. Those dimples always made a nigga weak in the knees. Damn… Aris looked even better than she did five years ago. I was so speechless that I couldn't do anything but stand there and stare at her. Even dressed in a simple black and white zebra stripped backless long maxi dress that tied around her neck and a pair of black Chanel sandals, she was still breathtaking.

"Yo, party people! Let's get this party started! Queen B has finally made it home! Time to turn up! I got the drinks. Who got the weed?" Kelly shouted excitedly. I couldn't do shit but double over laughing. Out of everybody that I know, Kelly is the only one who loves to get her party on and turn up at any time of the day. Her ass would wake up out of her sleep trying to turn up. She was definitely the turn up queen. It ain't a party 'til her ass walked in and got it started. Me bursting out laughing caught the attention of both her and Aris.

Both Aris' and Kelly's eyes bulged and mouths dropped opened in shock at me standing in the kitchen after being away for so long. They both looked like they had just seen a damn ghost fly by.

Kelly blinked her eyes twice before pinching the bridge of her nose and wiping cold from her eyes.

"Damn, I think that Mary Jane is still fucking with me. I'm hallucinating shit now," she said, making everybody laugh. Even ma burst out laughing which surprised the shit out of me. I was expecting her to go off on Kelly like she did with me and Kam when we cussed.

"Nah sis, you're not hallucinating. It's me," I said folding my arms across my chest with a smirk on my face.

"Brother!" Kelly screeched as she dropped whatever bags she had in her hand onto the floor and rushed over to me to pull me into a hug. "Oh my God, it really is you!" she screamed as she tightened her grip around my waist. I laughed while nodding my head up and down to confirm her answer.

"In flesh and blood, baby."

My gaze went from Kelly to Aris who hadn't moved from her spot by the door. Her face contained so many emotions that it was hard to tell which one she was feeling at the moment. She went from being surprised, to happy, and finally sad. It hurt me like hell to know that I'm the reason that she's not running over towards me, hugging and kissing on me like she would normally do when we were younger. The whole kitchen went into silence and everyone's attention was on me and Aris now. It was so damn quiet that you could hear a fly land and take a shit.

Finally building up the courage, I decided to speak first and break the tension in the room.

"Hey Aris."

She smiled softly and waved at me. "Hey. Welcome home, Rome," she said it so low that I could barely hear her. Just getting her to speak to me and smile a little sent an extra boost of courage through me. I finally released my hold from around Kelly's waist and slowly began to make my way over towards her. I wanted to grab her and kiss her so badly that it was taking everything in me not to run over there and do it. Just when I was in arm's length from her, this nigga Q stepped in front of me grabbed Aris by her chin and planted a wet kiss on her lips. I instantly came to a halt as I looked back and forth between Aris and Quamir's bitch ass.

"Hey baby. I missed you," I heard him say to Aris.

Aris gave his lips one last peck before she turned her attention back onto me with a guilty look on her face. Since the first time since she had been standing there, I noticed the little boy sleeping in her arms and immediately thought the worst. The mixture of hurt, anger, and jealously hit me from nowhere. I felt my blood pressure rise and my heartbeat accelerate. Q turned around to look around and flashed me this cocky ass smirk that I wanted to shoot the fuck off of his face. My fists started balling up at my sides and I was just about to make due on my thoughts when all of a sudden Kamron and Landon both grabbed my shoulders and gave them a squeeze.

"Not here, bruh. Not now," Landon whispered in my ear, squeezing my left shoulder.

"Yea, let's not do this shit in front of ma. You just got out enjoy your freedom a little longer before you end up doing something that's going to send yo' ass back there," Kam whispered in my other ear and squeezed my other shoulder. It was a good thing that they decided to step up and play holy because I had about four little devils sitting on my shoulders trying to convince me to say fuck everything and beat that nigga's ass. I inhaled deeply then exhaled sharply to calm myself down. Once I was calm enough to think for myself I flashed Aris and Q a nasty ass mug before turning on my soles and walking out the back door.

## Chapter Seven

**ARIS**

Coming in from the store and seeing Rome standing in the kitchen looking so goddamn sexy with that sexy ass smirk on his face had me thinking I have done hit my head somewhere and was dreaming at that moment. I wasn't expecting to see him at all. All of the emotions and feelings that I had for him and thought I got rid of a long time ago instantly came back at full force hitting me like a ton of bricks falling from the sky. They say milk is supposed to do the body good but I think hard time in jail does muthafuckin' wonders. Damn, Rome was looking good enough to eat. I instantly became wet on sight. I mean my thong was fucking soaked with my juices and the inside of my thighs were clammy. Rome is the same height as my brother six-foot-two with a dark caramel skin that turns mocha in the summer time, hazel eyes, tatted arms and a body that the Gods perfectly sculpted. Oh my God, the white Givenchy V-neck t-shirt that he had on wasn't doing anything to hid that beautiful body of his. His eyebrows, long eyelashes, chiseled jawline, nose and thick, soft pink lips only added to his sex appeal. And let's not forget that this nigga is bowlegged! Oh my fucking God! To put it in the simplest form, Rome was a walking orgasm!

I was staring at Rome so damn hard that I had quickly forgotten that Q was even standing a couple of feet away from me. It was like the moment our eyes connect everybody else in the room disappeared. It wasn't until Q walked up to me, grabbed my chin and pulled my face into his that I was brought back to reality.

"Bitch, do not make me show my ass in front of everybody. The fuck is you staring at ole boy for when yo' nigga is standing right here? Don't make me have to go upside yo' shit because you being very disrespectful as fuck right now. Do you fucking understand me?" he whispered harshly in my ear before forcing a kiss unto my lips.

Q was gripping my chin so fucking hard that I couldn't even reply to him.

"Hey baby. I missed you," he said putting up a front in front of everybody. I looked at him through slit eyes and he looked back down at me with his pissed off ones. I don't know what the fuck is wrong with this nigga or why he is acting like somebody is going to take me from him but I'm sure am going to check his ass for the stunt he just pulled as soon as we get home. Not to alarm my brother or anyone else that something wrong just happened I went ahead and planted a quick kiss onto Q's lips and at the same biting the shit out of his bottom lip. He flinched but didn't do or say anything.

Ignoring Q's little rant from just a few moments ago I turned my attention back onto Rome. All of a sudden I began to feel guilty like I was caught with my hand in the cookie jar. I had to remind myself that we were no longer together and that Quamir was my man now. Judging by the look on his face, I already knew that Rome was pissed and his feelings were hurt. I kind of expected him to bum rush his ass over here and beat the fuck out of both me and Q's ass but I was surprised as shit when he turned around and stormed out of the back door.

***

It was ten thirty at night and the party was going in full swing like muthafuckas ain't have kids that they needed to get home to. You should've seen how many people were packed in this backyard. What was normally a Sunday dinner that my family and a few close associates of my brother have every once in a while turned into a full blown out welcome home party for Roman. Word got back quick that Rome was finally free and everybody and they momma came to welcome him home. It looked like damn near everybody that ran in my brother's crew and their women came to our convention. It was so many people here that the food me, ma, Mo and Kells slaved in the kitchen all day for was gone before one o'clock. We had to call a food catering place and order large amounts of food just to feed everybody.

So many women where running round dressed in mini dresses that barely covered their ass cheeks, skirts, coochie cutters and bra's for tops that I suddenly felt like I overdressed and out of my own element. Even dressed in an all-white high waist swim suit bottoms and bikini top from the Robyn Lawley collection with a white mesh tunic dress and white Michael Kors flip flops I still felt overdressed.

After seeing Rome tonight, I was so ready to go home. I didn't even feel like being here anymore. Seeing him was too much for me, hence the fact that I was still hurting from catching him with a bitch that I hated with a passion together. To this day I'm still healing from the pain. And then to find out that this bitch might had his first born cut me deeply. That was like adding salt to the wound. I have always pictured myself having his babies, but this bum dusty bitch beat me to it. Seeing and being in the same space as Rome had so many unwanted feelings souring through me. I was going to leave when Roman's mother, Carmen, left earlier to go back to her hotel but after being threatened by both Mona and Kells, I had no choice but to stay and suffer this torture alone.

I was sitting on the other side of the pool with my girls, the whole time staring at Rome holding a conversation with the thirsty ass broads surrounding him. I couldn't help but feel jealousy and anger overcome me. I know I shouldn't be in my box about Rome talking to other women, but I couldn't help it. He was mine first. I was so fucking pissed that my heart was beating wildly in my chest. I had the urge to walk my ass over there and beat every fucking bitch down that was flashing all thirty-two at my man. All day long we'd been stealing glances at each other and turned our heads when we thought that the other was looking. I caught him staring one time too many and whenever our eyes would connect, he would smirk and lick his thick lips at me, getting me all hot and bothered. Just seeing him rubbing this bitch's bare thigh had me ready to go the fuck off.

"Aris… heelllooo, earth to Aris! I know this bitch hears me? Ari!" Mona said, snapping her fingers in my face breaking me from my trance.

"Huhn?" I said, finally tearing my attention away from Rome and towards them.

"What the fuck is wrong with you?" Kelly asked me, her and Mona giggling.

"Nothing," I spat out, taking a sip from the same strawberry margarita that I have been sipping on for the last two hours. I didn't try to come off so nasty, but I was deeply in my feelings.

"Bitch, please," Kelly said laughing.

"We see you over there watching and clocking Roman's every move," Mona added, laughing right along with Kelly.

I sucked my teeth and rolled my eyes at them. "Bitch, please! Why would I be worrying about what Rome is doing when I got a man?"

Mona and Kelly gave each other a knowing look before looking over my way with their lips tooted to the side as if to say 'bitch, really'?

"Who the fuck does she think she tryna run game on?" Mona asked Kelly.

"I have no fucking idea, but I know for a fact that she can't be tryna run game on us. We know that heffa better than she knows her damn self," Kelly replied. They were actually carrying on a conversation about me like I wasn't sitting right here.

"Fuck what you tryna say we know you better than that. You still love him, don't you?" Kelly quipped with a wide grin.

"No. I have love for him because he was my first at everything but I'm no longer in love with him," I said, lying through my teeth. Was I still in love with Rome? If you were to ask me that question before seeing him today, then I would've honestly answered no, but after seeing him again after so many years have passed, I realized that my feelings for Rome has never went away.

"My heart has a new occupant and that occupant is no longer Rome. I'm in love with Quamir. Me and Rome's ship sailed a long time ago and is never to return to land. Quamir has my heart now," I said unsure of my feelings my damn self. I loved Q no doubt, but my feelings for Rome would always overpower the feelings I have for Quamir. But I would never tell them that.

"Bullshit," Mona and Kelly said at the same time.

My head quickly snapped up as I looked them in the face.

"C'mon Ari, it's us you talking to. Yea, you love Q, but Q is not my brother. We peeped how you was looking at Rome earlier today in the kitchen. Those feelings that you tried so desperately to get rid of over the years while he was away came rushing back the very moment you guys' eyes connected. Hell, everybody in the kitchen had peeped that shit."

"Q most definitely peeped game. That's why his ass has been walking around here with a damn attitude all day today and acting insecure as hell. That nigga became your second shadow," Kelly said laughing.

I swear I tried stopping my eyes from rolling and my face from frowning when the mentioned Q's behavior today, but ended up failing miserably. That's another thing. Me and Quamir had been arguing nonstop all damn day today over Rome. We would go from arguing about Roman and my past to him suddenly wanting to start arguing about my swimsuit. The same kind of swimsuit that I wore on any other given day.

For most of the day, he had been on me like white on rice. If I was to get up to go to the bathroom, then Q would stop everything and escort me to the bathroom. A bitch couldn't even get up and make her own plate. He made it for me. I was so aggravated and annoyed with him being all up under me that I was four seconds away from snapping on his ass. If it wasn't for my brother dragging his ass over to the table to play Spades earlier, then he would probably still be here sitting underneath me like I needed a babysitter.

"Ugh… can we please stop talking about both Rome's and Quamir's ass. I'm getting a headache," I said, finishing up my the last of my margarita. I heard the both of them snickering behind me and chose not to say anything. "I'mma go grab another margarita from the freezer. Y'all need something?" I asked looking back and forth between Mona and Kelly.

"No," they both answered at the same time.

I nodded my head and took off into the kitchen. Unlike outside, the inside of the house was much quieter. I was bending over reaching down in the freezer, when all of a sudden I felt somebody standing in the kitchen with me. Closing the freezer, I turned around to see Roman standing near the kitchen island, staring at me with his arms folded across his chest and a small smirk on his face.

"Why did you move? I was enjoying the show."

I sucked my teeth and rolled my eyes at him in irritation. I don't know why seeing him got me both irritated and turned the fuck on at the same time, but I was. I ignored him, grabbed my margarita, and was on my way out the back door when Rome gently grabbed my arm and stopped me.

I threw my hands up shrugging his hold on me off and turned once more to continue my walk outside, when once again I was snatched back by my arm.

"What the fuck do you want?" I snapped while snatching my arm out of his hold.

"Can we talk?" he asked me, ignoring my attitude. The arrogant smirk he just had on his face was gone and his tone was very serious and thick with frustration.

"I don't think I have anything left to say to yo' ass."

"Well I do. And your ass is going to listen to me whether you like it or not. I've been tryin' for years to get this shit off of my chest and you avoided me each fucking time. Now that I'm out, yo' ass no longer have the choice to decide," he said, grabbing me by the elbow and forcefully dragging me upstairs and into one of the guest bedrooms. Once inside, he closed the door behind him, locked it, and stood in front of it to keep me from leaving.

I let out a loud dramatic sigh filled with irritation and stood in the middle of the floor with my arms folded under my breasts. Rome just stood there and said nothing as he continued staring me down. I waited for a few minutes to give him enough time to gather his thoughts, but after five minutes of silence and still nothing, I was beyond annoyed with his presence.

"Oh my God! Any time before Christmas!" I exclaimed, throwing my hands up in the air with annoyance. "You dragged me all the way in here to talk but still nothing yet has been said. You wanted to talk, so talk!" I said with my voice going up in a higher octave and cracking with emotion. All day long, I'd been fighting internally with myself to keep my emotions in check and so far I'd been doing a damn good job keeping everything in order. But after being locked in this room with the man who had caused me so much hurt and so much pain in the past, the tables had been turned and I was quickly losing control. I didn't want to show any emotion in front of Rome, but my heart was betraying me like always.

I was breathing hard and my throat was burning with raw emotion. I felt the tears gathering up in the corners of my eyes but willed myself not to cry. It took me a few minutes to calm down, but after doing a few breathing exercises I was able to calm my breathing and heartrate down. I looked up and saw the guilt and hurt in his eyes. It felt good to know that I wasn't the only one hurting. I inhaled one more deep breath and cleared my throat.

"I'm listening, Rome. Say what you have to say so I can close this chapter and continue on with my life. You want me to listen?" I stood in front of him and folded my arms across my chest. "You got my undivided attention. Talk."

Rome sighed as he ran his hand over his head then down his face in a frustrated manner. "First off, I wanna say that I'm sorry. I'm so sorry for all the pain, all the tears, and all the heartache that I caused you for all of these years. But I never thought that you would leave a nigga hanging like that. Especially when I know that we are better than that," he paused for a second to shoot me a very hurtful look before he continued on with what he was saying. "I needed you. I needed you, the one woman who is able to keep my mind clear and calm down the beast that's inside a nigga, but you left me. I want to be mad at you. Scream at you and blame you for leaving me there to rot, but I can't. Especially when I'm the one who caused you so much pain. So from the very bottom of my heart, I apologize," he said genuinely.

I could tell by the look on his face that his words were coming straight from the heart and that he meant it. Roman took a step closer towards me, getting all in my personal space. I didn't want him to see the tears that began to well up in my eyes, so I turned my head and dropped my chin into my chest. I was so scared to look him in the eyes. Because I knew the moment I did, the hard front that I'd been putting on all of these years would immediately crash and all of my emotions would come out.

I felt Rome reach out and pull back a strand of my hair and tuck it behind my ear.

"I loved you, Ari. Hell, I still am deeply in love with you, just as I was all of those years ago. I love you with all my heart and since the day you left, my life has been nothing but sad and gloomy. I have a void in my heart that can't be filled by nobody but you. I can't live without you, girl. You are my rib, my heart, my soulmate, the woman God made just for me. I love you more than anything in the world and would do whatever it takes for you to be mine again. If I could go back in time and change shit, then you know I would, Ari. I hate seeing you cry. You know that I would kill anyone who would try to hurt or bring any harm to you. And it's fucking with me to see you like this knowing I'm the reason behind it."

By now, the front that I tried so hard putting up instantly came crashing down and I was in a full-blown, ugly cry. I mean my face was fully wet with tears, snot was coming out of my nose and I was doing the hiccup cry.

"Why?" I whispered in an inaudible tone. I cleared my throat and tried again. "If you love me so much, then why did you do it?" I asked him, this time looking him dead in his eyes so that he could see just how hurt I still was behind his actions. "Why did you do it, Roman? You promised me when we made it official that you would never do anything to break my heart. You swore up to God and in front of my father that you would protect me, love me, and cherish me until the day you breathed in your last breath, yet you still cheated on me. Not only did you cheat on me, but you did it with somebody who I hate with a passion, your ex! If it was anybody else, then maybe I could get over the pain, but it was your ex! A bitch you had history with! You knew sleeping with her was going to break me, yet you did it anyway. I made sure I did everything in my power to make you happy. I cooked, cleaned, did laundry, made sure the house stayed clean and made sure you never left the house with a heavy nut sack, yet I still got cheated on. Not only did you cheat on me but you made a baby on me as well? Why did you do it, Rome? Was I not enough for you? Huhn? Answer me!" When he didn't respond, I spazzed out.

"I swear I fucking hate you! I hate you, Roman!" I screamed as I ran up on him and repeatedly hit him in the chest. Rome just stood there for a minute with apologetic eyes, letting me take my anger out on him. After a couple more hits to his chest, he grabbed my arms, pinned them at my sides and pulled me into a bear hug.

"Let me the fuck go, Roman!" I screamed out. By now, my face was wet with a mixture of snot and tears. Rome continued to ignore me, holding me tighter in his arms while whispering in my ear how sorry he was. My legs ended up giving out on me and I fell to the floor with Rome. I tried one more time to get myself free from his embrace, but it was pointless. I had no energy in me, none whatsoever. All the pain was hitting me hard as hell at once. I was hurting so much I began to hyperventilate. Rome tightened his grip around me and held me as I cried like a baby. He was rubbing small circles in my back and apologizing. After crying for what seemed like forever, I was exhausted. I literally had no energy left in me.

"I am truly sorry baby, but that shit that happened with Ebony was not what it looked like. That bitch set me up and trapped me with a baby," he spat heatedly.

"Rome, I don't car–," I started to say, but was cut off.

"Nah. You need to hear this shit, Aris. Unless I get this shit off of my chest, I won't be able to move on."

I sighed and didn't say anything else.

"Aris, you should know that I would never do anything to intentionally cause you any harm. I would never cheat on you willingly. I took everything that I vowed up to God and in front of you father seriously. My word is bond, ma. I never been the type of nigga to lie. I always kept it one hunnid and you know that," he said seriously, staring me in the eyes. By now my curiosity was piqued. *What does he mean that would never cheat on me willingly?* I asked myself.

"That night that all of that shit happened I was mad as fuck. I was upset because the first thing I see when I stepped in the club is my wife dressed up as if she was some hoe grinding her ass all up on her ex nigga. Pissed was an understatement at how I was feeling at that moment. I was ready to body the both of you muthafuckas, real talk. I already fucked up ole boy and was trying to my hardest to keep from putting my hands on you, but you continued pissing me off by not dropping the fucking subject. So to avoid me doing or saying some shit that I would regret later on, I dropped you off at home and went back to mine in attempt to calm myself down.

"You know how my temper is and with the way I was feeling that night, I was ready to jump in my car and kill this nigga whole fucking family. I began tossing drinks back like I was drinking water and before I knew it I was slopped. Somebody knocked on my door and me thinking it was you, I snatched it open without looking through the peephole. I had no idea it was Ebony's ass until she came barging in. She tried to get me to talk to her, begging me to take her back, but as I told her I didn't want anything to do with her ass. She tried kissing me and I pushed her ass back, making her hit her head against one of the end tables. Although I'm in the streets, I'm no heartless nigga and instantly felt bad. Her head was bleeding so I had her sit down while I went into the bathroom to retrieve the first aid kit. I came back into the living room and cleaned up her wound making sure she didn't need any stitches. When I was finished I told her ass that she had to go."

"After much arguing, I dragged her outside and slammed the door in her face. I was still pissed off and my only goal for the night was to drink until I fell unconscious. There was a brand new bottle of Henny sitting on the coffee table that I don't remember sitting there. I wasn't thinking at all so I popped it open and took the shit to the head. A few minutes later I started to get woozy and everything went black. When I finally came to, Ebony was sitting on top of me, riding me like a jockey in a horse race and you were standing there with tears streaming down your face. I tried to get up and stop you from running out, but because I was so drunk I tripped over my own two feet. That didn't stop me from trying to get to you, though. I hurried and threw something on and jumped in my car. I was breaking every traffic law rushing to get to you to explained the shit that had happened. By the time I noticed the police sitting off to the side in an empty parking lot with their lights off, I had already sped past them. That was the night that I lost both you and my freedom, all because of a bitch that spiked my drink and trapped me with a baby that I'm not even sure is mine."

I looked at him in disbelief. Not because of the story he told me, but because that was just some shit that I could see Ebony's desperate ass doing. When me and Roman got together, she tried to do everything in her power to break us up and get Roman to be with her, but of course he chose to be with me. After hearing his side of the story, I felt a little better knowing what happened but I also felt bad as hell. I practically gave him my ass to kiss and let him rot in jail. All because I assumed that he cheated on me willingly when the whole time Ebony's sneaky ass had something to do with it. I felt terrible but it was already too late to feel sorry. As I told Kelly and Mona, our ship had sailed a long time ago and I was now in a relationship with Q. I sighed and shrugged my shoulders.

"Whatever, Roman. I am honestly too exhausted to give a fuck. That is all in the past and I'm truly over it. I moved on with Quamir. He is who I love now and want to be with," I said feeling as if I was trying to convince myself more than I was trying to convince Roman.

I felt Rome tense up the moment I let Q's name roll off of my tongue. I could feel the anger bouncing off of him and for the first time in a long ass time I was scared to look him in the face. Rome had an unpredictable temper. I looked up and he was biting his inner cheek in anger and his cognac-colored eyes were dark.

"Yea ok," he scuffed. "I let that nigga borrowed my spot while I was away because I know how you hate being alone. I ain't never the type to break up a 'happy home' so I'mma be a real nigga and wait until you come back to your damn senses. You know that with me is where you belong. I peeped the way you've been staring at me all day today. I see the love that you still have for me in your eyes. Your eyes will always be the stairway to your soul, Aris. You claim that you love him and all but you know that he will never have your heart the way I had it. Hell, I still have ownership over that muthafucka. I'm the only muthafucka that can make that bitch beat the way it does. He has you for now but now that daddy's home, his time is almost up," he said in a matter of fact tone getting off of the floor.

I just sat there looking up at him dumbfounded. Exactly what right did he have to come into my life and make executive decisions like that? He doesn't! And if he honestly thinks that I'm going to leave Q for something we had over five years ago, then he was honestly mistaken.

"I think you should hurry up and get downstairs before yo' man comes up here searching for you. I don't know how well he will take it seeing us together alone."

I took my time climbing up to my feet and dusting my ass off. After wiping my eyes for any evidence of me crying, I slowly walked passed Rome with my head held high. As soon as I walked past him, he slapped me hard on the ass. Rome then wrapped his arms around my waist and placed his head at the crook of my neck inhaling my scent and placing soft tantalizing kisses behind my ear. The feeling of his strong arms around me and his chest against my back had my heart beating fast. I missed him like something terrible, but I wouldn't dare admit it. I felt his breath on the spot behind my ear and instantly got goosebumps. The hairs on my arms began to stand up and a jolt of electricity shot straight down to my essence. My palms started to get sweaty as my heartrate picked up. He always had this kind of effect on me and it was killing me slowly.

"I'mma give you all the time that you need to have your fun and come to your damn senses on your own. Until then, don't keep me waiting. I'm a very impatient and selfish man. Wait too long and you might just find ole boy's remains floating in the river somewhere. That's if the alligators don't get to him first," he said in a low, stern tone. I could tell by how heavy his tone was that it wasn't just a threat, but a promise that he was going to keep.

And with that he gave me a kiss on my cheek and left out of the room. It took me a minute to come back to my senses, because for a minute, I was dazed. After I calmed down, I went into the bathroom and splashed water on my face. I had to get myself together before anyone noticed that I was most definitely in heat. Damn, Rome had me ready to chase his ass down the stairs, drag his ass back upstairs, and fuck the shit out of him. My body was craving him. I checked my appearance in the mirror one last time before leaving and going back downstairs. I was coming down the stairs and was about to walk through the kitchen's double doors when all of a sudden I was roughly snatched back by my arm and pushed up against a wall.

"¿Qué coño?!" (What the fuck?!) I yelped out in shock.

"What the fuck was you doing upstairs with that nigga?" Q asked angrily through clenched teeth.

My mouth opened but hurried up and closed when words wouldn't come out. "Wha… what the fuck is you talking 'bout? I wasn't upstairs with anybody," I lied. A bitch was so nervous I was shaking. Did Q see Rome coming down the stairs?

"Don't lie to me, Aris!" Q bellowed. "I just saw that nigga come down the stairs grinning like he had just hit the muthafuckin' lottery and minutes later yo' ass comes down looking all shriveled up. The fuck is y'all doing upstairs together? You fuck that nigga, E? You gave that nigga my pussy?" Q asked me, looking possessed. He was gripping my arm so tight my blood circulation cut off.

"Ouch, Quamir! Stop! You're hurting me!" I whined while trying to pry his fingers around my arm loose. I guess he noticed how much pain he was causing me because he suddenly let go. I looked down at my arm and saw a red handprint. I started rubbing the spot, hoping the mark would go away before anybody else noticed it. I could only imagine what Kamron, Landon, and even Rome would do when they figured out that the mark came from Q. Hell, I could even picture Kelly and Mona's crazy asses wilding out with them as well. What the fuck is wrong with this nigga?

"Let's go!" Q demanded, chewing on his inner jaw. He grabbed my hand then started dragging me towards the front door.

"Wait a minute," I snatched my hand away from him. "Let me go tell my brother and them that I'm leaving," I turned around to go out the back door but was once again snatched back by my arm.

"I said let's fuckin' go!" Q yelled as he dragged me out of the house and to the car. Opening the passenger side door of his Benz he roughly tossed my ass into the car and slammed the door shut. He then quickly jogged over to the driver's side, jumped in, and pulled off.

I was pissed off because lately he had been using unnecessary ass force with me and I didn't play that shit when it came to people putting their hands on me. As soon as we got home I'm going to dig all into his shit about that. The whole drive home the car was awkwardly quiet. Q was fuming the whole fucking way, too. I didn't know what the fuck he was so mad for, but the nigga was. I could see the smoke coming out of his ears. I just shrugged my shoulders and got comfortable on the way home. After the day that I'd had I was too tired and exhausted to argue. I just wanted to go home and sleep my problems away.

# Chapter Eight

**QUAMIR "Q" MYLES**

I swear I was fuming the whole fucking way home. Aris had me so fucking mad right now playing dumb and shit like I was some fuck ass nigga and didn't know what the fuck I was talking about. I know what the fuck I saw and she was still sitting up here saying some other shit that I didn't want to fucking hear. Seeing that ole extra cocky ass muthafucka coming downstairs with a smirk on his face and minutes later she brought her ass downstairs looking all out of place was enough to send me over the fucking edge. I wanted to beat her ass every time I took my eyes off the road and glanced her way. She looked so bored and so unbothered in the passenger seat that I was pissed off. Her ass thought I didn't know that all day today she had been staring at that fucka. I'd been peeped game and picked up the undeniable chemistry between the two. It was something about the way her eyes would get whenever she was looking at dude that had me feeling some type of way. It doesn't take a fucking genius to figure out that those two used to have something going on.

I admit that I am one jealous ass nigga, but that's because Aris has made me this way. Before hooking up with her, I didn't give two flying fucks about another nigga looking at mine or mine having a simple conversation with next muthafucka. Knowing that the next nigga is envious about the bad bitch that I had on my arm used to swell a nigga's head up. But as soon as I got with Aris and got a sample of that gold mine sitting in between her legs, all of that shit went out of the fucking window. She could be dressed in a pair of sweat pants, oversized t-shirt, and a pair of flip flops and still be outshining most of these bitches that spent their whole first of the month check on Brazilian and knock-off brands. Aris is so fucking beautiful that it was hard as fuck for a nigga not to look and stare at her. I know for a fact that it was hard for me when her brother first introduced us. A nigga was straight drooling at the mouth.

It was a thirty-minute drive from the party house to the spot I had out in Miami Lakes. I owned a beautiful and comfortable, two-story, four in a half thousand sq. ft. mini-mansion. This mansion was rebuilt only a few years ago from the ground up and as soon as I came to Florida and saw it for myself, I bought it for 1.2 million in cash. The mansion came with five huge bedrooms, his and hers walk-in closets, three full bathrooms, with his and hers sinks, separate tub and shower, marble floors, foyer entry, wet bar, washer and dryer unit, family room, formal dining room, gourmet kitchen with all the top of the line LG appliances, closet cabinetry, two garage spaces, attached garage, in-ground pool and a lakefront view. The house wasn't as big as Kam's or the girls' mansion, but it was enough space for me until I started building my family with Aris.

Pulling into the circular driveway, I tossed my car into park and shut the engine off. Looking over at Aris, I noticed that she had fallen asleep on the drive home. My face relaxed and the attitude that I had instantly went flying out of the window. She looked so peaceful that I forgot all about the shit that had happened earlier. That was until her ass started mumbling this nigga name in her sleep. Anger flashed over me quickly like an old bitch catching a hot flash in her menopause stage.

"Yo, Aris, wake up," I said slapping her hard as fuck on the thigh. I wanted to do more but was struggling harder than a fat bitch on a strict diet not to put my hands on her.

She groaned then rolled over onto her side before opening her eyes and sitting up. "Where are we?" she asked, rubbing the sleep out of her eyes.

"Home. Where else?" I spat sarcastically as I opened the door and got out, attitude and all.

Aris sat all the way up in her seat and began looking around as if she didn't believe me. Yo, I could've sworn I just saw her ass roll her eyes and kissed her teeth, before hopping out of my car and slamming my door so damn hard that I thought the glass shattered. I went around my shit to double check and what the fuck you know? There was a long ass crack going down the middle.

"Man, what the fuck? Really? Ka'Mya?!" I yelled out, running my hand over my head before storming her way like a bull on a rampage.

"Could you shut the fuck up, stop complaining, and open the fucking door before I call Kamron to come and pick me up. It's only a fucking crack!" she spat back at me.

I had to stop and take several deep breaths before I ended up hitting her in the mouth. Being around Kelly's ratchet ass, she had picked up on some shit that she should've left wherever the fuck she got it from. Grabbing my keys from out of my jean pocket, I unlocked the door, and pushed it open. Aris rolled her eyes at me and with an attitude she pushed past me. I slammed the door shut, locked it, and followed her ass right upstairs to my bedroom.

"Yo, what the fuck is yo' problem?" I barked, walking behind her and shutting the bedroom door.

Aris simply ignored my ass and continued digging in my dresser drawers for something to wear. She searched for a little while longer until she found what she was looking for. A pair of my basketball shorts and a tank top. Still ignoring me, she went to walk into the bathroom to shower. "Aris, do not fucking play with me. You hear me talking to you! Da fuck is yo' problem?" I yelled, snatching her back to me by the elbow.

"No, nigga, what the fuck is yo' problem?" she yelled back, snatching her arm out of my grip and getting in my face.

"Ain't shit wrong with me. Yo' ass is the one who has been acting all funny today! Since that nigga came home you've been walking around with a fucking attitude!" I screamed at her.

Aris looked at me with her head cocked to the side and scoffed. "Me? Attitude?" she said in disbelief. "You wanna know why I got an attitude, Quamir?" she asked me calmly.

"Nigga, you're the reason why I have an attitude! I got a fucking attitude because all damn day today you have been on my ass like a shadow! Like, damn I'm tryna breathe here and yo' ass still want to walk around tryna start some shit you know you can't finish!" she spat heatedly, pushing me back or at least she tried to.

"Man, quit putting your hands on me."

"I just don't see what the fuck your problem is with Roman. Ever since he came from prison and showed his face today, you've been acting really fucking shady like somebody took a shit and you walked in on the smell. What has Rome ever done to you besides breathe the same oxygen you breathe?"

"First off, I just don't like the nigga. He too fucking arrogant, walking around this muthafucka like he God or some shit. Second off I –, wait I ain't got to explain shit to you! Why the fuck is you tryna change the fucking subject and shit? This shit ain't about me and him, but about you and that nigga."

"There ain't shit to talk about because nothing fucking happened!" she yelled, sounding fed up.

"Oh yea? So tell me why the fuck was y'all upstairs for?" I asked her with my arms folded across my chest and head cocked to the side. I was just waiting to hear the lie that was about to roll off of her tongue.

"You dumb ass! I just told you that I wasn't upstairs with nobody! I was in the damn bathroom! If you so fucking worried, then why you ain't ask him what the fuck he was doing up there when he brought his ass down," she screamed out louder.

"You must think I'm really fucking stupid, don't you? Yo' ass could've used the damn bathroom downstairs, so bitch try again! You want that nigga? Is that what it is? What, y'all used to fuck around or something?" I asked her heatedly and through clenched teeth as I walked up on her, getting all into her personal space. We were so close that our noses were touching. Just the thought of them being together before me had my trigger finger itching. When we first got together, Aris told me that she wasn't a virgin but had only been with one man in her life. It would kill a nigga's ego to find out that bitch ass nigga got to the gold mine first.

"There is nothing going on between me and Roman!" she yelled out in frustration but I knew right off top that was a lie. She had that fucking look in her eyes again.

"Bullshit! I've seen the look in your eyes when you looked at that nigga earlier. You want him, don't you?" My jaw was clenching so tightly that I was tasting blood.

"You know what? Think what the fuck you want to think I don't give a fuck anymore. You know just like I know that if I want Rome I can have him. Ain't fucking shit to it. Keep on acting like you are so fucking insecure and I'm going to end up leaving yo' ass. If I wanted kids, then I would had my own to raise, not trying to babysit your overzealous ass."

I cocked my head to the side and looked at her through tiny slits. "Oh really?" I asked her calmly.

Just that quick I snapped. Everything went into black and when I came to I had my hand around Aris' throat pinning her up against the wall behind her.

"On my life, Quamir. If you don't get your fucking hands off of me –," she tried to say but my grip tightening around her throat cut her sentence short.

"What the fuck you gon' do? Tell yo' brother? Bitch, if you think I'm anywhere near fucking scared of Kamron's bitch ass then you seriously got me fucked all the way up. If you think, I am then gon' 'head and tell him and watch what the fuck happens. That nigga bleed just like I bleed. Ain't nobody scared of Kamron's pretty boy ass!" I barked with spit flying out the corners of my mouth, my grip tightened more. I was trying to squeeze the fucking life out of her ass.

Aris' eyes widened in shock as her hand shot up my mine. "Let. Go. Of. Me," she groaned out breathlessly as she tried to claw at my face.

"Let me tell yo' ass something right fucking now. If you think that this shit is anywhere near over, then you are sadly mistaken. Don't fucking try to switch up now that fuck boy is out of jail. I will fucking kill the both of you bitches and everyone else that you love before I let you leave me. Don't. Fucking underestimate, me, Ka'Mya. Now play with that," I growled through clenched teeth in a tone so fucking evil and dark that even I didn't recognize myself. I squeezed her throat a little harder, cutting off her air supply just to get my point through before I let her go. Aris immediately collapsed onto the floor gasping for air all dramatically like I really did something to her ass.

The vibration from my cell phone ringing pulled my attention away from Aris. Reaching in my pocket, I answered it without looking to see who was calling first.

"Yo!" I spat heatedly into the phone.

Before the caller even got a chance to respond Aris had already regrouped on my ass and two-pieced the fuck out of me, making me drop my phone onto the floor.

"Bitch ass nigga, I know you didn't just put your fucking hands on me! Do you know who the fuck I am?" she screamed sounding all deranged and shit as she charged at me. I was still a little dazed from the two-piece she gave me so I didn't even have enough time to react. Aris swung catching me with a right hook to the eye and a left to the jaw.

A nigga ain't even gon' lie. Those punches were fucking hurting like hell but the last one really sent me over the edge. Before I could even stop myself, I ended up pushing her ass into the dresser making her gasp out from pain and fall to the ground.

"The fuck wrong with you? Bitch, you don' lost your muthafuckin mind putting yo' hands on me!" I snapped as I wiped my lip with the back of my hand. Looking down at my hand I noticed blood. My breathing quickened and my chest caved in and out from anger.

Aris slowly climbed up to her feet using the dresser as support. "An eye for an eye right?" she said with a slick grin on her face. The look she gave me pissed me off so fucking bad that I was ready to box this bitch all over this house. "Let me get the fuck away from you before I end up doing some shit that's really going to hurt yo' feelings," I warned her as I bent down to pick up my phone from off the ground. Inspecting it for any damages I noticed that the caller had hung up on my ass. Good, because I don't even feel like talking to anybody any fucking way.

I spun on my shoes to leave out of the door. I haven't even made it out when a vase went flying past me missing my head by a couple inches. I looked back at Aris and she stood there with a grin on her face and her arms folded across her chest. "That's for pushing me, pussy!" she spat, spitting on my floors.

I couldn't do shit but shake my head. "Fucking crazy bitch!" I yelled at her before walking out of the room and closing the door behind me.

***

After I left the crib, I swung by my side chick Kia's house to release some much needed stress. Aris had me fucking stressing and ready to wring her fucking neck because of that fucked up attitude she picked up on fucking around with Kelly. I truly wish that she would stay away from those bitches. Kelly's ass is too fucking ghetto for me and I can't stand her smart mouth as just like she can't stand mines. Parking my Benz in her driveway I jumped out of my car and used my key to let myself in the house. I walked into the living room and there she stood in the front room stacked and made thick like a stallion.

Although she was a little bit on the chubby side Kia was bad in every sense of the word. She was five-six with smooth chocolate skin, huge 48DDD titties, thick juicy thighs and enough ass to go around and feed Africa with. She had her hair done in faux locs hanging down her back and framing her chubby cheeks. To sum it all up Kia was gorgeous! But of course Aris looked way better.

"Wifey acting up?" She said to me after exhaling a thick cloud of smoke out.

"Bitch, I didn't come over here to hear you talk about her." I spat as I took my jacket off and took a seat on the couch.

"Then why the fuck are you here, Quamir?" She asked taking a seat across from me.

"The fuck you think?" I asked her sarcastically.

"You know what the fuck I want. Nigga, gon head and toss that shit on up." She said with her hand out.

I reached inside of my pocket and pulled out a wad of money, an eight ball of coke and throwing it on the table.

A smile about a mile-long crossed Kia's face. Typical for a money hungry ass hoe. I watched her as she licked her lips before standing up and seductively walking up towards me before climbing down on her knees in front of me. She gave her thick succulent lips one last lick as she reached down in my jeans and pulled my semi hard dick out.

"Mmm… daddy." She moaned as she rubbed my mushroom tip against her lips.

"Quit playing and swallow this muthafucka." I said as I wrapped her faux locs around my fist before shoving my tool down her throat without any mercy. Her eyes watered at first but soon she got over it and was sucking my shit like a pro.

"Shit, girl! That's it… do it just like that! Fuck!" I hissed as I caught onto the little rhythm she had going on and started thrusting in and out of her mouth.

I guess me groaning was her motivation to go harder because she started sucking me feverishly. Her licks were perfectly synched with my gyrating hips as I made love to her tonsils. Her not once gagging damn near sent me over the edge and made me pick up speed.

"Fuck! Open the fuck up." I growled through clenched teeth as I tilted her head back.

She being the good girl that she is obliged and opened wide for me. With one hand holding my dick and the other cuffing the back of her head I slowly slid my length down her throat one inch at a time. She gagged a few times because of my size and quickly grabbed my hips to slow me down. She then relaxed her throat muscles before taking my full length all the way down to the base deep throating my shit.

With her eyes staring deeply into mines, she gathered all the spit in her mouth and spits on my shit before relaxing her throat and taking my meat all the way down her throat. Up and down her head slowly bobbed. Each time she came down the deeper my shaft went down her throat.

"Mmmm… shit! Damn girl! That's it! Mmm, yeah," I hissed as I ran my hands through her hair holding her head still while I pumping my shaft deeper and deeper into her mouth.

I felt the tip of my dick throb and I knew then I was close to my release. She must have felt it too. Knowing I was close to cumming, she made no attempt to move or even to slow down her stride. If anything she started sucking me harder and faster than ever before. Her small hand wrapped around the base of my shaft as she stroked it in perfect rhythm with her suckling mouth.

"Fuck!" I groaned. On some G shit my toes started curling up and cramping in the soles of my shoes.

"Shhhhiiiittttt! I'm about to cum!" I yelled out as my shit started throbbing intensely.

She suddenly stopped right before I was ready to feed her these vitamins, wrapped my mans up and slowly slid down on my dick. Her walls wrapped around my dick sucking me deeper into her abyss.

I grabbed her ass checks, spread them open and lifted her up a little and slowly slid in and out of her. Soft wails of pleasurable moans escaped from her pouty lips. Her pussy muscles clenched tightly around my dick, gripping me tightly and trying to pull me in deeper inside of her.

A groan escaped my lips at the feeling. Soon my slow strokes became faster and I began rocking in and out of her so hard and deep that she yelped with both passion and a hint of discomfort.

"Mmm… shit… Q wait!" She yelled out as she sat her hand on my abs trying to slow my thrusts.

I quickly slapped her hand away and pushed myself deeper into her. "Nah, fuck that! This is what you want isn't it? Don't try to run now. Take all of this dick!" I demanded grabbing her by the hips and slamming her down onto my shaft.

I went from slowly stroking her pussy to picking up speed and knocking the bottom of her pussy out. She was so wet that all you heard was the sounds of her pussy was making and skin slapping against skin.

"Oooohhh shit nigga! Yes! That's it! Just like that baby!" She screamed out as her muscles contracted around my shaft. Grabbing her by the waist I picked Kia up and carried her into the bedroom laying her back on the bed with her feet pinned up behind her head. I would slam all ten in a half inches inside of her and slowly slide out. I repeated this move a few times all the way up until her body was violently convulsing.

"Shit. Shit. Shit. Shit. Shit. Shit. Shit. Ohhh fuck!" She chanted out breathlessly.

I grinned wickedly as I started pounding in that pussy fucking up all of her walls and knocking shit out of the frame. She let out an ear piercing scream just as her body tensed up and she started shaking.

"OH! MY! FUCKING! GOD! QUAMIR!!!" She screamed out in pure pleasure.

"Mmm… damn girl! This is some good ass pussy! Shit!" I groaned out in passion as I sunk my teeth into my bottom lip to keep from screaming out like a little bitch.

I reached in between me and pinched her hardening clit while thrusting deeply inside of her. My toes started curling, my knees buckled and my stomach started bubbling. My nut was approaching and fast. I closed my eyes and tilted my head back while punishing her cervix.

"Shit girl! I'm about to cum inside of this pussy. You ready? Here it comes!" A few hard violent thrusts later and I was shaking and spilling my seeds deep inside of the condom. My body shook so hard that I thought I was having a seizure.

"Fuck, Kia," I groaned while slowly stroking my semi hard dick out of her. I was so fucking tired that I couldn't even move. Kia had to pull the condom off and flush it down the toilet. By the time she came back with a hot soapy rag to wash my dick off I was drifting off into la la land. At the moment I was like fuck everybody and they fucking feelings. Including Aris' ass too. Until her ass comes back the fuck around a nigga was about to do him for the time being. It ain't like I never stopped any fucking way.

## Chapter Nine

**ROME**

"I 'preciate each and every one of you for attending tonight's meeting on such short notice," Kamron said from his seat at the head of the conference table. There were about seventy niggas that were of some type of importance to this operation scattered about all throughout the warehouse. Each nigga was a stone cold killer with deep loyalty tendencies. Some of these niggas I've been knowing since the sandbox days and some faces were new to me.

Of course, I was sitting on that nigga's right side and Landon was on his left. Q's bitch ass was leaning up against the wall with his arms folded across his chest and his face in a deep scowl. He was feeling some type of way all because I was sitting on Kam's right and not his bitch ass. As I stared this punk muthafucka in the face, I was shaking my head at the same time. What the fuck Ari saw in this nigga was fucking beyond me. He was a straight bitch ass nigga with hoe tendencies. There was nothing real about this muthafucka. I'mma have to talk to Kam about his boy a-fucking-sap. It's something about that nigga that was rubbing me the wrong way. And I ain't just saying that shit all because he got my bitch. It's because real recognize real and this muthafucka was looking real un-fucking-familiar right about now.

"I called a very special meeting today because now that my nigga Rome is back home, a lot of shit is about to change. Rome –',"

"Exactly what kind of changes are you talking 'bout Kam?" Q asked dryly, his sudden outburst cutting Kam's sentence short.

"If would let me get to it first then you will know, stupid dumb muthafucka!" Kam barked heatedly at Q. Anybody that knows Kamron knows that he hates it when muthafuckas cut him off. His retarded ass would go from zero to a thousand really quick. Me and a few other niggas in attendance started snickering with humor at the way Kam just checked his ass.

Anger flashed in Q's eyes as he clenched his jaw in and out. He looked like he had some shit that he wanted to get off of his chest, but decided to keep his mouth closed. I was just waiting for fuck boy to get out of pocket, just so that I had a reason to go up upside his shit.

"Now back to what the fuck I was saying before I was rudely interrupted. Now that Rome is home, he will officially become my second hand in command as well as my right hand man and Landon's still my left hand. Anytime y'all can't reach me y'all can always go to him and Lay for some shit. The same loyalty and respect you show me, you will show it to these two. Anybody got a muthafuckin' problem with that or questions that they want to ask regarding my decisions?" he asked as he looked each soldier in the face, his own face serious and at the same time emotionless with murderous intent.

"I fucking do," Q spat while pushing off the wall. "How the fuck this nigga who just came home from doing a stint yo' right hand man when I'm yo' right hand?"

"Damn nigga, is it that fucking hard to comprehend?" I asked him with my feet sitting on top of the table and crossed at the ankles. "Yo' ass just been demoted," I said, laughing cockily.

I noticed Q tensing up and bucking at me like he was really going to do something but my nigga Teddy grabbed him by the shoulder, holding him back. It was a good thing my nigga did, because I was about two point five seconds away from putting a hot one right in the center of his head.

"Yo, Q, you my homie and all but you gonna have to chill out on all of that extra ass shit you doing. This shit here is business so don't take nothing personal," Landon said, turning his attention to him with a mean mug on his face and his hand near his waist. Once things started calming down, Kam continued on with the meeting.

"Shit has changed a lot since you went in, bro. Bricks here go for twenty thou, eight balls are a buck fifty, and rocks are fifty. Nothing more. Nothing less. I buy at least three hundred keys whenever we need to re-up and collection day is every third Monday of the month," Kamron said to me.

I just nodded my head as my brain processed everything he was saying. My niggas Kam and Landon really had come the fuck up since I'd been locked up. "Q will be in charge of collecting and drop offs for anyone who's low on work. It will also be his responsibility to make sure that all of my money is on point. One cent missing and it's off with yo' muthafuckin head. Ya heard me?" Kamron said, looking Q right in the eyes. Q mumbled something under his breath but made sure it was kept to himself, otherwise he knew what the fuck would happen.

"Shy I still want you to run the traps on the south and east sides of Hialeah and Cario you will be the new leader to the trap houses in Little Haiti. Malachi will run the traps in Overtown and Sabrian will stay in Aventura. B-Free I will leave Carol City in your care. You are in charge of everything surrounding that city. Brayton will be taking over Dee's spot in the Pork & Beans as the new leader with Dee as second command and Tae, you're in charge of Opa Locka since that's where you're from," Kamron announced out to everyone.

"Hold on youngin'," this older cat by the name of Demarious said out loud as he stood up from his seat. I remember his old ancient ass. Nigga been hustling since my daddy and 'em was running shit. "No disrespect, but I'm in charge of the north and west sides. How in the fuck you gon' give this young muthafucka my shit?" he questioned with an attitude.

Kam's face contorted into a hard scowl as he looked up and down like he had done lost his muthafuckin' mind. I could tell by the way his breathing picked up that he was pissed the fuck off.

"Nigga, you want to know why the fuck I gave Shy yo' shit? It's because that nigga name ring bells in these streets and yours ain't rang shit in I don't know how many fucking years. Yo' ass can't even control the young niggas you got under yo' belt right fucking now. You slacking while he picking up yo' muthafuckin' weight and making sure my money is on time. Since you want to question me about my shit and the way I run shit then yo' ass just got demoted back to being a corner boy with Cario as your boss. Work that position for a little while. Once I feel like money has once became your motivation again, then I might promote yo' ass again."

Demarious' mouth opened as if he was going to try to argue but the murderous look in Kamron's eyes shut his ass up real quick. Without another word, Demarious sat back in his seat pissed the fuck off.

"All lieutenants of each team will meet here every Friday at eight o'clock sharp. No exceptions. Any tardiness is an automatic demotion. Anyone else that wants to question how the fuck I run my shit or with the changes I made is free to walk the fuck up out of here right now. You're free to leave, but I can guarantee that you wouldn't make it out of the driveway with your life," he said, aiming his last statement directly at Demarious' and Q's asses.

Kamron's grayish-blue eyes scanned the whole room, giving those who wanted to add their two little cents in or those who had any objections, enough time to speak up. When no one said anything, he adjourned the meeting. Q's and Demarious' punk asses were the first two to fly up out of that muthafucka. As everyone piled out, niggas started cheering and slapping my hands, welcoming me back with open arms. Now that that part of business was over with, it's time for me to pop up on Ebony's hoe ass and see about my son.

***

I had been out of jail for two weeks now and let me say that a nigga was certainly enjoying his freedom. Damn, it feels good as fuck being home. I never wanted to end up back in that shit hole. I spent the past two weeks getting shit in order for myself. The first thing that I did was cop me a whip to get around in and a spot downtown Miami. I'd managed to get a three bedroom three bath condo right off of the shores of Biscayne Bay. It was an alright spot. Couldn't really complain it's better than staying under the same roof as Kamron. Don't get me wrong, Kamron is my brother and all but I cannot stay with him. A nigga like me like to walk around the house with his nuts swinging. Can't do that when you staying in somebody else shit.

After making sure that I was straight, it was back to business and to the real grind. I already handled my business part earlier now it was time to handle Ebony's ass and see about my son. Knowing the type of bitch Ebony was, I knew that her momma would probably have RJ in her care while she out popping pussy for any and every muthafuckin' body that was willingly to show her basic ass some attention. I rolled my eyes and instantly got irritated just from the thought of that bitch. I know Ebony's type too fucking well. Sad to say it, but I came across a lot of the bitches in my young life.

Ebony was not the motherly type at all. She would rather party the fucking night away before making sure her son has been fed, bathed, and clothed. She's the type of mother who would sell her food stamps and WIC coupons just to make sure that her Brazilian was on fleek. The type that would be fly as shit, but her kids be looking dusty as fuck. Yo, I swear if lil' man is actually proven to be mine then I will be getting full custody of him and cutting all ends that attach me to her ass. Ain't no way in hell am I leaving him with his unfit ass mother. Would you believe me if I said that once upon a time I was actually feeling her ass? It was way before I started recognizing my true feelings for Aris.

Ebony was nothing like she was when we first met back in high school. Wait, I'll take that back. She has always been a damn thot. She was just good at keeping the shit on the low. I ain't even gon lie; Ebony had my ass fooled. When I first met her, she was what every nigga wanted and what every bitch hated. She had all the qualities in life to be someone great. She was smart, pretty and bad as fuck. That smooth, silky brown sugar skin, slanted eyes, and fat ass were what caught a nigga's attention in the first place. It wasn't until some of my homies pulled me to the side and hipped me up on the real with her ass. After that I fell back and started watching her ass. It didn't take long for the real Ebony to come out and play.

I was out cruising the streets with my niggas Kam and Landon when I watched her climb out of some other nigga's car wiping white shit away from the corners of her mouth with a wet wipe. It didn't take a rocket scientist to know that the bitch just got done sucking dick for that new Gucci bag. After that, I started fucking with her ass the long way. Somewhere in that delusional ass mind of hers she had confused me bussing down her throat every night with a relationship. Delusional muthafucka.

Thirty minutes later, I was pulling my customized Audi R8 into Ebony's mother's driveway. I cut the car off and slowly climbed out. Ebony's mom, Ms. Doris, was sitting outside on the porch smoking a Newport on the cordless phone running her damn mouth as usual. Ms. Doris was ratchet as fuck. She was fifty something years old and acted as if she was still in her early twenties. A pack of Newports and a thirty pack was her best friend. She was certainly a wild one. She popped her oldest child out at fourteen and Ebony in her early thirties. Ms. Doris also liked 'em young. Sometimes so young that right after she get done feeding them, she had to burp them. When I first met Ms. Doris she was drooling at the mouth and damn near throwing me the pussy. But y'all already know my ass wasn't catching. Ma would've whipped mine and

Doris' ass all over Miami if she ever found out we got down on that kind of level. She don't play that shit.

"Hey, Ms. Stevenson."

"Girl, let me call you back!" she hurried and spoke into the cordless phone as she quickly hung up the phone, never giving whoever was on the phone enough time to say bye. "I know that ain't who I think it is? Roman?" she asked with excitement in her voice and a wide ass grin on her face.

A cordial smile tugged at the corners of lips as I walked up the porch's stairs. "Hey, Ms. Stevenson. How are you doing today?"

"Ms. Stevenson? Now when in the hell did you start callin' me that? You know that you can call me Ms. Doris or Doris, boy. C'mere," she said, pulling me in for a hug. "I ain't seen yo' young ass in I don't know how long. I'm so mad at you! I thought we were better than that Roman," she said while squeezing me and at the same time trying to feel me up on the sly.

I went ahead and let her hug me for a lil' second before pulling away. "Ms. Doris, I was in jail for the past four and a half years. I just got out the other day."

"Damn, jail sure as in hell can do the body some justice," she tried mumbling under her breath while biting her body lip. The lust was evident in her eyes. I cleared my throat and looked at her with a raised eyebrow.

Caught red handed, Ms. Doris tried to smile and play it off like she just wasn't eyeing a nigga like he was a big, juicy T-Bone steak. "In jail? Damn, forreal? I didn't know. Ebony told me that you had just gotten her pregnant in one night of unprotected sex, said fuck her and that baby, and ran off into the sunset with the white bitch. Ebony never told me that you was in jail serving time," she said lighting up another Newport.

Was that what muthafuckin' Ebony's ass was running around telling everybody? Oh bruh was I hot! I was taught to always respect my elders so I tried biting my tongue to keep me from snapping on Doris' ass. Hell she was just the messenger, no need to kill the messenger.

"Nah. It's not even like that, Ms. Doris. And what white bitch?" I asked through gritted teeth.

"That little home wrecking bitch that came in between you and my baby. Aries? Aris? Whatever the fuck her momma named her. Her," she responded while pulling a long drag on her cancer stick and blowing the smoke out through her nose.

For Doris to even sit up here and call Aris out of her name was enough to make me lose the little respect that I had left for her ass. Aris was both classy and better looking than what her and her daughter would ever be. My jaw tensed in and out in anger. I had to put my hands in the front pockets of my pants before I fucked around and did some shit that I wouldn't regret. Real shit, I just saw myself wrapping my hands around her old sagging ass neck and choking the shit out of her ass. Ms. Doris' mouth was what got her ass kicked by the neighbors.

"No disrespect Ms. Doris, but don't believe shit your lying ass daughter says when it comes to me and mine. There wasn't shit going on between me and your daughter but fucking. Two grown muthafuckas casually fucking with no strings attached. If you really want me to be blunt, Ebony wasn't shit to me but a muthafuckin' head doctor that I would see, whenever my other head began to swell up and I couldn't get in contact with my other doctors. Yo daughter is a hoe. She done already fucked every nigga in the borough before I busted her ass down with this grade A meat. Ain't no fucking way will I ever wife a hoe and turn her into a housewife. Aris was and is my only girl and when we made shit official, I cut all strings loose with her ass," I ain't never been the one to hold my tongue and beat around the bush, so I didn't have any problems giving her that shit raw and uncut, not really caring if my words stung or not.

Doris' mouth opened and closed in a motion resembling a fish out of water. I guess she was surprised to hear how foul my mouth had gotten over the years. Or maybe she was shock about how I was talking about her daughter. Who the fuck knows. I didn't give a fuck.

"Matter of fact, the only reason I am here now is to see about this supposed to be son of mine that I just found out about a little while ago and to put my size twelve boot up Ebony's ass. She here?" I asked her as if I didn't just threaten to kick her daughter's ass.

"N…no. I ain't seen here since earlier."

"What about lil' man? He here or does she have him?"

"Yea, hold on. RJ! Bring yo' ass here!" she screamed inside of the house. I looked at her like she was crazy before shaking my head. Like who in the fucks talk to a four-year-old like that.

"Ma'am?" A little voice called back, followed by some little footsteps running.

I'm not even gon' lie and say that a nigga's heart wasn't beating fast as fuck in his chest. I was scared as shit. I always wanted kids, but I didn't see myself having none with nobody but Aris, and further down the line in the future. I guess the reality of me being someone's daddy was starting to hit my ass. Damn, I'm somebody's daddy. Maybe.

I looked down to see a little body running up to the door and to mine and Doris' direction. Ms. Doris bent down and swooped the little boy up into her arms.

"Look at who's here," she said pointing at me. It was like the moment my eyes caught sight of him, I started looking for any signs of myself inside of him. He was so small in Doris' arms. A light chuckle escaped my mouth as I stared at him. There was no denying this baby. He was the exact replica of Ebony's ass. He had the same brown sugar skin tone as her, her slanted shaped eyes, and her nose. He did look like somebody that I know, but I just couldn't quite put my finger on it.

RJ peeked up at me and smiled shyly before laying his head on her shoulder. "Yes," he answered in a low tone while playing with the transformer toy in his hand.

"Then who is he?" Ms. Doris quipped.

He looked up at me then back to Doris who nodded her head as if to tell him 'go 'head'. Looking back up at me, he smiled, flashing off a perfect set of tiny white teeth.

"Daddy!" he yelled excitedly as he jumped from out of Doris' arms and into mine. The little action took me by a complete surprise. Just hearing lil' man calling me daddy had me speechless.

"Ebony shows him pictures of you all the time so he's familiar with who you are."

Although I was nodding my head at her, my attention was on little man. I needed to hurry up and get a test done on lil' man ASAP. Ebony had his ass wearing a dingy ass white shirt, Walmart sneakers, and a pair of flooding ass shorts. How the fuck, do you flood in shorts, I have no fucking idea. Lil' man needed a haircut as well. This thick ass wild fro that he had on top of his head was not going to work with me. Lil' nigga look like he had a matted mop sitting on top of his shit.

"Aight, Ms. Doris. I'mma take Junior off your hands for a couple of hours. Take him shopping and get this shit cut off," I told her. Yo, I can't believe she straight got my jit out here looking like this. Man, I can't wait to see her ass. I promise you, word to my momma, I'm fucking her up.

"I don't know about all that, Roman. I think you should wait until she comes back before taking off with her son," she said apprehensively while flickering her cigarette into the yard and pulling another one from behind her ear.

"He's my son too, right?" I asked her with a raised eyebrow.

"Yes. Of course he is. I just –',"

I scoffed and quickly cut her ass off. "Bullshit. If he's my son like y'all claim him to be, then he's leaving with me. End of discussion. Like I said, I'll have him back in a few hours," I spun on my heels and began walking to my car with RJ securely tucked in my arms.

I was snapping RJ's in with the seatbelt when Ebony finally decides to show her ass, looking like the fucking neighborhood hoe dressed in a pair of shorts too fucking short for her ass and a t-shirt showing off her stomach.

"Roman? Wha…what are you doing here?" she asked as she approached me sounding as if she was surprised to see me.

I slammed the back door closed after making sure RJ was safely secured in his seat. I took one look at Ebony and saw the little suck mark on her neck and blacked the fuck out. When I came to, I had my hand wrapped around Ebony's throat, lightly squeezing her shit. Y'all just don't know how bad I wanted to choke her ass out, but just off the strength of my son being in the car, I didn't. Her eyes had widened from the shock of me putting my hands on her. Her hands were clawing at mine trying to loosen my grip on her while Ms. Doris was in the background screaming for me to let her loose. All of that shit went into one ear and out of the other as my anger had gotten the best of me. This bitch had the fucking nerve to have Brazilian in her hair and my son was dressed like one of those fucking kids in the feed me commercials.

I picked Ebony up by her neck and slammed her on the hood of the run down ass Civic she was riding around in. With my hand still around her throat, I pulled Ebony closer towards me so that she could hear what I was about to say very loud and fucking clear. "When I come back yo' ass better be here. Do you fucking understand me?" I growled through gritted teeth.

Ebony was so damn scared that she was nodding her head up and down so damn fast I thought the muthafucka was about to fall off. I gave her neck a quick squeeze before pushing her the fuck away from me. Ebony fell to the ground, holding her neck and inhaling air in all dramatically like I was actually choking her ass out.

"I'm not playing witcho stupid ass, Ebony! Don't be here when I get back and I swear I'm fucking you up!" I shouted over my shoulder as I climbed inside of my car and pulled the fuck out.

The first thing I did was have my homeboy Devin down at the DNA Diagnostics Center swab me and RJ. I was serious as fuck when I said I was going to get him tested. I would never in my life again trust a desperate bitch like Ebony who had to drug a nigga and steal the dick over the paternity of mine. A part of me felt bad as hell while Devin swabbed us. Questions like, what if RJ was mine swarmed through my head. If RJ is mine, then I'm gonna most definitely man up and take care of my responsibility, but if he isn't… then I'll feel really bad for lil' man. Because Devin's strict asshole of a supervisor wasn't going on vacation until next week, I wouldn't get the results back until damn near two weeks from now. That was cool with me because I was going to spend these two weeks getting to know lil' man and making up for lost time.

After leaving the DDC, I went to the mall and bought Junior a whole new wardrobe. I didn't want to see him in none of that outdated, outgrown ass shit Ebony had him in no more. At first Junior wasn't really fucking with me like that. He kept a safe distant away from my ass and everything was responded with a head nod. But as soon as I took his ass to Toys 'R' Us and cashed out in that muthafucka, his whole damn attitude switched up on me. Now I can't get the little nigga to slow down. I had to remind his ass to breathe he was talking so much now. It warmed a nigga's heart up to see his eyes light up at all of the shit I had bought him, though.

After getting Junior fresh gear to wear and that damn fro cut off, he was actually starting to look like a human and not like a damn escaped zoo animal. The shit Ebony had on him was tossed clean the fuck out of the window the moment we left the mall. I had RJ matching my fly. We both had on matching black and white Adidas fits, matching fresh out of the box all white shell-toe Adidas low top sneakers, and diamond stud earrings.

Thirty minutes after leaving the mall, I was pulling up into my sister's driveway and knocking on her door. I was wondering how she was going to react to being an auntie. I just knew that she gon' be pissed. Especially when she found out who's RJ's momma was. I already knew that it's gonna be a fight as soon as I stepped through the door. Although I'm Mona's only sibling you can't tell her shit when it comes to E. She treats Aris as more of a sibling than she does me! She was so overprotective of her. Someone pulling on my pants leg snapped me back into reality and cause me to look down.

"Daddy, who's house is this?" RJ asked me with curious eyes as they looked back and forth from me to the house.

I opened my mouth to respond but before I was able to answer his question, the front door was swinging open. I looked up from RJ to see my beautiful sister standing there, holding my nephew Levi. Yeah, that's right. I found out that the baby Aris was holding onto yesterday wasn't hers and Q's, but was my sister's son. I ain't even gonna sugarcoat shit. A nigga felt like a huge jackass for getting mad and jumping to conclusions. Even though I was relieved that Ari didn't have that fuck boy's kid. I was also mad as fuck because I never knew Mo even had a baby.

After me and Ari broke up, Mona was so pissed off at me that she quit talking to my ass. Don't get me wrong, when I was locked up she would always write and visit me while I was in there but we never really talked about what was going on with her. Although Mona was mad at me she was also my informant when it came to Aris. Yeah, she told me about Aris messing around with this new nigga but it was never supposed to be that serious. So imagine my surprise when I found out that the new nigga Ari was messing around with was that bitch ass nigga Quamir. I was pissed off at her, Kam, and Landon's ass for not telling me. When I asked them why they just shrugged their shoulders and said it wasn't their business to tell.

Mona's eyes darted from me to RJ hiding shyly behind my leg then back up to me. "Wassup, big head. Whose kid you don' kidnapped?" she asked me in a tone so serious that it made me burst out laughing.

"Why I gotta be the one to kidnap somebody's kid?" I asked her laughing.

"Boy, quit trying to beat around the bush and tell me. Whose kid is that?" she asked me again sounding irritated.

"Well, damn crazy girl. Can I come in first then explain? It's hot as hell out here."

Mona moved away from the door and walked off towards the kitchen. I grabbed RJ's hand and followed her. The first thing I see when I entered the kitchen was fat ass Kelly and Ma at the kitchen table scarfing down buffalo chicken Philly Cheesesteaks and cheese fries like it was their last meal.

"Hey baby!" Ma said, hopping off of her stool and making her way towards me.

"Hey beautiful. What you still doing here? I thought that you'd been left for home. Lord knows that you can't stay that far away from Pops too long," I joked laughing and wrapping my arms around her body pulling her in for a hug.

She laughed pushing me in the chest. "Boy, shut up. I'm still here because I'm trying to spend more time with my kids before I go back to boring ass Columbia," I watched her step back and her eyes immediately dropping down to RJ. It was like she had frozen in place she was so still.

"Whose baby you don' kidnapped?" she asked calmly her eyes still on RJ.

"Same thing I asked! Ro is going straight back to jail! Kidnapping is a serious offense, you know. You better hurry up and drop little man back off wherever you picked him up from before his real parents figure out he's missing," Mona said while taking a big bite out her philly cheesesteak and feeding Levi a french fry. Her retarded ass remark had Kelly choking on her soda.

"Yo! Bruh robbing cradles and shit now! I know times are hard, but damn I didn't know you was struggling like that," Kelly said laughing while wiping her nose with a napkin.

Momma finally broke her gaze from RJ and cut her eyes over at Kelly. "Kelly Re'Nae."

"I mean stuff. Roman robbing cradles and stuff. Sorry, ma."

"Man, what the hell is y'all problem? Why I gotta kidnap somebody's kid for?"

"Cause ain't nobody dumb or desperate enough to let you babysit they kids," Mona retorted laughing, momma and Kelly laughing with her.

"Well, sorry to crack all of y'all salty faces, but according to Ebony this is my son Roman Cayden Clarkson Jr," I boosted bending over and picking up RJ so that they could get a better look at him. I was straight warming up to the idea of being a father. It seems like once I let those words escape from my mouth, all laughter ceased and the tension became serious.

"So what you're telling me is that is your son?" Ma asked me again pointing at RJ who had his head laid on my shoulder. I just nodded my response. Ain't no need to keep repeating it over and over again.

"I got another grandson?" Ma asked me for confirmation, her eyes twinkling with excitement and again I nodded.

I looked up over towards the girl's direction and watched Kelly looked over at Mona, shooting her this look that I couldn't translate and

Mona shot it back at Kells. The both of their lips were tooted up at the side.

"Can I hold him?"

"RJ go to your grandma. Show her the toys that we picked out together at the mall," I said while trying to hand him to my momma. RJ looked at me and shook his head no, his tiny arms locking around my neck.

"C'mon dude, you'll be ok. She won't bite. After you show her all of your toys she might give you some ice cream," I assured him. RJ's eyes widened with excitement just at the mere mention of ice cream as he looked up from me to momma then back at me again. I nodded my head is if I was telling him to go 'head.

"C'mon RJ. Show me your all of your toys and I'll give you some ice cream right after we're through," Momma said with her arms out, waiting patiently for him to jump into them.

"Pinky promise?" RJ said in a tiny innocent voice with his left pinky out. His facial expression made momma, Mo, and Kells squeal in delight.

"Oh my God! He's so cute!" Kells squealed.

"Yes he is! Who on this Earth can say no to a face like that?" Mona added.

"I promise. Girl Scout's Honor," Ma replied wrapping her pinky around his and bumping fists. RJ's eyes lit up brightly like a Christmas tree. He didn't hesitate to jump into her arms right after she said that. Levi stopped chewing on the fry that he was eating on and frowned. It was as if on cue he tossed the wet mashed French fry onto the floor and started crying, reaching out for momma to pick him up.

"Aww… look, he's jealous. He doesn't even mess with me like that, but as soon as he sees me holding somebody else, he wants to act jealous," Ma said laughing. "Come here grammy's dooda," Ma cooed, picking up Levi with her other arm.

"Can Levi play with your toys, too?" Ma asked RJ on her way out of the kitchen. RJ nodded his head up and down vigorously passing over the toy truck in his hand. Levi just looked at RJ with his face frowned up.

"What the fuck is a dooda?" I asked Mo and Kells, my eyebrows dipped in confusion. They looked at each other then back at me and fell out laughing.

"A nickname, duh!" Kells replied smartly.

"A name Aris came up with."

That explained it. Aris was always giving somebody some type of fucked up nickname when we were younger. When we were younger Mo was Lovebutt and Kells was Bubblebutt. "Y'all know he's going to hate y'all for calling him that shit, right? That shit doesn't sound right at all," I shook my head.

Mona and Kelly started laughing even harder. "No, he's gonna hate Ari for that shit. She the one named him that," Kells laughed. "RJ's cute, though."

"Did you get the test done?" Mona asked me, her tone all of a sudden very serious.

I walked over to the fridge and grabbed a bottle of water out. "Now you know that I did. I had Devin swab us. The shit felt weird as hell, though. Hell, that was the first thing I did before taking little man to the mall. I had to fucking get RJ a whole new fucking wardrobe. Y'all should've seen the shit Ebony had him dressed in earlier. Lil' man was looking like he deserved to be in on one of those Feed My People commercials," I spat heatedly, slamming the fridgerator closed. Mona and Kelly were doubled over bugging the fuck up. They were laughing so hard that they had tears in their eyes and were breathing heavy as fuck.

"Nigga, my ribs!" Kelly yelled out breathlessly, still laughing.

"I gotta pee!" Mona added, bending over holding her bladder and crossing her legs.

"I'm talking 'bout clothes old, dirty, dingy and too fucking small. Had lil' man walking around looking like he was still stuck in the slavery days. Afro all the way out here and nappy as fuck. I had to buy the barber a new pair of blades when he was done cutting that shit off," I went off, getting angry all over again just thinking about it.

"You going to hell man," Kelly exclaimed, wiping the tears from her eyes and at the same time sucking in huge amounts of oxygen in.

"I think I peed on myself," Mona mumbled lifting her shirt up and looking down into her sweat pants. Me and Kelly's head quickly snapped in her direction our faces frowned up in disgust. "Eww bitch, too much info! Pissy ass hoe."

"Anyway!" Mona sung stretching the word out as she rolled her eyes at Kelly and flicked her off with both middle fingers. "When did Devin say that the results would be coming back in?" she asked me.

By then, I had already opened my bottle of water and was guzzling that shit down. My throat was drier than a bitch. I waited until the bottle was empty before responding. "Two weeks," I said with a slight belch.

Mona's and Kelly's eyebrows dipped into confusion. "Why two weeks, though? Can't you get them back sooner than that?" Kelly asked me first. "I know people who got their results back the next day, three days' tops."

"Yea. But I couldn't. Something about I had to wait until his supervisor goes on vacation sometime next week or some shit like that. It's whatever. I don't mind waiting as long as Ebony stay her dramatic hoe ass far as fuck away from me. I damn neared killed that bitch earlier. I can't stand her ass and that's The Gospel Truth."

"So what you gonna do when Devin comes back and confirms that he is yours?" Mona questioned, taking a huge bit out of her sandwich.

I leaned across the counter top and stole a cheese fry off of her plate. "What you mean what I'm gon' do? I'm going take care of mine. Even if that means that I got to deal with Ebony's ass for the next fourteen years, then so be it. I know what I am gon' do, though. The day I get those results back saying that Roman Jr came from my nut sack, I'm taking my ass down to the court house and filing for full custody. Her ass is unfit to be somebody's mother."

"I can respect it," Kells said nodding her head and scarfing down the rest of her food.

I reached out to grab another fry off of Mo's plate and she slapped my hand away hard as hell.

"Nigga, make your own," she yelled, moving her plate far away from me. The way her face scrunched up and her eyes glared at me as if I did something wrong should have been illegal in all fifty states. She looked like she was about to kill a nigga over her food.

"Man, quit being so damn greedy and let me get half of your sandwich," I begged, feeling drool running down my chin. That sandwich looked good as fuck and a nigga was hungry.

"Nigga no!"

"That's why yo ass fat now," I said, feeling defeated as I sat back down in my seat.

Mona picked up a fry from off her plate and threw it at me, hitting me dead in the eye. "Bald head trick," she mumbled rolling her eyes.

I laughed, picking the fry off of the floor and tossing it into the trash can. "Honey, please. My hair longer than that nappy shit on yo' head. Yo' ass just jealous," I joked, running my fingers through my curly fro that grew out back when I was in jail.

"Maybe in your dreams you do, but this is the real world boo boo."

"Yo, chill with those gay ass nicknames," I said. The seriousness in my tone made them laugh.

Mona picked up a knife off of the countertop, cut her sandwich in half, sat the other piece on a paper towel, and handed it to me. No lie, a nigga's eyes lit up like it was Christmas. I didn't hesitate to grab the sandwich out of her hands and bite into it. "Damn, no fries?" I asked with a mouthful of food.

Mona's face frowned and she looked at me as if she had an attitude. "Damn, nigga no," she spat heatedly. I just shook my head and raised my hands up in mock surrender.

Kelly started laughing, getting up from the table to throw away her empty plate. "So what you gon' do when the test comes back that your soldiers lost the battle to safety?" she asked me, making my ass choke from laughing. Like who in the fucks makes a reference like that? Only Kelly's mentally challenged ass.

"Safety? More like a danger zone," Mona cracked. "I'm surprised any sperm even made it. I use to think that her hot pussy ass worked better than any other birth control, but I guess I thought wrong," she cracked again.

"The both of y'all are wrong," I said laughing.

They looked at each other and started laughing. The fuck had they been smoking on?

"If RJ didn't come from my sack of loins, then I would feel hella bad. In the few hours that I did have RJ today, I kind of grew extremely attached to little dude. I was actually going around telling everybody that he is my son. If the results determined that he isn't mine, then y'all better go tell that bitch Ebony to run far the fuck away from me, hell move out of the country, because I'm deading that bitch on sight. Ruining my fucking relationship over something she couldn't have."

"Holl up, holl up, holl up nigga," Mona said with her hand up as if to tell me to stop talking. "Although I don't or can't stand that bitch," she paused and rolled her eyes hella hard, "You just can't put all the blame off on her. It takes two to tango, nigga."

"Right," Kelly cosigned.

I looked at the both of them like they had lost their damn minds until it dawned on me that they didn't know the shit Ebony pulled to get me to fuck her ass. I took thirty minutes out of my time and ran down the whole story to them about what happened. The same story that I had told Kam, Landon, and E, I told to Mo and Kells. When I was finished their mouths were dropped open, touching the countertop. No exaggeration.

"Yo, I swear I'm fucking that bitch up for hurting my best friend!" Kelly yelled, jumping up from her seat and pace the kitchen floor.

"Man, I heard of someone being thirsty but what the bitch did was some deranged desperate type shit. I'm with Kelly, that bitch got some muthafuckin heat coming her way. Bitch had my sister crying her ass off and made my brother out to be the bad guy. Her ass gots to go," Mona spat out venomously.

"Does Ari know?" Kelly asked me, stopping in midstride.

"Yea. I told her at the BBQ."

"Good," she said, going back to pacing the floor.

"As a matter of fact," Kelly stopped again and looked at me. "Nigga, you know where that bitch stays. Have momma watch RJ and Dooda for us, grab the keys, and let's go beat this bitch ass!" Kelly said, hyped. She started jumping up and down in the same spot popping her knuckles and punching the air. "I owe that bitch an ass whooping for thinking that she could threaten me and live to tell it.

Mona eyes grew wide with excitement and the next thing I knew, she was jumping up and down popping her knuckles and slap boxing with Kelly. "Oohhh bitch! Fuck yea! Bitch got away with five years for that shit. It's time to pay the muthafuckin' piper. She deserves this ass whooping. C'mon, Rome. Get yo' shit and let's go!"

I started laughing at them. I swear those two will go to war for Aris and likewise. "Aight now. Calm down, bulldogs. Ebony's time will come."

Right after I let that shit slide from my mouth, Mo's and Kells' slap box match immediately came to a stop. They looked down at me with their faces tighter than a bitch with Botox. They were pissed that I'd rained on their little parade. I couldn't do shit but laugh and ignore the glares of death that they were giving my ass.

"Bitch ass nigga," Kelly and Mona mumbled under their breaths, rolling their eyes at my ass.

I kicked it with Mo and Kelly for a little while longer just talking shit and trying to catch up on everything I'd missed out on in the last five years until it got dark outside. To be honest, the whole reason I even stayed around that long was because I was waiting for Aris to come through those doors. It crushed my soul when she never showed her face. When it was time to take RJ home, he begged and cried that he wanted to stay with me. He told me that he didn't want to go home that his momma would only make him stay in his room and yell at him when he asked for something. It pissed me off when he told me that all Ebony does is drink, smoke, and party all fucking night long while he's trying to sleep. What type of 'mother' throws a fucking house party there with her kid in the other room?

I had to promise RJ that he could stay the night with me just to get him to stop crying. I swear, wait until I got RJ to lay down and go to sleep, I was going over to Ebony's house and wring her fucking neck loose.

# Chapter Ten

**EBONY STEVENSON**

I huffed out a very heavy, irritated sigh as I got up and blew out the candles pissed that I had cooked a meal fit for a king all for nothing. Grilled lemon pepper steak, sliced potatoes, green beans, and chocolate dipped strawberries all gone to waste. It was going on eleven o'clock and Roman still hadn't showed his ass. If I knew that his ass was going to stand me up, then I wouldn't have told my dick that I had on standby not to come. A bitch was both pissed and horny at the same fucking time. As the time on the clock ticked by, I was getting even angrier knowing that Rome's ass was probably laid up with that ugly ass mutt and not here with me where he belonged. I swear that bitch Aris made my muthafuckin' ass itch. I just wished she would go lay down somewhere and fucking die. Then I could have Rome all to myself.

I was making my way upstairs to retire to bed early and use my battery operated boyfriend, B.O.B., as I liked to call him, just so that I could go to sleep when there was a knock on the door. Thinking that it was probably my momma's ass leaving the house without her keys like she always did, I opened the door without looking out of the peephole. Imagine the surprised look on my face when it was Rome standing there and not my momma.

Damn… Rome was looking good as fuck right about now. He must have changed, because the Adidas fit that he on earlier was gone. He wore a white wife beater that had his muscles flexing without him even trying, a pair of grey sweat pants, and a pair of Jordan slides. He had me salivating at the mouth. His print was clearly visible in his sweats. I had to hold onto the door to keep my knees from buckling he was so fucking fine! I loved everything about this man. Everything from his body, to his cognac-colored eyes, and of course that twelve-inch pole that I fell in love with the first time he blessed a bitch with it. Oowweee.

"Is you just going to stand there with your shit all out in the open and drool at the mouth or are you gonna move the fuck back so that I can come in?" His deep baritone voice brought me out of the little daydream that I didn't know I'd slipped in. Cheeks turning red in embarrassment, I moved to the side to let him in. Rome stepped in and closed the door behind him, lancing around the front room like it was the first time he had ever been there. I walked up behind him and wrapped my arms around his waist. It felt good to be this close to him.

"I'm glad that you came. I cooked your favorites for you. Lemon pepper steak, potatoes, green beans, and I even got chocolate strawberries for desert," I said trying to sound sexy and seductive my hands rubbing against his abs.

I heard Rome smack his lips before prying my arms from around his waist and turning around to face me. "Cut the bullshit out Ebony. Yo' lazy ass ain't cook shit. I've seen the Styrofoam plates outside in the trash can with Big Mama's Soul Food engraved on the top," he said with an arrogant ass smirk on his face. The smile that I had on my face immediately went away and my face flushed red. Fuck, I did leave those plates out!

Shaking any embarrassment away, I shrugged my shoulders. "Ok. You caught me. I didn't have time to cook so I bought something. Are you hungry?" I asked him, wrapping my arms back around his neck.

"No. I already ate," he said to me in a bland ass tone.

Fuck, there goes twenty-six dollars that I didn't have down the fucking drain. Do you know what I could've did with twenty-six dollars?! I thought to myself. "Well good. Now we can just skip straight to dessert," I said with a sexy smile.

"Ebony, I didn't come over here to fuck you. I need to talk to yo–',"

His sentence was caught short by me reaching into his sweats and grabbing his dick, giving it a hard squeeze. "What you wanna talk about?" I asked him mischievously as I continued stroking his beast and feeling it grow in my hands.

"I –','"

"Shush," I shushed him, slowly climbing down onto my knees. "Let me give you your welcome home present first," I said pulling his sweats down. I was anticipating his large tool in my mouth, when all of a sudden I was grabbed by my shoulders and yanked up to my feet. Grabbing me, Rome pushed me up against the wall. I would have been turned on by his roughness if it wasn't for the murderous look he was giving me. Fear instantly took over my body.

"I just fucking said that I'm not here to fuck you!" he spat through clench teeth. "I want to talk about what the fuck is this shit I hear about you yelling and putting your hands on my son all because he asked for a glass of water and the fucking house parties you throw when my son is in the other room!" he yelled angrily and at the same time was shaking my ass.

"Wh...what?" I asked him, feigning ignorance.

"Don't fucking play stupid with me, Eb. You heard me correctly, now answer my question," he barked spit flying out of his mouth. No lie, I was so fucking scared I almost pissed on myself. I had never seen Rome this mad before.

"Rome, I didn't whoop him. I hardly whoop that little boy. The only time I whoop RJ is when he asks for water when it's time for bed, knowing that he's going to piss in bed if he drinks before bed," I said lying through my teeth. I swear I'm beating RJ's ass. Always running his fucking mouth. Ass needs to stay in a child's place.

"You gon' sit up in my face and fucking lie?" he asked me sounding as if he was in disbelief. I just bit my tongue, refusing to answer his question. That was my story and I was sticking to it. "Ok," he said nodding his head up and down and letting me go. "Since your ass wanna fucking lie and shit, then don't expect RJ to be home anytime soon," he said heading for the front door.

I panicked. And it wasn't about Rome keeping my son away from me. That was a good thing because now I was free to do whatever the fuck I wanted to do. Truth be told, I never did want any kids. I despised them. The only reason why I kept RJ was because he was the key to my meal ticket. Don't get me wrong, I tried to fall in love with RJ, but I just don't have that mother instinct in me. As long as I could convince Rome that RJ came from his nut sack, then I would be using RJ to my fullest advantage. At the time, I wasn't even thinking about RJ. All that was on my mind was Rome going back home to his mutt bitch. "Where are you going?" I asked him, running up behind him and grabbing his arm.

"Home," was his reply.

"But…but…but you just got here," I stuttered. "Don't leave yet. I miss you. Please stay here," I said, practically begging him to stay.

Rome let out an irritated sigh. "Man go on somewhere with that bullshit, Ebony!" he yelled, yanking out of my hold and turning around to go back out of the door.

"You're going back home to be underneath that bitch, ain't you?" I spat with jealousy, folding my arms across my chest.

Rome stopped and turned around to look at me. "And if I was that ain't none of your fucking business, now is it? You ain't my girl. I ain't gotta tell you shit," he spat with his face contorted into a hard frown.

"Why are you treating me like this? I went through nine months carrying your son for you and being there for you! And this is how you treat me? The mother of your child!" I yelled through blurry vision as the waterworks started flowing. To say that I was hurt was an understatement. I really hated her ass! "I fucking love you and you left your family to be with that fucking mutt bitch! I hate her! What does she have that I don't have! I have always been there for you since day one. When you needed someone to hold your drugs for you, I was the one who offered my house as security! When you needed shit moved, I didn't hesitate to push that shit up inside of my pussy and travel across the fucking states for you! So why does she have you and not me?" I screamed out being all dramatic.

"Bitch, you will never be my girl!" he snapped at me with disgust. "Every nigga in the fucking hood has ran through your ass. The first time I met you, you sucked my dick behind the school bleachers. The only reason I kept you around was because you had a good head on your shoulders and knew how to make a nigga toes fucking curl. Yo' ass had to fucking drug and rape me just to even get me to run up in that jungle pussy! How else am I supposed to treat a thirsty, desperate, deranged ass hoe?"

His words stung and hurt me like hell. I couldn't believe that he'd just said that shit to me. I was really stung. Rome looked me up and down with his face still contorted into a frown, looking at me as if I disgusted him. "You got your priorities all fucked up, ma. You worrying about some dick that don't even belong to you when you should be asking me where your son at," he said shaking his head from side to side. Rome turned around once again to opened the front door but stopped. "Oh, and another thing. I went ahead and got Junior tested. You know since you act like you're too busy to do it," he announced his tone laced with sarcasm.

I instantly snapped out from my little trance that his words had sent my ass into. My eyes bulged from their sockets and my palms began to sweat. "You…you did," was all I managed to get out. I tried to appear as if I didn't care, but on the inside I was shitting bricks. Fuck!

Glancing back at me with dark murderous eyes Rome said, "Yea. You better pray and hope that RJ came out from my nut sacks. I'm pretty sure you know what's going to happen to you if I find out that he didn't," he said calmly. Although his voice was calm and collected, I heard the murderous intent loud and clear.

My knees waited until I heard the door opened then slammed closed before they finally gave in on me and I collapsed to the floor. My breathing picked up and I started hyperventilating. I guess it's time for me to state the obvious, huhn? Confession time! RJ does not belong to Rome!

# Chapter Eleven

**MONAE "Mona" CLARKSON**

"Bitch, there he goes get down hoe!" Kelly whispered harshly, as she grabbed me by the shirt and pulled me down in my seat. We both ducked just time to see Rome's car drive past us. I know y'all probably like 'Wtf… did these heffas really follow Rome to that girl's house?' Well, to answer y'all question. Yes, the fuck we did! Kelly and I were serious as fuck earlier, and Rome wanted to laugh it off like what we said was a joke. We were dead muthafuckin' serious. That bitch Ebony needed her ass whipped.

I know that Aris should be the one serving Ebony the ass beating of the century, but we already know that she ain't gonna do it. Aris was the true meaning of being a sweetheart. If you look up the word in the dictionary, I'll guarantee you that her picture is right under it. It's just not her personality to do something like that. With Aris' personality, she's just going to keep letting that hoe slide with all the shit that she does until she finally snaps. Of course, she has an attitude problem and can get saucy at the mouth, but it never goes beyond that. It takes a lot to upset E and push her to the point where she said fuck talking and began throwing blows. E isn't a very violent person and would rather talk things out first; only resorting to violence when she absolutely has to. In clearer words, when muthafuckas start messing with her family, that's when she gets violent. The beef between Ebony and E didn't just start with Rome. This shit goes way back to elementary and middle school. It was like the shit has been predestined for them. They were destined to become each other's enemies. Ebony has always been a hating ass bitch who is extremely jealous over Aris and anyone else who was better than her.

Back in high school, Ebony and her little flunkies were always fucking with E, but no matter what they did Aris wouldn't beat the living daylights out of her ass. Instead, she would turn and walk away, shrugging the situation off of her shoulders, giving Ebony a chance after chance. Ebony knows that Aris isn't going to fight her, that's why she keeps fucking with the girl.

Aris is the calm collected one out of the trio. Me, I'm in the between. I can control my anger, but only for so long. I'm not so violent and would love to stay drama free, but at the same time, I don't take shit from nobody. Growing up, my father instilled the importance of respecting someone and someone returning that same respect. If I feel like I'm being disrespected, then I'mma let that person know. With me, I give one warning and one warning only. If that warning continues to get ignored, then it's lights out. Kelly, on the other hand, is a very violent muthafucka. Her ass has a very short temper and doesn't hesitate to pass out ass whoopings. Any and everybody can get it when it comes to her. She and Kamron seriously belong together, because they act the same damn way.

Nobody can stand Ebony's ass. Each and every one of us has a reason why we should beat her ass. I've owed that bitch since we were in middle school when the bitch stole my diary out of my desk and began reading it in front of the class when she was supposed to be presenting her science project. I swear I wanted to die right then and there when she went to the page I wrote for my crush. It was a corny ass poem that I wrote for my entertainment only and that bitch read it to my crush. I swear if it wasn't for Mr. Samuels protecting her ass, I would've killed that bitch right then and there. The icing on the cake was when she started fucking with the boy I was crushing on. That was the straw that broke the camel's back.

I wanted her ass bad, but E always kept coming to the girl's rescue and stopping me. Even after all of that shit that Ebony has done to E, she still forgave her and continued to let her slide. Aris needs to beat her ass from all the nick picking the bitch did. Kells has wanted to beat Ebony's ass just because she couldn't stand her ass. We've given Ebony chance after chance to leave us the fuck alone all for the sake of Aris coming to us and begging us not to beat her ass. But now the bitch is getting what's coming to her. Especially when Roman admitted the real reason he and Aris broke up. The ass whooping that she was going to get tonight is just karma coming back around to finally get her ass.

Hence, the reason why Kelly and I are outside, parked three houses down, stalking this bitch's house in our beat-a-bitch's-ass gear. We were dipped in black from head to toe. We both wore black sweat pants, black hoodies although it was damn near eighty degrees tonight, black Timbs, and our hair braided straight to the back.

"Alright, he's gone now," Kelly breathed a sigh of relief, as she leaned up in her seat. "Are you ready?" she turned in her seat to ask me as if she was making sure that I was down and not gonna back out at the last minute.

Instead of answering her question, I just pulled my hoodie over my head and got out of the car. The first thing I did was look around for any nosy ass neighbors before jogging towards Ebony's door with Kells right behind me. Kelly looked at me, nodding her head towards the front door. Slowly, I raised my hand and knocked three times hard on the door.

BANG! BANG! BANG!

"Who is it?!" her irritating voice had me rolling my eyes and sucking my teeth in irritation. When I heard her heavy footsteps coming closer towards the door, I placed my thumb over the peephole, just in case she tried looking out of it first. The locks turning on the door was our signal to get ready.

"I just knew you were coming back! I knew you wanted this while you were playing so hard to get," Ebony said sounding like a true thot opening the door with this big ass grin on her face. Wrong fucking move. The moment that she saw it was us, and not my brother, her eyes widened with fear and her mouth fell open in shock.

"Wrong nigga, bitch!" Kelly snapped as her hand went back and her fist went flying dead into Ebony's face. Kells had hit her ass so damn hard Ebony went flying off of her feet and across the room. We hurried and stepped inside the house, closed the door, and locked it.

"Didn't think I was coming back to tag that ass did you, huh, bitch?" Kells asked Ebony kicking her in the side. Ebony gasped breathlessly. Her hands immediately went to her side where Kells had kicked her. "Don't nobody threaten me and think they gonna live and tell it!"

After saying that Kelly went into commencing a good old fashion ass whooping, doing nothing but face shots. When her arms got tired, she started stomping her ass. I was just standing there watching thinking to myself like damn, my bitch got it, she got it. I couldn't jump in even if I wanted to. Kelly handled that shit. No lie, with each cry for help and groan I was starting to feel bad for Ebony, but not so bad to where I wanted to jump in and break it up. Nah, fuck that. She was going to have to learn one day. I must admit Kelly was fucking her ass up. She was damn near unrecognizable. Blood was dripping out from the corners of her mouth. Purple and blue bruises immediately began forming all over her skin.

"You steady fucking with Aris like she ain't got hittas that would straight go hard for her on her team! Bitch, you got me all the way fucked up if you thought that we were just gonna sit back and let you keep fucking with my girl. You've been fucking with her for the longest. Bitch, it's time for you to take this ass whooping like a true muthafuckin' woman. Aris ain't here to save yo ass now. Bitch every time I see yo' ass, I'm tagging you!"

Kells went on and beat her ass about five minutes nonstop until she got tired. "Man, this shit is boring as fuck! After all of that big shit she was talking the other day, I would've expected some type of real fight. This weak bitch just laid down curled up in a ball crying and shit! If you don't have a bite to match that bark, then your weak ass shouldn't have said shit and stayed in a weak bitch's lane," she spat, bending over holding her knees panting heavy. "Shit. I'm tired. Those muthafuckin' sandwiches getting to my fat ass now," she said, making me laugh.

It took Kelly about two minutes to catch her breath. "Are you done?" I asked her with my hand on the door.

Kelly looked at me, down at Ebony, then back up at me again. She lifted her foot and kicked Ebony in the stomach one last time before saying she was done. I couldn't do shit but shake my fucking head at her extra ass. We walked out that bitch and back to our car parked down the street like we didn't just get done kicking somebody's ass. Kells climbed into the driver's seat and burned rubber. Hopefully, Ebony gets her shit together and thinks before opening her mouth talking slick to a muthafucka.

# Chapter Twelve

**ARIS**

It's been two and a half weeks since Rome has been out of jail and since Q put his hands on me. Meaning I have been stuck here in this house underneath this nigga for two and a half weeks straight! To say that I was very irritated and aggravated would be putting it very lightly! I was about to commit a murder being all underneath Quamir's ass all day long. His clinginess is suffocating me! I would leave and go home if it wasn't for the big bruise on my back from being pushed into the dresser and a red mark around my neck from Q choking me. The bruise on my back was so big there was no way to hide it. For some reason, it was taking my body a lot longer to heal than normal. When I do get a bruise from bumping into something, it usually takes anywhere between three to five days to go away. I guess because the bruise covered up the majority of my back, it took longer to heal.

The night that Quamir and I had that big argument that led to us putting our hands on each other, Q disappeared and didn't come home for three days. He didn't call or text me the whole time he was M.I.A. Not that I gave a fuck anyway. I was actually happy that I could relax with the house all to myself. The day he did finally come home to show his face, he tried apologizing by buying me expensive ass gifts. He bought me a seven-karat diamond princess cut ring, a pair of Christian Louboutin red bottom pumps, and a Burberry handbag, thinking I was going to just accept it and forgive him for putting his hands on me. I told him to go fuck himself with a sick crackhead's dick and take those gifts and shove it up his ass.

I took the ring, shoes, and handbag and sold that shit on EBAY for half the price he paid, then turned right back around bought the same pair of shoes and handbag, in a different color. Yep, I was being queen petty, but ask me if I gave a fuck about his feelings. I don't want shit from Q's ass.

As sad as it is for me to say, I already found myself falling out of love with him. And I'm not saying that just because Roman is out and walking amongst us. I figured that out a few months ago. It took me a while, but I had finally opened my eyes and admitted that my love for Quamir just wasn't there anymore. His insecurity and possessive ways had pushed me far away and to be honest, I'd had enough of feeling like I needed to put up with the bullshit when I obviously deserved better. I finally came to the decision to end our relationship. It'd already run its course. I had plans to tell Quamir how I felt and end this. By tomorrow I'd be a free woman and would start back focusing on going to school like I originally planned on doing before meeting Q's sorry ass. Ugh.

When I woke up this morning, I was on a mission. The mission to finally dead what Quamir and I called a relationship and start my life fresh as a single woman. When I got up this morning, Q was nowhere to be found. I was pissed that I couldn't just get this over with, but at the same time, I was somewhat relieved. Lord knows I wasn't ready to have this conversation yet. This was going to be hella hard. Especially when I just found out yesterday that I was pregnant. Yep. You heard me right. Quamir finally trapped my ass with a baby. I had took the pregnancy test where it tells you how far along you are and come to find out I became pregnant the first time Q came inside of me without using any protection. I made myself a memo that night to get a Plan B bill from Walgreens and fucking forgotten. Now look at me. Pregnant by a nigga that I don't want shit to do with any more.

Determined to get out and enjoy myself after being hidden away for two long weeks, I decided that today I was going to pamper myself. I called the girls to see if they wanted to join me for my girl's day out, but Mo already had made plans with Landon to take Levi to Chuck E.

Cheese's, and Kelly didn't answer her phone. So, I guess I was going to be by myself today. The first thing that I did was treat myself to a full body hot oil massage at my new all-time favorite spot Beautify my Beauty. It had just opened a few months ago, and the place stayed busy. It was so packed there that you have to make appointments ahead of time, and quick too, unless you had connections like me. I met the owner a while back when the place was still it's renovation stage.

I had been eyeing this baby for a long time in hopes of purchasing it and turning it into a beauty parlor myself. Kelly was a beast when it came to doing somebody's hair. She was Mo's and my personal hairstylist because we didn't let anybody else touch our shit. Kelly always wanted to open up her own hair salon, but never had the chance to. So, Mona and I took the initiative to start looking around for buildings. We wanted to surprise Kelly with it for her twenty-first birthday. But, before I was even able to come up with all of the money for the building, someone had already beat me to the punch and purchased the place.

The owner was really chill and laid back. Although when I first met her, she had that look like she was not to be fucked with and wouldn't hesitate to beat a bitch's ass, she was a cool ass chick. We talked that day and found out that we had a lot of things in common. We exchanged numbers that day and had been texting each other ever since. She wasn't from around this way nor lived anywhere close to her business, but she always flew down here at least once a month to check on it. She went by the name of Slim.

Now I'm not a hater and would admit if another woman was pretty or not, so I'm not afraid to tell y'all that Slim was drop dead gorgeous. Light-skinned, crystal clear emerald green eyes, and long, pretty curly hair. Slim could stop traffic if she wanted to. She really had me questioning my sexuality, she was just that pretty. We made plans to meet up again once she was in town. I was going to introduce her to the girls. I knew that if I liked her, Mona and Kelly would too. She was just that down to Earth and cool to chill with.

Whenever I came here, I would always get the De-Stress Spa package and the Ultimate Spa experience. The prices were very high, running me almost seven-hundred dollars, but in the end, it was well worth it. When I walked out those doors, my body would feel like I was flying and my skin would have a beautiful, radiant glow. I was feeling like a million bucks and all the previous stress that I carried had melted away.

After leaving the spa, I ended up stopping by a shoe outlet and showed the fuck out. I was on my way down to the nail spa when I came across the shoe outlet. I wasn't trying to stop by that store, but as you know shoes are every woman's weakness, and they had a pair of boots that I knew that I had to have. I ended up buying a nude pair of designer pumps with a gold ankle strap, a pair of brown knee-high stiletto boots, a red pair of ankle booties with golden strap buckles and a black pair of snakeskin open-toed stiletto booties with the cut out heel and added them all to my sick shoe collection back at home. I had everything from the sexiest pair of pumps to style in, from boots to flats and owned every Jordan that was ever released. I was a versatile girl who could rock stiletto heels and tennis shoes at the same time.

It was five o'clock when I finally made it back to Quamir's place. It was then I realized that Quamir had not made one attempt to call me the whole time I had been gone. To say that I was shocked would have been an understatement. I was flabbergasted! I pulled into the driveway and noticed that his car was parked outside, meaning that he was home. For a while, I just sat in my car, trying to decide whether I wanted to give our relationship one last try or just wave the white flag now and call it quits. An hour later, I finally made my decision. I was going to keep my man and work on our relationship. We'vdbeen on this thing for two years now, there's no way I could just turn my back and walk away. I'd invested too much of my time into this. Of course, this time around there were going to be some major changes that I would be addressing tonight. Starting with Quamir's possessive and jealous behavior.

With a smile on my face, I grabbed my Burberry satchel from the passenger seat and proceeded to climb out of the car and go into the house. The first thing I noticed when I walked inside was the smell of delicious food cooking. Following my nose into the kitchen, there was dinner for two. Quamir cooked our favorite which consisted of creamy garlic shrimp alfredo, cheesy garlic bread, and a fresh salad. Rose petals decorated the dining table, wine was chilling on ice, and low music played in the background, setting the scene.

"Aww… he's so sweet! Who knew that behind that rough thug ass shell was a romantic, loving dude," I said, walking over to the stove and opening it to check on the alfredo and garlic bread which was sitting in the oven to keep warm. Grabbing the oven mitts, I slipped them on and took our food out and set it on the table.

"Let me go find this man so that we can eat. I'm starving!" I said to myself as I was walking up the stairs and towards our bedroom where R. Kelly crooned from the speakers, telling somebody to keep it on the down low. Pushing the door open, I was not prepared for the shock that I was about to receive. I opened our bedroom door in hopes of seeing my man waiting for me butt ass naked, ready to give me what I was craving the moment I walked in the house and saw dinner ready along with the roses and wine. Instead, I'm standing still, frozen in my spot with the bedroom door now wide open, watching my man have sex with another woman in the bed that we share. They were so focused on each other and into it that neither even saw or heard me come into the room. It was like déjà vu all over again.

Quamir was laying on his back with his knees bent upwards, his ass lifting off of the bed, with his hands holding securely onto the girl's hips as he pounded in and out of her in a fast rapid motion. I couldn't stop the aching in my chest even if I wanted to. That shit hurt so fucking badly that I instantly stopped breathing. I was in so much pain that I began to hyperventilate. I felt like I was about to have a heart attack when all that was happening was my heart breaking for the second time by someone whom I loved dearly. I couldn't believe that after all the shit that we went through, him accusing me of fucking around on him, the whole time it had been him fucking around on me! It was as if someone switched on a light switch and the sweet, calm, and collected person that I am disappeared, and this mean I'm about to beat a bitch's ass bitch came out. The pain immediately melted away and was replaced by anger and hatred for this man that I'd spent two years of my life with.

I picked up the first thing that I saw, which was a picture of Quamir and me posing at the park, and tossed that bitch across the room, hitting the woman in the back of her head.

"Ow! What the fuck!" she yelled, grabbing the back of her head. Me throwing the picture and hitting old girl upside the fucking head caused them to jump away from each other as if someone had suddenly lit a fire and turn their attention towards the door. The shocked look on Quamir's face was so comical that I wished at that moment I had walked in with a camera.

"So, this is why you haven't been blowing up my phone today, " I said calmly as I stood at the end of the bed with my arms folded across my chest. I was so calm that even I shocked myself. "You got to be kidding me, right?"

"Aris, b…baby! I… I can explain!" he said, making the woman he was fucking's face frown and causing her head to snap in his direction.

"Why the fuck you need to anything explain to her? You need to be explaining to me, your wife, what the fuck is going on and why is this bitch in our house!" she screamed at him.

"Your wife?!" I screamed at him in disbelief.

"Yes, bitch his wife," she stressed while waving her ring finger in the air, displaying the huge rock that sat pretty on her finger.

Quamir's eyes immediately went black, and if looks could kill, old girl would have been outlined in chalk.

"Are you fucking serious?! Is this shit true?!" I screamed at him, at the same time fighting to hold my tears back. Quamir never answered my question and just looked at me with apologetic eyes. His eyes confirmed everything she said to be true, but I wanted to still hear it out of the horse's mouth.

"Answer me muthafucka!" I spat heatedly at him.

"Bitch, don't be talking to my husband like that!" Quamir's wife yelled at me, at the same time jumping up with her fists balled up at the side like she was going to do something.

"Bitch, sit yo' silly rabbit looking ass down somewhere before I beat your ass down! My beef ain't with you, it's with your supposed husband, but you can guarantee that you can get these hands, too. My hands don't discriminate. Male or female. I will beat yo' muthafuckin' ass! You better ask around about me!" I spat so venomously that you could see the fear in her eyes and the shock on Quamir's face.

"And you got one more time to call me out of my name! Now back to your friendly ass. Is it true?"

Quamir sighed in defeat. "I'm sorr,y E. I never meant to hurt you, but to answer your question yes, this is my wife of seven years and the mother of my two children, Monica. You were actually supposed to be a one-night stand, a casual fuck, while I was out here trying to get my feet wet in the game before moving my family out here, but I ended catching real feelings behind your ass, girl. I'm so fucking sorry man," he said with sad, apologetic eyes.

*SLAP!*

"You bitch made ass nigga! You really gon' sit up here in my face and admit to having feelings for this bitch! I should beat your muthafuckin ass!" Monica screamed as she pounced on top of Quamir and began raining blows all over his head and face. Quamir just balled into a fetal position on the bed and lied there, trying his best to protect his face.

I was honestly shocked. To hear the man that you have given two years of your life to just admit to living a double life is enough to turn a sane bitch crazy. I just stood there in a daze about five minutes, watching them fight and go back and forth with each other, before I had seen enough of ass and titties jumping around. I quickly took the key to Quamir's house off my keychain and tossed it, knocking him upside of his head with it. "Bitch ass nigga, lose my fucking number and stay far the fuck away from me," I said to him one last time before spinning on my heels and walking out of his life for the last and final time.

***

"There goes my budda butt! I missed you stinky!" Kelly screamed as she ran to me with her arms opened wide, hugging me tight.

"Damn Kells, the girl just got home from being locked away for two weeks, let her breathe and enjoy her freedom before the warden comes back," Mona said, laughing coming out of the kitchen with Levi in one arm and a baby bottle filled with apple juice in her hand.

"Shut up, Monae," Kelly laughed, letting me go. "Girl, I thought I was going to have to go up there and kidnap you from Q's ass. Don't you ever leave me in this house alone with that bitch ever again. You know we can't stand to be in the same room together without arguing," Kells said jokingly.

"Oh, shut up thot. I should be the one complaining. Between you and Kamron's nymphomaniac asses I ain't had a decent night of sleep since the last time E was home," Mona countered, laughing.

"What's wrong, Aris?" Mona asked me once she got closer to me. Her sudden and random question had Kelly looking me dead in my face. You could see the worry and concern in their eyes.

"Nothing, " I said as I leaned in and planted a kiss on Levi's forehead. He looked so peaceful sleeping in the comfort of his mother's arms.

"Then why are your eyes puffy and red?" Kelly asked me after grabbing my chin and expected my face. "You've been crying?"

I pulled my head out of Kells' grasp and let out a nervous laugh. "Girl, no. My eyes are red because I just got through smoking on a big, fat ass blunt before coming here and I don't know why my eyes are puffy. Maybe it's because I'm sleepy, " I lied to them.

Mo and Kells looked me in my face with a facial expression that said that they knew I was lying, but instead of being persistent, they just left it alone. "Well, if you say so," Mona said skeptically.

"What are you about to do?" Kells asked me.

"I'm tired, so I'm about to go lay down and go to bed."

"Since you're tired, you wouldn't mind watching Levi for me. I already gave him a bath, and as you can see, he is asleep."

I looked back and forth at Mona and Kells with slanted eyes. "Where is your hot in the pants ass about to go?" I asked with a raised eyebrow.

"Well if you must know… Kells, Landon, Kam and me are about to go down to the sport's bar for a couple of drinks and a few rounds of pool."

"And y'all don't invite me? Ok, I see how y'all do it now. I'm hurt," I said jokingly with my hand over my heart, faking as if I was truly hurt.

"Boo, please," Kells laughed with a roll of her eyes. "Your warden ain't about to let you out to play with us unless he's there to babysit. And besides, why should we invite you to come along when all you're going to do is turn around and go back home once Rome comes."

"Rome's going?" I asked them.

"Yes," they answered in unison.

I sucked my teeth and rolled my eyes, "Never mind. I would rather sit home by myself and babysit than sit and watch Rome flirt with other women." I didn't realize what I said or how jealous I sounded until the words had already left my mouth. I looked at Mona and Kelly snickering.

"I don't know why you don't just drop Quamir's tired ass and get back with yo' boo, " Kells said laughing.

"Ha! I'll think about giving Rome another chance when she," I pointed my finger at Mona, "admits that she likes Landon more than what she is letting on and you," I pointed my finger at Kells, "quit playing with my brother and make it official," I said leaving them with their mouths hanging open. I laughed and grabbed my nephew and baby bottle out of Mona's hands.

"I guess it's just you and me tonight little man," I cooed into his ear as I kissed the top of his head. "Have fun girls!" I yelled over my shoulder as I walked up the stairs.

Kelly and Mona left an hour ago, and I was still lying awake in the middle of my bed with Levi curled up on the side of me deep in my own thoughts. My heart was still hurting from all of the shit that I found out about Q earlier, but I'd stopped crying. I sat outside in the driveway and cried for an hour straight before saying enough. To be honest, I was more hurt when I caught Rome and Ebony together than I was catching Q and his wife. I'm more shocked than hurt finding out about Q's double life. Since leaving Q and his wife back at his house, Quamir had been blowing up my phone with back to back calls and texts begging me to answer the phone. I was so over and done with Quamir's ass that I called my phone company and got my number changed. I even had it set up that all unknown numbers would be automatically blocked. I laid in bed until sleep finally took over me.

***

You know how you get that feeling that you are being watched? Well, that's how I was feeling even while I was asleep. I was lying in a deep sleep when the sound of my bedroom door opening and closing, waking me. I didn't think anything of it because I honestly thought it was Mona or Kelly coming in to check on me. I continued to lay with my eyes closed until the strong scent of weed and alcohol insulted my nostrils. Waking up, I looked up to see Quamir standing over me with red, bloodshot eyes. I knew right then he was either high, drunk, or both.

Leaning up, I wiped the sleep from my eyes before checking the alarm clock. It was only a little after twelve, so I knew that Mo and Kelly weren't back yet. The sports bar doesn't close for another three hours from now, and knowing them heffas and my brothers they are going to stay until the bar closes. I looked to the other side of the bed for Levi and noticed that he was gone.

"I took him to his room," Q said right before I was about to start panicking.

"What the hell are you doing here, Quamir? How in the hell did you get in?" I asked him in a groggy voice as I pressed my back against the headboard.

"Why haven't you been answering my calls? I told you that I had something important to tell you, and I needed to talk to you?" he said taking a seat next to me at the edge of my bed.

"I have nothing to say to you, Quamir. Didn't I tell you to stay far the fuck away from me and to leave me the fuck alone? Whatever you and I had is over! I'm moving on, and it's time that you do the same with your real family."

"What the fuck you mean it's over!" he yelled, shooting me this deadly deranged look that I had never seen before. "It's not over until I fucking say it's over, ya hear me?"

This time, I looked at him with my head cocked to the side and through tiny slits. My anger immediately shot through the roof. "Are you fucking serious?! You are fucking married! I don't belong to you! I'm not your fucking property and now that this shit is over with I can do what the fuck I want to! I do not want to be with your tired, lying, cheating ass, son of a bi—',"

*SLAP!*

The slap to the side of my face was so unexpected and came out of nowhere that the only thing I could do was look at him with my mouth hanging open in shock. I finally snapped out of my state of shock and slapped his ass back which was returned with an even harder slap to the other side of my face, busting my lip in the process.

"Bitch, you must have bumped your fucking head somewhere and lost your fucking mind. I'm tired of you trying to play me as some type of fuck ass nigga who is so scared of your bitch ass brother that you think that I won't put my hands on you!" Quamir spat in my face spit flying out from the corners of his mouth. I looked at him and at that moment it was like staring at the devil himself. His eyes were bloodshot red and completely cold and dark. He was looking like he was straight possessed or something.

"Do you honestly think I'm just going to let you leave me just so that you can get into the arms of your other nigga?" he asked me in a dark, cold tone.

"Wha…what are you talking about?" I asked him, honestly confused. As far as I was notified, I didn't have any other nigga, so what the fuck was he talking about now?

"You know exactly what the fuck I'm talking about so don't fucking play dumb with me!" Quamir spat, his grip around my neck tightening with each word that came out of his mouth. I looked at him with wide eyes and instantly began clawing at his hands as he continued to choke me. I felt myself about to pass out but found the strength to fight when my thoughts drifted off to Levi and to the unborn baby that I had just found out about a few days ago. I looked around the room for something, hell anything I could use to get this big nigga off of me before he ended up killing me.

"You want that bitch ass nigga Rome, don't you?" he asked me through clenched teeth. "Well, bitch, too muthafuckin' bad that nigga ain't here to save yo' hoe ass! Because bitch, you about to die tonight," he yelled in my face, his hands crushing my windpipe.

Just then my eyes landed on the picture frame of my brother, my dad, stepmom and me at his mansion in Columbia sitting on the nightstand next to my bed. I desperately began reaching for it but couldn't quite touch it. I bucked my body against his one good time, and when I felt my fingers grazing the cold metal frame, I quickly picked it up and hit him in the back of his head with it splitting his shit wide the fuck open.

"Ah! Fuck!" he screamed out as he released me to attend to the wound on the back of his head. While I had the chance, I quickly rolled over onto the other side of the bed where I began sucking in deep breaths of air to calm down the burning sensation in my lungs.

"You fucking bitch! I'm about to kill your ass!" he said evilly.

I tried to make an attempt to make a run for it when Quamir grabbed me by my hair and slammed me face down on the hardwood floor. I cried out in excruciating pain. I felt the blood gushing from my nose and my nose snapping.

"You want to leave me to be under that nigga! Bitch, I will fucking kill you before I let that shit happen! Yo' ass belongs to me, and you're not going anywhere unless I fucking say so!"

"Quamir pleased stop!" I cried weakly as I curled into a fetal position to protect my unborn baby. "I'm pregnant!" I blurted out.

"Fuck you telling me for? That ain't my fucking baby!" he spat in pure disgust.

What he did next broke my heart and crushed whatever feelings that I did have left for him to itty bitty pieces. As I was recouping from the last hit my face had taken on the hardwood floor; Quamir raised his foot up and violently kicked me in the side of my stomach knocking all of the wind out of me.

"Aaaaarrrrgggghhhhhhhhhh!" I screamed out in pain as I felt a sharp pain shoot through my stomach then followed by a warm liquid running down my inner thighs. My baby!

Quamir grabbed my hair, turned me onto my back where he mounted me and wrapped both of his hands around my throat again. Once again I felt myself about to pass out. The sharp pains I was feeling ripping through my stomach was enough to make me pass out and succumb to the darkness. As much as I want to close my eyes and drift off somewhere else the baby inside of me made me want to go harder. With whatever energy I had left remaining I lifted my knee up and violently kicked Quamir in his nuts bringing the big giant down to his knees. Literally.

"Aaaarrgghh! Fuck!" he yelled out breathlessly as his hand left my neck and went to his balls.

I leaned up and pushed him the fuck off of me and at the same time sucked in quick breaths of air. It took every ounce of my strength to get off of the floor. I tried making another run for it, but Quamir grabbed me by my ankle making me fall down on my knees.

"Let me the fuck go!" I screamed as I raised my free leg up and kicked him as hard as I could in his face.

"Aaargh!" Quamir screamed out in agony releasing my ankle.

I climbed back on my feet again and made a sprint out of the room as if I was competing for first place in the Olympics. At that moment the only thing that was on my mind was getting downstairs to the phone and calling for help. I ran downstairs with one hand nursing my throbbing stomach taking three steps at a time. I made a swift dash to the kitchen where the cordless phone sat on the counter top. I heard the floors upstairs creaking alerting me that Quamir was up and right behind me.

My heart was beating fast as hell as a light sweat broke across my forehead. My chest clenched tightly with fear as I tried to dial the first number that I could think of. My hands were so shaky that I ended up dropping the phone onto the floor.

"Shit!" I yelled as panic sat in.

I hurried up bent down and dialed a number up. The phone rang about three times and on the third ring somebody picked up.

"Hello," a deep baritone voice said smoothly into the phone. You could hear the music playing lowly in the background.

"Oh my God! Kamron! Please help me!" I cried desperately, my hands shaking and chest caving in and out in fear.

"E?" The voice called out to me. It was then I recognize that voice to be Rome's.

"Oh my God! Roman! Save me! Please, you have to save me! He's after me. He's gonna kill me!" I screamed hysterically into the phone. I was so hysterical and paralyzed with fear that I was spitting out my words so fast that they were coming out in a slur.

You could hear Roman get up from wherever he was and move into another room where it was much quieter at. "Calm down Aris. Now tell me who's after you? Who's trying to kill you?" he asked me in a calm tone. You could tell that Rome was trying to stay calm just to calm me down, but you could still hear the panic in his voice.

"He's gonna kill me!" I screamed crying harder.

"Who gonna kill you?!"

"Qua-,'"

*CRASH!*

Quamir appeared out of nowhere and with a glass vase he busted me in the back of my head with it cutting my sentence very short. My body instantly went crashing to the floor making the house phone slide out of my hand and across the floor. I was in so much pain that I could no longer cry, and my body was going numb. I swear I saw black spots behind my eyelids.

"What the fuck?! Aris? Aris!" I heard Roman screaming through the phone.

Through half-closed eyelids, I saw Quamir walk over to where the house phone slid, pick it up and just stared at it. He looked back and forth between me and the phone a few times before ending the call. The last thing I remember was Quamir ripping my clothes from off of my body and him entering my bleeding vagina before everything went black.

## Chapter Thirteen

**ROME**

*"He's gonna kill me!"* Aris screamed loudly into my ear through uncontrollable sobs.

"Who's gonna kill you?!" I yelled. The alarm and seriousness in my voice had not only gathered the attention of other patrons but Kamron and them as well. I watched out the corner of my eye, Kamron threw the pool stick across the table and run over to where I was standing.

"—,"

*CRASH!*

"What the fuck?! Aris?! Aris!" I screamed into the phone.

I heard heavy footsteps approaching then someone picking up the phone. I heard someone breathing heavily into the phone. I was trying my hardest not to fear the worst and think that this was some type of sick ass joke Aris was trying to play, but once I heard the heavy breathing on the other line I knew something bad had happened.

"Aris!" I had screamed one last time before I was left with the dial tone.

"Yo, what the fuck is you yelling for? What is wrong with my little sister?" Kamron asked me his deep voice was laced with panic and concern.

"I don't fucking know! But, we need to get to the girl's house pronto," I said as I made a dash for the exit door. Hearing the sound of heels and tennis shoes running behind me let me know that my team wasn't far behind me. We all hopped in Kam's truck and burned rubber. I had Kamron breaking all kinds of traffic laws while I used his phone to call Aris hoping that E will pick up. I swear my heart was thumping loudly in my chest. Each call that went unanswered took whatever hope that I was holding onto with it. I felt it in my gut that something was wrong.

"Did anybody get in touch with E?" I turned in my seat and asked the girls.

Kelly and Mona face with masked with worry and concern. They looked at each other then up at me. "No. She's not answering her cell phone either," Mona answered sadly.

I leaned forward and punched the dashboard with my fist in frustration. "Kamron drive this muthafucka!" I screamed at him. Kamron's foot pressed all the way down on the gas pedal pushing one hundred on the speedometer. Twenty-minutes felt like five hours. Kamron didn't even have the truck all the way in the park before I jumped out that bitch and took off running towards the house. Kelly had already beaten me to the door and by the time I was on the porch she had the door unlocked and was rushing inside.

Kelly had made it in the house first and worked her way further into the front room.

"Aris!" Kelly yelled out, but no answer in return.

The house was too fucking quiet. I knew off the bat something was wrong and immediately went for my gun. Carefully everybody filed inside of the house with their guards all the way up. Kam, Landon and me had our guns out with the safety off ready to shoot anything moving whilst Kelly had a metal baseball bat, and Mo had her Taser. If the situation wasn't so serious, I would have fallen out laughing. Like what in the hell was a Taser gonna do?

Mona gasped. "Oh my God! Look, there's blood!" Everyone turned and looked in Mona's direction and just as she said, there was a small trail of blood leading from the stairway towards the kitchen. With Kelly in the lead, we followed the trail of blood. Opening the kitchen door, Kelly was the first to step inside with Mona right on her heels.

"Aaaaahhhhhhh!" They screamed together in horror. "Aris!" Kelly cried out with tears streaming down her face. She and Mona made a quick dash around the kitchen island before dropping to the floor.

Landon was right behind them and whatever he saw made him gasp with his hand covering his mouth. Judging from the look in his eyes whatever we were about to see wasn't pretty. There was nothing on this earth that could have prepared me for what I was about to see. The love of my life was lying naked in a puddle of her own blood. Her long, beautiful black hair looked like somebody had taken a pair of scissors and just hacked her shit off, her eye was black, her lips and nose were bleeding profusely, and she had thick blood clots running down her inner thighs. Her face was so swollen that you could hardly recognize her, and her golden skin was covered in purple, blue bruises. There was blood everywhere! Kamron, who was the last person to come into the kitchen pushed past everyone and ran over towards Aris.

"What the fuck! E!" Kamron yelled out dropping down to his knees and swooping Aris' still body into his arms. "Aris, please baby, wake up! Please get up!" Kamron begged with tears the size of gumdrops falling down his face.

It broke my heart seeing her like that. My breathing started shallowing out, and my chest felt like something heavy was sitting on top it.

"Please, girl don't do this to us!" Mona cried out sitting on the floor beside Kamron running her fingers through Aris' bloody hair.

Rocking back and forth with Aris in his arms, Kamron held her body tightly in his arms as if he was afraid that she was going to disappear and letting his tears fall. In all of my years knowing Kam this is my first time ever witnessing him cry. And this wasn't just no a couple tears here and a couple of tears there. No, he was in a full blown out ugly cry.

Kelly grabbed Aris' wrist checking for a pulse. "She still has a pulse! It's faint, but she is still breathing! C'mon Kam. We have to hurry and get her to the hospital. If we don't hurry, we won't be able to save her!" She screamed.

Kamron just sat there holding onto Aris' body with a far off and glossy look in his eyes. It was like his body was there, but his mind was somewhere else.

"C'mon Kam! We need to get Aris some help right now!" Landon yelled causing Kam to jump out of whatever trance he was in.

"Hold on my baby!" Mona yelled out in panic as she jumped up from her spot on the floor and ran upstairs with Landon right behind her.

"Get me a blanket or something," Kam said to Kells while swooping Aris up in his arms and making a dash for the door. I was right behind my brother. He ran out of the house carrying Aris and put her in the backseat of the truck with me jumping in right behind him with Aris' head in my lap. After making sure E was straight Kamron hurried and jumped in the driver's seat already shifting the truck into drive just as he was getting ready to pull out, Kelly jumped into the passenger seat with a cotton blanket in her hand.

"Here," she said handing me the blanket. I hurried and took it from her wrapping the blanket around Aris' body.

"I already told Lay and Mo just to meet us at the hospital. Take her to Jackson Memorial."

I looked down at the love of my life just barely hanging on and couldn't stop the tears from falling. "C'mon, Aris baby, open your eyes. Please, baby Kamron, Kells, and Mona needs you. I need you," I whispered softly into her ear while stroking her hair. I felt like I had let her down… once again. I promised her father that I wouldn't let nobody bring any harm to his baby girl and I did. I wasn't able to protect her, and that shit hurts like hell.

"Kam! Please hurry!" I yelled from the backseat before looking back down at Aris. Five minutes later Kam was swerving into the hospital emergency entrance. I picked Aris up and jumped out of the truck running into the hospital and towards the nurse's station.

"Please! Someone help her!" I screamed in a panic-stricken voice. The nurses immediately jumped into action running around the station with a gurney. I carefully laid Aris body down on the gurney and watched them feel around for a pulse before placing an oxygen mask over her face. Two female and two male nurses began running back to ICU, and I tried following them but was stopped by one of the nurses.

"Please sir wait right here."

I couldn't do shit, but stand back and helplessly watch the doctors rush Aris to the back. Right then and there I dropped down to my knees and prayed that God spared Aris' life. We still had so much shit to do together. I wasn't ready to give up on her yet.

***A Few Hours Later….***

"Family of Ms. Miller."

My head instantly popped up at the sound of the doctor's voice. Kam, Mona, Kells, Landon and I jumped to our feet and damn near bum rushed the doctor.

"Are you the family of Ms. Miller?" he questioned, looking up from his clipboard.

"Yes," Mona answered before everybody. "We are her sisters, those are her brothers, and this is her fiancé," she said pointing at me.

"Hello, I'm Doctor Evans," he said sticking his hand out for a handshake. Mo and Kelly shook his hand, but Kam and I looked down at it as if he was contagious or some shit.

"Yo, doc. I'm not tryna be rude or anything, but I ain't got time to shake yo' hand, bruh. All I want to know is my sister's condition. How's my sister? Is she ok?" Kamron asked with concern etched all over his face. Dr. Evans inhaled deeply before exhaling it out very loudly. His eyes connected with everyone in the room before answering the question that was heavy on everybody's mind.

"Well, I'm sorry to inform you, but your sister has suffered from several serious injuries. Ms. Miller suffered several cracked ribs, a fractured jaw, a broken nose and a miscarriage.

Beca-,"

Kelly and Mona's gasping cut the doctor's sentence short.

"Wait a minute! A miscarriage?!" Kamron asked out loud in disbelief.

Dr. Evans looked at all of us with sympathetic eyes before continuing his report. "Yes. Because she was brought in naked, we had a rape examination done. I'm sorry to inform you, but Ms. Miller was raped. Her vagina and anus were split open and judging from the excessive bleeding her attacker raped her while she had the miscarriage. Because she was in so much pain, we had to put her into a medically-induced coma so that her body could properly heal," Dr. Evans said.

Hearing the doctor admit all that shit broke my fucking heart into a million pieces and made me feel worse than I was already feeling.

"No. This shit cannot be fucking happening!" Kamron screamed before punching a hole in the wall and falling to the floor crying. Kelly immediately rushed over to him and wrapped her arms around him, comforting him. She was rubbing small circles on his back and rocking him back and forth.

"Can… can we see her?" Mona asked Dr. Evans, her voice cracking with emotion.

Dr. Evans nodded. "I will have someone escort you all to Ms. Miller's room. Again, I'm sorry," he said sympathetically before walking off. Minutes later a nurse escorted us to Aris' room.

The tears that I was fighting so hard to hold back immediately came running out when I walked in that hospital room and saw her hooked up to all kinds of machines and tubes running through her body.

Seeing her like that made my heart hurt even more. I felt like a complete failure for letting this happen, and I just knew that it was killing Kamron as well. This was his baby sister, his heart laying right there. Kam walked in the room and quickly turned back around to walk right back out. It was too hard for my boy to see his baby sister like that. I stood back watching Mona and Kelly run to Aris' bedside and cry. After letting everybody have their alone time with Aris, it was finally my turn, and I was by myself. Slowly walking over to Aris, I sat in the chair next to her bed and grabbed her hand.

"I'm so sorry, baby. I wasn't there to protect you. It's all my fault you're in this position now. Please forgive me baby and come back to me. We need you, Ari. It's not your time to leave us yet. Despite everything that has happened, I still love you, ma. Please come back to me and I promise you that I will never let anyone hurt you again," I said kissing the back of her hand. "Ari, baby, I need you to wake up for me and tell me who did this shit to you. Tell me baby and I promise that I will kill that muthafucka for you. I won't rest until that muthafucka is dead. I promise you that, ma," I laid my head in the palms of my hands, thinking real hard on who wanted to harm Aris when I felt somebody grab my shoulder and gave it a squeeze. Thinking it was Aris somehow waking up from her coma, my head quickly shot up only to be disappointed. Aris was still knocked out. Turning to look behind me, I saw that Kamron was in the room with me as well.

I looked around the room expecting the girls to walk in, but they didn't. "Where are the girl's?" I asked him.

"I went ahead and sent them home. Levi was becoming a little too cranky and because we just rushed out of the house earlier, Mo forgot to grab his diaper bag that had his bottle in it," he answered solemnly, standing at the end of Aris' bed. Kamron really looked like he was about to break down and cry, but was fighting hard not to.

"You know I had to call the old man and tell him what's going on with Ari right?" he asked me with his tone low and his eyes on Ari.

I just nodded my head and swallowed whatever little spit that I had left in my all of a suddenly dry mouth. Now, I don't fear any man, but knowing that Kamron had talked to Killa and updated him on Aris' condition had me feeling some type of way. That is one nigga that you do not want to fuck around with, especially when it comes to his family. That nigga will fucking kill everybody that walks in front of him when he's emotionally unstable. Killa was a cool, calm, collected ass dude, but hell let's be real here, everybody knows that the nigga is just dangling over the borderline of being a psychopath. Back in his day, he would kill a muthafucka just for breathing the same air as him. He plays no games.

"And how did that conversation go?" I asked Kam, already knowing the answer to it.

Kam scoffed, chuckling lightly finally taking his eyes off of Aris' still body and turned his attention towards me. "You already know how that went. The nigga flipped! Cussed my ass out six different ways to Sunday before threatening my life and yours. And nigga I'm his son!" he said, making me laugh.

I shook my head. "Man, I already know."

"Yo, where the fuck is Quamir's punk ass?" I asked Kamron, expecting him to know since that was his boy. "Aris has been in the hospital for over six hours and that bitch ass nigga still ain't been here to see her yet. What da fuck is up with that shit?" I spat.

"I don't know what da fuck is wrong with tha nigga, but I know as soon as I run into his bitch ass I'm knocking his ass clean the fuck out!" Kamron snapped angrily with his fists clenching at his sides. "I tried calling him earlier to tell him about what happened with Ari and the nigga ain't never answered the damn phone. It rang a few times before going to voicemail. I tried calling again and this time, it just went straight to voicemail, meaning that the nigga had turned his phone off."

I watched from the corner of my eye at Kamron gritting his teeth in anger. "Ole bitch ass nigga. Ain't shit more fucking important than the well-being of my sister," Kam spat heatedly, he was breathing in and out really fast, indicating that he was beyond pissed. "I'm about to call his ass again," he said as he reached inside of his pocket for his cell phone.

"Nah, leave that bitch ass nigga right where da fuck he at!" I yelled, stopping him from calling Q.

"Ari don't need his ass when I'm sitting right here. Fuck his ass man, and I mean that shit. I was tryna be nice to the black ass nigga by letting him play house with my girl a little while longer before I shitted on his muthafuckin' dreams. But his ass done fucked up royally by not being here when Aris needs him the most. It's about time I come back home and claim what's rightfully mine any fucking way. Nigga, probably still pissed off 'cause his ass got demoted and shit. That's the only good, acceptable explanation as to why his ass is ignoring everybody," I spat, equally pissed off. Even I will admit that I sounded hella jealous. If I had just taken Aris away from Q's bitch ass the first day that I came home, then she wouldn't be in this situation right now. It's obvious that Quamir's punk ass can't be here when she needs him to be to protect her. But nah, I had to be a good nigga and try to let Aris find her way back home to me. Never the fuck again.

I guess my little jealous outburst was funny as fuck to Kam because when I finished ranting and raving, Kam was bent over bugging the fuck up. I tried to keep a hard face but couldn't around that idiot.

"Fuck you, man, " I said laughing.

Kamron continued laughing until he couldn't breathe. Yeah, he was laughing that damn hard.

"Damn bruh. I needed that laugh," Kamron said, wiping the tears from the corners of his eyes.

I just nodded my head in response. I'd tuned out Kamron's idiotcy and focused back on the rising and falling of Aris' chest.

"Man, I'm about to head on out of here and go check on Kelly's emotional ass. Her crazy ass was ready to go question everyone in a fifty-mile radius on what happened tonight. She plays no games. Between her and Pops, I don't know which one is more serious and overprotective when it comes to Aris," Kamron announced, walking to the other side of the bed. He leaned down a placed a soft kiss on Aris' forehead.

"Yea. I'm still trying to figure out who the fuck could have done this shit to Aris, man. As far as I know we not beefing with anybody and Aris ole friendly ass doesn't have any enemies. Everybody loves her, so it's really fucking me up in the head."

"You just don't know how hard I have been trying to come up with an answer to that question as well. Let me tell you now. Forget about trying to figure out who. You'll fuck around and get a headache from thinking too hard."

"All I can say is wait until Aris wakes up. Only then will we know."

I nodded my head in agreement. "Yeah you're right. Hopefully, she'll be able to tell us the answers that we so desperately need."

Somebody barged into Aris' room, causing our heads to snap up and look in that direction. My head snapped so hard I thought my ass had whiplash for a second. It was Landon walking inside of the room with the ugliest mug expression on his face. His facial expression and aura gave off that murderous vibe.

His expression alarmed me and had me sitting straight up. I didn't like the vibes I was getting from him, and it had my ass curious as fuck. "What's wrong? Why you looking like that?" I asked him.

Instead of responding, Landon just passed me his cell phone. With a confused and still puzzled look on my face, I hesitantly took the phone out of his hand and looked down at the paused screen. Kamron got up from his spot on the other side of Aris to come around to where I was to watch the video as well. I pressed play and immediately knew that it was the security footage at one of our main profitable houses.

"What the fuck is this shit?" I said, already alarmed. My stomach had started tightening as an uneasy feeling filled the pit of it. My gut was trying to tell me that something was terribly wrong. I had that same feeling in my gut when I had gotten that phone call from Aris earlier that day.

At first, everything seemed fine, and nothing was out of the ordinary. With it being so late at night, there were only three goons present getting shit prepared for the next day. Kam and I didn't let the workers sell drugs out of the trap house after three a.m. We wanted all of our workers to be on alert at all times. Niggas can't do that shit when they are sleep-deprived.

The lieutenant that's in charge of the house stays back and makes sure that the count was correct before locking everything up. Now what the fuck they do on the outside of those doors I don't care, but the trap closes at three. No more sales out of that house after three. Shy and two other goons that I remember, whose names were Spyder and Jeremiah, were sitting in the front room passing a blunt around while Shy did the count. Everything seemed fine until there was a knock and Spyder stood up to answer the front door. It was like time stood still and shit happened within the blink of an eye.

Five masked men busted through the door and lit that bitch up like was the Fourth of July. Poor Spyder didn't know what the fuck happened. He didn't even get a chance to react. As soon as that front door opened up, his fate was sealed. Miah went to pull his gun out, but was too slow. One shot to his shoulder made him drop his gun. He went down quickly, but a bullet to the middle of his chest silenced him. Shy was successful enough to grab his gun and take down two gunmen before the AK47 riddled his body like Swiss cheese. With all three men down, it was easy for the intruders to run in, grab the rest of the drugs, and money from the table. One of the masked men ran to the back of the house and returned later with black duffle bags, letting me know that this was an inside job, which only pissed me off even more.

"You gotta be fucking bullshitting me!" I yelled out in blood-curdling anger.

I took Landon's phone and threw it across the room in a raging fit. Kamron was just as pissed as I was and punched a few holes into the hospital's cheap drywall while yelling obscenities. Landon just stood back with a blank expression on his face as if he was used to seeing us acting that way. The nigga wasn't even mad at me for breaking his phone. It was like he expected that to happen. I honestly didn't mean to throw his phone across the room, but I was so pissed off that I had to take my anger out on something and quick. Unfortunately, Lay's phone was the sacrificial lamb.

"Muthafuckas is really trying to send me on a goddamn war path!" I yelled through tight jaws as I jumped up from my seat and began pacing the floor with my hands on my hips.

"What's the loss?" Kamron asked Lay in a shaky breath. He was trying his best not to explode, but the look in his eyes said otherwise. He was ready to paint the city red.

"Well as you could tell from the video Jeremiah and Spyder are gone. But Shy is still hanging on despite taking that many bullets to the chest. The paramedics found a faint pulse and rushed him here for immediate surgery."

My head snapped up Lay's direction as my eyebrows raised in shock. "Shy's here? In this hospital?" I asked him, almost in disbelief.

Lay nodded. I exhaled a sigh of relief glad that my nigga Shy was still holding on to his life.

"What's the substantial amount that we lose?"

Lay hesitated before answering Kam's question. "They were able to run off with thirty bricks and took over two hunnid."

"Hundreds?"

Lay shook his head no. "Nah man. Two hunnid thou."

I stood in the middle of the room with my arms folded across my chest in deep thought trying to piece everything that happened tonight together. First, it was the attack on Aris, then our most profitable spot getting hit when we ain't even beefing with anyone, and lastly Quamir's disappearance. The more I stood there and thought about it, the clearer shit had become to me.

"Yo, when's the last time anyone has seen Quamir?" I suddenly asked them, my question catching the both of their attention.

Landon's eyebrows dip downwards in confusion as he looked up at Kamron, then at me. "I haven't seen him much lately, and I haven't spoken to Q since we had that meeting. Why what's up? Is there something I'm missing?" he asked looking back and forth at Kamron and me for answers.

"You think Q's disappearance has something to do with the spot getting hit?" Kam asked me.

"I'm not saying that it does, but it sure as in hell sounds suspect to me," I answered him while taking my seat back in the chair near Aris' side. "I mean I know that's y'all boy and all, but something ain't right. Like I'mma need y'all to really think this shit through. We don't have no beef in these streets as of yet, so who else would hit our shit? And do it just out of the blue? Who else would have known that only a few people would be at the spot counting money and getting shit ready for the next business day when we keep shit tight?

"Nobody knows any of this shit unless they are from our circle. It's obvious that those muthafuckas in the video knew exactly where the drugs were. They didn't ask for shit when Spyder opened that door, niggas just got to bussin', ran in grabbed the money and the drugs, and got ghost in less than five fuckin' minutes. It was a simple in and out a job that was executed perfectly."

"All I'm saying is that shit ain't adding up and with yo' boy missing right now just makes him seem suspect as hell to me. That's all that I gotta say, and I'm just going to leave it at that. I spoke my piece," I leaned back in my chair with my arms folded across my stomach, trying to get comfortable.

The room fell into a deep silence as each man had gotten lost in his own thoughts. I could tell that my accusation had the air thick with tension and had really given them something to think on. I ignored it and focused on the rising and falling of Aris' chest. About five minutes had passed, and still, no one said anything. Landon looked sort of spaced out with a blank facial expression, while Kamron continued to angrily pace the floor.

"Boy, sit yo' ass down somewhere before your shoe soles take flight," I cracked, trying to lighten up the situation. Kamron stopped pacing for a few seconds to shoot me an ugly glare. Landon cracked a smile and tried to stifle his laugh.

I balled my fists up and playfully bucked at Kamrom. "Nigga, the hell you keep looking at me like that for? Feeling froggy, then nigga jump."

Kamron continued glaring at me. "How in the hell can you continue to joke when the situation is as serious as it is?" he asked me, referring to Aris being attacked and the spot getting hit up.

I just solemnly shrugged my shoulders as I redirected my attention towards Ari. "In regards to the spot getting hit… there isn't shit that we can really do besides put our ear to the streets and see what we can come up with. We gonna have to take those thirty bricks and two hunnid thou and chalk that shit up as a loss until we can find out who the fuck was bold enough to rob us. In the meantime, while we are waiting, we need to shut shit the fuck down for a few days. Switch shit up, changing every fucking thing around. Everything from new trap houses to days the shipments arrive and changing the routes we normally use transporting drugs. There's a snake in the camp, so only a few selective people should know this shit. That's all we can do. Ain't no use in crying over spilled milk. All a nigga can do is get up and get another cup and be careful not to spill that muthafucka. We go around on a killing spree, and we won't have anyone left guarding the frontlines," I said to him. "Now the situation with Aris… you and I both know that there ain't nothing we can do right now. We just had that conversation not too long ago. For both situations, all we can do now is play the waiting game and keep our eyes and ears open. Believe me, somebody is gonna slip the fuck up and spill the beans."

Kamron let out a loud irritated sigh while he ran his hands across his face. "You're right. But you know I'm an impatient muthafucka. I don't like to wait."

I chuckled while shaking my head. I couldn't agree more. Kamron expected everything to be up in his face easy and hated to wait on certain shit. He was an impatient little fucker.

"Aight man. I'll listen to you and fall back… for now. In the meantime, let me do what I said that I was going to do and check up on Kelly's ass," he said walking up to me and slapping hands.

Landon laughed. "Good luck with trying to calm her ass down."

Kamron started laughing, too. "Nigga, I'm gonna need all the luck that I can get," he said, slapping hands with Lay as well.

"I'm about to get out of here as well. I'm about to go check the streets and see what everybody is talking about. I'll let y'all know if I find something. See you later bruh, and keep your head up."

After coming up to me and slapping hands with me, Landon left with Kamron, leaving me alone with Aris. Grabbing her hand, I brought it up to my lips, kissing the back of it after making a vow to never make her sad ever again. No matter what, I was going to stick by her side and be the man that she needed me to be because she deserved it. I promised myself that shit would change after today.

*"Sometimes you must HURT in order to KNOW; FALL in order to GROW; Lose in order to GAIN because life's greatest lessons are learned through PAIN." -- Unknown*

# Chapter Fourteen

**ARIS**

*One Year Later…*

The rays of the sun slipping through the drapes and shining brightly on my face caused me to stir in my sleep. Groaning in irritation, I rolled over and pulled the covers over my head, not really wanting to get up from my comfortable California King-sized bed. I balled up in a fetal position, trying to fall back asleep when all of a sudden I felt somebody staring at me. Pulling the covers back, my eyes met with a pair of light brown eyes staring back at me. Just like that, my irritation melted away, and my heart swelled up with love.

"Good morning, Mommy."

"Good morning, baby, " I said back to him in a groggy voice. Leaning up, I wiped the sleep from my eyes before checking the alarm clock. It was only a little after ten in the morning. I'm normally up much earlier than that, but I guess my ass was tired as hell last night. It took me a minute for my eyes to adjust to the lightening of the room, but when they finally did, I finally glanced around the room. RJ was on the other side of my bed, half of his body out from under the covers, still dressed in his pajamas eating a big ass bowl of cereal.

"What are you doing in my room and where is your dad? I know your dad did not make you that big bowl of cereal, did he?" I asked him as I pressed my back against the headboard.

RJ shook his head no while taking a big bite of his Captain Crunch cereal. "Daddy left earlier this morning with Uncle Kamron, and I made myself breakfast."

"Why didn't you wake me up RJ if you were hungry?"

"Daddy told me not to wake you up and let you sleep longer."

I forced a faint smile at him while cussing Rome's stupid ass out in the back of my head. He could've at least made RJ's breakfast before running the streets with Kamron's dumb ass. Finally finding the strength and forcing myself out of the bed, I tossed the covers back and climbed out. As soon as my feet sunk into the soft carpet, I stood up to stretched and let out a loud, tired ass yawn. I wanted so badly to climb back into my bed and go back to sleep, but knew that I couldn't because of RJ's hyperactive ass. That boy had so much energy that I could barely keep up sometimes. Leaving RJ to his cartoons, I walked across the room and into the adjoining bathroom. Pulling my underwear down, I sat on the toilet and breathed a sigh of relief as I relieved my bladder. I've been holding my piss in for so long that my stomach was cramping. Once I was finished, I grabbed some toilet tissue and wiped myself clean. After washing my face and brushing my teeth, I felt so much better. I went from having no energy at all to feeling revived and rejuvenated.

"Did you brush your teeth this morning?" I asked RJ once I was back in my bedroom.

"No, ma'am," he responded.

I turned to look at RJ through tiny eye slits. He knows damn well that I don't play about hygiene in this house. "Are you almost finished eating?"

"Yes, ma'am," he said while drinking the milk out of his cereal bowl. When he was finished, he burped and sat his bowl on my nightstand. "I'm finished!" he exclaimed cheerfully, tossing his hands up in the air in victory.

"Boy, come on and let's go brush your teeth and run you some bath water, " I said, shaking my head and laughing.

After putting Jay in the tub, I grabbed his cereal bowl to take it to the kitchen and to put it in the sink where it really belongs and not on my nightstand. Seeing my kitchen in the state that it was in, anger flashed through me like an old woman going through menopause. RJ had cereal and milk all over the damn place.

"I swear I'm cussing Rome's dumb ass out! He should've fucking woke me up if he wasn't going to make Jay breakfast," I fussed, grabbing the dish towel and cleaning up the mess that was made. By the time I was finished, Jay had finished bathing and was ready to get out. Getting him out of the tub and drying him off, I lotioned his body from head to toe, then put him on a pair of denim True Religion jeans, a white Armani Exchange V-neck t-shirt, and a pair of his white Air Force Ones. He wasn't going anywhere as of yet, but you never know what Rome has planned. I might take him out later on and do something.

"Mommy, can I go outside and play in the backyard?"

"Yes, baby. As long as you don't get dirty."

"Yay!" he yelled out in excitement as he ran across the room to get his basketball and ran out of the back door.

Laughing, I opened the fridge to find me something to put in my stomach. I really wasn't that hungry, but at the same time, Rome would chew my asshole out if he found out that I hadn't eaten. After searching the fridge for something really quick to eat, I decided on a fresh bowl of diced fruit, orange juice, and an egg and cheese bagel. I moved effortlessly around the kitchen to gather all of the supplies that I needed to cook my breakfast. As I stood there cooking my breakfast, my mind took a trip down memory lane dating a year back.

It's been exactly one whole year since Quamir had almost beaten me to my very last breath and one whole year since anyone had seen or even heard from his bitch ass. According to what my brother told me, Quamir didn't even come to the hospital to see me not one time while I was in a coma for three months. Which wasn't very surprising to me. That was some coward ass shit he pulled. When they tried calling him at first, he would just send them to voicemail or cut his phone off. The next day his number was disconnected and out of service. When Landon and Kamron stopped by his house, it was empty. He had just up and disappeared and to this day nobody knows why. But I do. I don't care where the fuck he flew to or what the fuck happened to him. I don't give a fuck if he was attacked by several rabid dogs and died before getting the vaccine. As long as he stays far the fuck away from me.

I never told anyone that Q was the reason why I was in the hospital suffering through so much. Both my brother and dad pleaded with me to tell them who was responsible, but I just couldn't bring myself to tell them. What happened to me would traumatize anyone. Call me dumb, stupid, or whatever you want to. I don't care. Y'all are not the one that has to live every day knowing that a man that you gave your heart to once upon a time had damn neared killed you and raped you while you were suffering a miscarriage with his baby. Y'all are not the one that has to go to sleep every night and wake up every morning screaming because you're having constant nightmares of what happened. But guess who has to? Me! I have to go through all of that shit plus more. And let me be the one to tell you that I have come a long way since then.

The days following me waking up from my coma and going home consisted of me leaving the home that Mo, Kells, and I once shared to move in with my brother. I just couldn't go back to that place after what happened. That one bad memory overpowered all of the other good memories my girls and I created in that house. Mona and Kelly couldn't either, so they moved out just weeks following. They now have their own places . I locked myself away in a dark room and cried my eyes out each and every day of the week. I was so depressed about losing my first born that I wouldn't eat, hardly slept because of the nightmares, and continued unintentionally pushing away and hurting those who were just trying to help me and make me feel better.

I was so hurt and stuck in my own funk that I refused to let Kells cut my hair. For months I walked around with my hair all chopped off and cut unevenly. I had my brother's neighbors filing police reports about an escaped mental patient. My life was spiraling out of control, and I couldn't stop it even if I tried. Before I knew it, I was overusing Percocet to help me numb the pain and after two failed suicidal attempts, Roman said that was enough and basically kidnapped my ass from my brother's house and forced me to stay with him.

On days that I would lock myself in my dark room, Rome would come and unscrew the door off of the hinges and take the curtains down. When I didn't feel like eating, Rome would force me to. Even if that meant t he would have to tie me down to the bed and force my mouth open, he would do it. Rome would drag me out the house by my bald ass head and force me to do something constructive. No matter if it was shopping, trips out of the country, or even going to the park for a little one on one in football or basketball. Just something to do just to get me out of the house. Rome fought me tooth and nail, always having a comeback for something. He helped build me back up when I was so broken down.

Rome was there to help me kick my drug addiction. He was there to collect the broken pieces of what used to be me, and delicately glued the pieces back together. Whenever I just needed someone to just hold me and tell me that it was going to be ok, Rome would stop everything that he was doing and be there for me. He got through to me when my dad, my brother, and even best friends couldn't. You could say that Rome and RJ together helped me back to normal. Never did I ever expect to take in Rome's outside child the way I did, but life has a funny way of changing shit. RJ filled in that empty void that I had in my heart from losing my first born, making me love him even more.

If it wasn't for my baby RJ and Rome's annoying ass, I probably would've overdosed on Percocet or even worse, actually succeeded in killing myself a long time ago.

A year later and I really had come a long way. I'd kicked my drug habit and my depression to the curb and was just about back to my normal, happy self. My hair was finally cut, styled properly in a sunrise orange shoulder-length layered, curly bob. Of course, Rome had to tie me to a chair so  Kelly could come through and do it for me. Otherwise, I probably would still be walking around her with a bird's nest matted to the top of my head. For once in a long ass time, I was back to being happy and just grateful to be alive.

The front door opening and closing loudly quickly snatched me out of my thoughts and back into reality. Just as I finished my breakfast and was about to sit down, in walked Rome and my brother. Still pissed off at Rome for running out of the house this morning without fixing Jay breakfast, I ignored him standing there staring at me.

"Wassup bald head," Kamron said walking up to me, grabbing me by the head, and planting a big wet, disgusting kiss on my forehead before playfully mushing me in the head.

I turned around in my seat and tried swinging on him, but he was too quick, running around to the other side of the kitchen.

"Quit playing all the damn time. I know damn well you saw me over here eating," I spat heatedly. I made sure that my attitude was apparent. Kamron plays too damn much.

Kamron started laughing like me suddenly having an attitude with him was funny.

"Technically, you just sat down and haven't even touched your food yet," he smartly replied with his arms folded across his chest. I picked up a grape and threw it at him, praying and hoping that I hit his ass. Unfortunately, my aim was off, and it missed him.

"Where is Jay?" Rome finally asked walking further into the kitchen and standing next to me at the kitchen island.

"Backyard," I said, keeping my answer short. To avoid any eye contact, I grabbed my cell phone and started scrolling through Instagram, trying to fake as if I was busy looking for something.

"I'm going to go play with Jay for a minute, " Kamron said, walking out the sliding door and into the backyard.

As I sat there chewing and eating my food, I continued ignoring the stares from Roman's ass. As I said earlier, I was still pissed at his ass from earlier, so I had nothing to say to him. I continued ignoring Rome until I was finished with my breakfast and even then I was still ignoring him, but for a totally different reason.

Being in the same breathing space as him and smelling his masculine Clive Christian No. 1 cologne always did something to me. I had my back turned to Rome and was putting the dirty dishes into the dishwasher when he wrapped his arms around my waist and pulled me back into his chest. My whole body froze as a familiar heat rushed straight down to my flower. My nose was suddenly attacked by the masculine scent of his expensive cologne mixed perfectly with the faint scent of his Ralph Lauren body wash. I closed my eyes and slowly inhaled. I swear I was in love with how he smelled. His scent alone was enough to release my floodgates and ruin the seat of my panties. Having me walk around the place looking like I'd pissed on myself.

"Why do I feel like you're ignoring me?" he whispered into my ear while grasping my hips and grinding his hard-on against my ass cheeks. I inhaled a sharp, shaky breath before slowly exhaling it. I was trying my hardest to keep my composure in front of him, but was finding it very hard to do. It's been a whole year since the last time I had sex and every day I spent hanging around Rome became a fight I could see myself losing in the long run. Lord knows I'm in desperate need of some dope dick.

Clearing my throat after finally regaining my composure, I turned around and pushed Rome away from me like I was annoyed with him or something, when that was far from the case.

"Why did you leave the house this morning without feeding Jay?" I asked him with a deep frown etched on my forehead and my arms folded across my ample breasts.

"Who said that I didn't feed Jay?" he asked me with his head cocked to the side and confusion written on his face.

"It wasn't something somebody said, but what I've seen this morning and how my kitchen looked when I came down. Jay was eating a big stupid bowl of cereal this morning and when I came downstairs the kitchen was destroyed. There were milk and cereal all over the damn place."

Rome chuckled. "Yo, I swear I'm kicking RJ in the ass when he comes in the house," he mumbled. "First of all, I did fix RJ breakfast before I left this morning," he stated matter-of-factly.

I looked at him with my head cocked to the side as if I didn't believe him. "Oh yeah? Then what did you fix him?"

"The same shit you woke up to him eating," he replied. "I fixed his ass two bowls of Captain Crunch this morning because that was what he wanted. Right before I left I asked the little nigga if he was still hungry and he told my ass no. If you don't believe me ask Kam. He'll tell you exactly how many bowls of cereal I made for Jay and everything."

I looked deeply into Rome's eyes for any signs of him lying, but knew immediately off the top that he wasn't.

"Whatever."

I tried pushing Rome back so that I could move out of the way, but he moved in closer to me, backing me up into the counter and trapping me up against it.

"Aww… what's wrong, baby momma? Yo' ass embarrassed, ain't you?" he asked me, laughing.

I rolled my eyes at him while trying to push him back some. Being that close up on me was not safe for me at all. "Move, ain't nobody embarrassed," I said, lying through my teeth. I was hella embarrassed.

Here I was, ready to chew Rome's ass out about not feeding my baby before leaving, and come to find out he already did. Jay was just being hella greedy and decided to take it upon himself and make a third bowl. I swear that I hated when I was in the wrong and he was right.

"Nigga, if you don't move on somewhere else with that bullshit. You better go find Ebony's ass because that's the only baby momma that you have around here. Ain't no kids coming out of me no time soon," I spat, annoyed because I was turned on and my hormones were driving me crazy. Y'all don't know how hard it is to fight against temptation when standing in front of someone so damn fine. Damn, Rome was so fine and was looking mighty delicious dressed in a pair of black basketball shorts with no t-shirt on. I just wanted to drop down to my knees and outline every ab and every pec that was perfectly sculpted on his body with my tongue.

I'm a female damn near in heat, so y'all already know where my eyes traveled off to once Rome came within my line of vision. Without me fully conscious of what I was doing, my top teeth sunk into my bottom lip and my thighs clenched tighter together to stop my wetness from running down my legs.

"Damn," I mumbled softly. It should be illegal to be this damn fine.

Someone snickering snapped me out of my daze and caused me to look up at Rome's grinning face. My head dropped to my chest, and my cheeks instantly turned red after realizing that I got caught staring at the man that I want so bad! That shit was so embarrassing!

Rome grabbed me by the chin and forced me to look at him. Just gazing into his cognac-colored eyes had my body shaking and caused my hormones to shift into overdrive. I had it bad for this man. I'm officially convinced that Rome had put some type of voodoo curse on me. Only staring in his eyes, or just being in his presence, could make my body do everything that I didn't want it to do. I had to remind myself that both my brother and son were outside and were bound to walk into this kitchen at any time.

Rome was well aware of the type of effect he had on me, that's why his ass was standing in front of me now smirking and shit.

"You already know what it is Ari, so I don't know why you want to keep playing with a nigga like that," he spoke softly so that only I was able to hear what he was saying. Rome's fingers left my chin and traveled up to my hair.

Softly he ran them through my hair before tangling his fingers up and gently yanking my head back, causing me to yelp out from being surprised. By now Rome was looking down into my soul with mischief dancing all in his eyes. His face was so close to mine that if I stuck my tongue out, I would be licking his bottom lip. My breathing hitched, and my body set aflame. That fight was becoming harder and harder with each passing second.

"The first chance I get back up in that thang, I'm knocking shit all out of the frame and rearranging organs, ya understand me? I'mma make sure that pussy remembers me and these long daddy dick'em down strokes." His deep and raspy voice whispered to me, causing chills to run down my spine and my juices to run down my legs. My heart was beating so damn loud in my eardrums that I'm positive that he heard it as well.

"You are right about one thing, though. When I do give you this dope D and fill you up with my babies, you won't be just another baby momma, but my wife. The only woman other than my mother and my baby sis to rock my last name and give birth to the rest of my kids. I'm planning on marrying you before you even give life to my seed. So, get to planning now Mrs. Roman Cayden Clarkson, because your time running away from me and playing these damn games is up. It's time for you to bring yo' ass home. I waited a whole year to get you to snap out of it and find yo' own way home, but now a nigga is starting to get very impatient. Starting today your time is up." Rome planted a soft kiss on my forehead before pulling away and leaving me standing there looking dumbfounded.

I tried thinking of a comeback for that one, but couldn't. Rome really had my ass speechless. It took me a minute, but when I finally thought of something smart to say, RJ came running into the kitchen with wide, scared eyes.

"Mommy! Mommy! Help me!" Jay frantically screamed out. RJ ran around the kitchen island towards his dad and me with his arms stretched out wide. "Momma! He… he trying to whoop me!"

"Who's trying to whoop you?" I asked him, bending down to pick him up. RJ wrapped his arms tightly around my neck. His light brown eyes looking back and forth between me and the back door.

"Him!" he exclaimed pointing at the door. Seconds later, a very pissed off Kamron came storming in. As soon as he made it through those doors, his grayish-blue orbs zeroed in on me and RJ. "I don't know why you ran towards her like she gonna whoop my ass. Aris can't save yo' ass from this ass whooping. Bring that ass over here, boy!" Kamron bellowed, making his way towards us. I could tell by the deep frown that was etched onto my brother's handsome face and the thick throbbing vein on the side of his forehead that he was pissed the fuck off and about to murder my baby.

"Uh huh! You are not about to beat my baby," I said laughing holding onto RJ tightly and running around the kitchen island.

"Fuck that! That little nigga needs his ass beat!" Kamron yelled out heatedly, running around the kitchen island on the side. Whatever RJ did to Kamron this time really got under his skin. He was really about to kill my baby.

I hurried and ran to the other side of the island, barely escaping from Kamron's clutches.

"What did he do?" I managed to ask him through my laughter.

"Little nigga called me a bitch after he kneed me in the nuts!" Kam bellowed out heatedly, making Rome fall over laughing.

My eyes widened, and my mouth dropped open in shock as I looked away from my brother and to RJ. "Roman Cayden, Jr! You did not!"

"No, I didn't!" Jay yelled at Kamron. He turned and looked at me with bright wide eyes.

"Him lying momma! He just trying to whoop me because I took my money back!"

Kam gasped out dramatically with his hand over his heart like he was hurt by RJ's accusations. "Why you little lying bas– Come here!" he yelled out taking three huge steps towards me.

"You better not hit my baby while he's in my arms! I will fuck your Adam's apple up if you even think about touching him," I growled at Kamron while at the same time looking him up and down, sort of daring him to touch him.

Kamron must have sensed how serious I was because he put his hand down and stepped back. I may not have gone through the morning sickness, weird cravings, weight gain, nine months carrying him in my womb, long hours in labor or gave him life, but I would fuck somebody up over this one, brother included. I have been raising and taking care of him since his momma refuses to unless Rome fucks her or gives her some money for the past seven months. And that's if she doesn't try to keep RJ away from Rome. She tried that shit one time and had almost gotten choked the fuck out. You could not tell me that he wasn't my child.

Kamron sucked his teeth and rolled his eyes at me. "Man, you always babying these boys! They are boys! They need some discipline. They gon' come out acting like little girls when they get older."

"You call punching them discipline? RJ is only six and Levi is about to be two. Wait until they are a little older before trying to kill them."

Kamron said something slick under his breath before dropping it and backing away.

"Mind explaining to me what happened?" I asked Kamron, finally setting RJ down onto his feet. Jay must've still thought that Kamron was going to whoop him because he stood at my side, holding onto my leg for dear life. Every now and then he would peak around me and mug Kamron, causing me to laughed. Since Jay had been in everyone's life, he couldn't stand being around Kamron. Kamron was always doing something to make my baby mad at him. They had that love/hate relationship thing going on. One minute they're cool as hell playing video games and slap boxing with each other, and then Kamron would do something that would aggravate my baby and they were back to hating each other.

"So look, check this out," Kamron started to say, but paused so that he could get water from the refrigerator. Taking the cap off, he took a swig while taking a seat at the kitchen island. "I go outside to see what Jay was doing, and he was playing basketball. I asked if I could play with him and the little nigga basically told me to put some money on the line first. So I did. Very long story made short, I was out there putting the heat on his ass, but because I had an unfair advantage against Jay, I decided to let up and let him win. There was about five hunnid on the line, and I gave all that shit to Junior. You know that there ain't a day that goes by that I don't fuck with him and teach him a life lesson all at the same time."

"What you do to my baby?" I asked him, grabbing a glass plate out of the cabinet, sitting a few chocolate chip cookies on it, and giving it to Jay along with a glass of milk to wash it down. Jay grabbed his plate from me and took a seat across from Kamron at the kitchen island. All the while smirking at him kind of taunting him on the low. Kamron sucked his teeth and grunted something under his breath before continuing on with his sentence.

"I snatched his money out of his hand and faked like I was going to take it. And just like I told and taught him, Junior got mad because I had taken his money and tried to fight me for it. I'm talking about the little nigga was out there really trying to box my ass for it. I'm laughing and shit talking about it was fair game."

I started snickering because I could just picture Kamron laughing and teasing Jay, rubbing in the fact that he took his money in his face and Jay running up swinging on Kam's big ass.

"You know me and how I do. I'm laughing and thinking that the shit was cute that the little nigga actually got some heart. I'm like that's what the fuck I'm talking 'bout! Don't let nobody just run up and take yo' shit and don't do nothing. I'm feeling like a proud ass uncle! I taught my little nigga good! Then all of a sudden the proudest moment of my life was interrupted when all of the wind knocked out of my ass and I dropped to my knees, groaning in pain. Jay caught my ass off-guard and uppercut my ass dead in the nuts!" he exclaimed animatedly.

Roman doubled over laughing hard as hell while I was trying my hardest to hold mine in. Kamron mugged Rome hard as hell before continuing with his story.

"That ain't the part that killed it, though," Kam said. "While I was at the weakest moment of my life, this nigga not only snatch back the five hunnid that I took from him, but he went inside of my pockets took whatever little cash that I had in there and snatched my chain off from around my neck and put that bitch on. The nigga straight robbed my ass clean. Right after he robbed me, he called me a bitch ass nigga, kicked my ass one last time, then took off running into the house."

I could no longer hold my laughter in and just had to let it out, bugging the hell up right along with Rome's ass. By the time Kam let that last sentence roll off his tongue, I was in tears and holding my ribs. I was laughing that hard. I looked up to see Kam's face contorted into the meanest and ugliest mug ever. Judging from how hard his face was tightened and the vein throbbing in his temple he was pissed at me for laughing.

"What? You thought that I was going to change my mind about you touching my baby after you told me your story, huh?" I asked him rhetorically, laughing at the duh expression on his face. I couldn't do nothing but laugh at him. "Nigga, salty face." I mocked laughing even harder.

"Yo, I swear I can't stand yo' bright ass," Kamron said to me with his face frowned up.

"Nigga, look in the mirror. Yo' ass is just as bright as me."

"That's what your ass gets," Rome said, wiping his face with the palm of his hands. "I told you to stop fucking with my son that he was going to get your ass one day. Lesson learned, huh?" Rome said, high fiving Jay before turning around to face Kam.

"Man, bring yo' cheating ass on back out here for a little one on one. I'm about to whoop yo' ass for the way you did my son out there earlier. Cheating ass nigga."

"Oh, nigga shut yo' big cry baby ass up. You know damn well I wasn't cheating! Jay ass just sucked just like his damn daddy does," Kamron said to Rome, laughing while following him out the back door. Right before he walked out, I popped him hard as hell on the back of his neck.

"You better put some respeck on his name when you're talking about that one," I said imitating Birdman while laughing my ass off. My imitation had both Rome and Jay laughing as well. The only one who wasn't laughing was Kamron's hating ass.

Kamron began to rub the back of his neck where I hit him and glared at me through tiny slits. "Bald head ass," he mumbled underneath his breath before running out of the sliding door, holding onto the back of his neck.

"Wish daddy luck," Rome whispered in my ear before planting a quick, discreet kiss onto my lips and slapping me on the ass. With that, he turned around grinning and followed Kamron out of the back door.

I ain't gonna even lie and say that my ass wasn't turned on because a bitch was burning up. My body was hot, and the seat of my panties was over with. I knew for a fact that I had to go upstairs and change clothes before someone else noticed. With the way, I was feeling I needed to go up to my room and pull out my battery operated boyfriend and put his ass to work. This shit was not just going to go away, that's how turned on I was.

"Ma. You okay?" RJ's little innocent voice asked me, snatching me out of my dirty thoughts about Rome.

"Ye…yea baby. Momma is fine. Why did you ask?" I asked him, kneeling down so that I was eye level with him. RJ reached out and wiped his hand across my forehead like he was checking my temperature or something. "Because you're sweating. Are you sick or something?" he asked me, his eyes and voice filled with concern.

I wanted to scream out hell yeah so bad but remembered that this was my baby talking to me. Hell yeah, I was sick. I was dick sick and wanted Rome in the dirtiest ways ever. Instead of speaking on my dirty thoughts I pushed them to the back of my mind and cleared my throat.

"Did you finish eating your cookies?" I asked RJ, changing the subject.

RJ smiled wide at me and nodded his head. "Yea. I finished. Can I have two more cookies?" he asked me sweetly while batting his long eyelashes at me.

I swear this little dude could eat. In an hour timespan, this boy had a big ass bowl of cereal, three cookies with some milk and is now asking for two more cookies. I swear it amazes me how big his appetite is. I took one look into his eyes and into that innocent face of his, and melted. My heart swelled with nothing but love for him. I was like putty in RJ's hands. Whatever he wanted he got from me when his dad wouldn't give it to him. Those light brown eyes, that adorable smile, and sweet innocent voice would forever be my weakness.

"Of course, you can baby. You can have whatever you like," I cooed, taking two cookies out of the cookie jar and sitting them on his plate.

"Thank you," he said to me, spinning on his heels to leave.

"Uh uh! Where you about to go with that cup, little boy?"

"I'm going back outside to watch daddy whoop Uncle Kam's butt in basketball," he tried to hurry up and say.

"Uh uh, little boy. Get back in here and finish those cookies. You know I don't allow you to take any dishes out of my kitchen," I said sternly.

I let Jay get off with a lot of shit, but my dishes aren't one of those things I'm just going to let him run off with. His ass was lucky that I didn't make him breakfast this morning. He would not have been in my bed eating and watching cartoons.

"Yes, ma'am," he said sadly as he sat back at the kitchen island. I didn't like the way he was sounding and was just about to cave in and give him a paper towel to put his cookies on when somebody started ringing the doorbell.

"Don't you leave that spot until I come back," I told Jay before going to the door to see who was laying on the doorbell like they were fucking crazy.

I walked to the door and opened it only to find out that it was Ebony's hoe ass on the other side of the door, looking as if she'd just left the damn club. I couldn't help but turn my nose up at her. Ugh! I couldn't stand this chick. Here it was going on twelve o'clock in the afternoon, and this bitch was dressed in a fucking dress that looked too damn small on her ass and had on some tall ass stripper heels with her weave all over her head in a messy ponytail and her makeup smeared. I could've sworn that I saw some dried up white shit by the corners of her mouth.

When Ebony saw that it was me who answered the door, her eyes went from being filled with hope to disappointment.

"Ugh! This ugly bitch here," she tried mumbling under her breath

I arched an eyebrow and looked this bitch up and down like 'really hoe'. "Bitch, only in your dreams. I could be sick as fuck with the flu, dressed in nothing but baggy ass clothes, and still be shitting on your dry weave having ass. Hoe, you wish you were me," I threw back at her.

Ebony sucked her teeth and rolled her eyes at me. "Why in the fuck would I want to be you? You ain't shit your damn self but a low key thot just like I am. I heard about you still fucking with Jacquese behind Rome's back. I always wanted to ask you. How do you like the taste of my leftovers?" she asked with a smirk on her face and her arms folded across her chest.

I burst out laughing hard as hell. My outburst took Ebony by complete surprise. Did this dumb retarded bitch just call herself a thot? Who in the fuck does that shit? I was laughing hard as hell at the dumb, confused expression on her face. I was laughing so hard that I was slightly bent over, holding my ribs. I couldn't breathe. After a few minutes of just straight dying I was finally able to stop and get myself under control.

"Trust me honey, ain't shit about you low key," I said wiping the corners of my eyes. "Everybody knows about you and your hoe tendencies. Someone had even made a Facebook page about you naming it, The Biggest Ran Through Thot of Miami. They got videos, pictures, and some more shit of you on there." Ebony's mouth dropped, and her eyes slightly widened a bit in shock. I could tell that she was trying to see whether or not was I lying to her. My right hand up to God somebody made a Facebook page about her, and some other ran through local thots of Florida. There was even a list of muthafuckas who had that shit made.

"Since you're so curious as to know why I think you wish that you were me, I'll spare a few seconds of my time and name the reasons as why. I'll make this quick for the both of us. It's simple actually, and even a blind man can see it," I chuckled a bit, leaning comfortably against the door frame and folding my arms across my chest.

"You want to be me so bad because I have the man, the house, and the life that you so desperately want. Everybody that comes across me loves me while not even your own mother could give a damn about you. Everything comes easily to me while you have to struggle to get anywhere near like me. I draw attention wherever I go without even trying to, while you have to be loud and promiscuous to hold a man's attention, and even that doesn't last long. I'm a go-getter and will work hard for my own money and not ask or beg Rome for it, while your lazy ass can't even tend to your own child properly. I'm wifey material while you… just aren't. I'm classy you're trashy. The list could go on and on, but I'm sure you get the point by now."

I smirked at Ebony's face turning beet red and the sound of her breathing picking up. She had her fists balled up at her sides looking as if she was ready to swing on me. I was just waiting for her ass to. I've been ready to tag her ass. She didn't have to say it out loud to admit that everything that I said was true. I could see the green all over her face. The eyes do not lie.

"I'm done talking. You can leave now. Get off my fucking porch. You're dismissed," I said turning around to dismiss her. I began to close the door in her face, but the hoe stopped me by trying to push through it.

"Where is Rome?" she spat, her hatred for me burning deep from within her.

"Like I'm going to tell you where my man is at. Bitch swerve," I said, putting extra emphasis on my man.

"Your man?" she asked me in a high octave voice as if she was shocked or something.

I looked up and saw the envy and jealousy written all over her face when I referred to Roman as my man and couldn't stop the arrogant smirk from tugging at the corners of my mouth. Although Rome and I had never officially gotten back together, she didn't know that shit. I opened the door back up and stepped outside onto the porch closing the door behind me.

"Yes bitch, my man," I stated matter-of-factly while hopping in her face. I'm so sick and tired of this hoe. The old me would have tried to ignore her pathetic ass, but the new me was like Kelly being reincarnated. And y'all know how retarded Kelly's ass is. I'm so ready to beat this bitch's ass.

"Funny that you call him your man. Was he still your man when he was at my house bending me over fucking the shit out of this good pussy?" she asked with an evil smirk on her face.

I took my time looking Ebony's ass up and down with a blank expression on my face before I fell over laughing. "Bitch, please. Rome wouldn't touch your dusty, dirty ass with a ten-inch pole if he had one. If I remember correctly, you had to drug Rome just to get him to fuck your loose pussy ass. Take that story and try to run it on somebody else that doesn't know any better. I'm hipped."

"Where's my son? I want my son!" she yelled out dramatically, while trying to push me out of the way to get inside of my house.

"You must be out of your rabbit ass mind if you think I'm just going to let you take RJ when you got some white dried up shit on the corner of your mouth. Take your unfit ass on somewhere Ebony, and try to sleep that alcohol out of your system."

Ebony tried running up on me, and I pushed her back, making her stumbling in those tall ass heels that she had on. The girl had impeccable balance because all she did was stumble.

"GIVE ME MY FUCKING SON! I WANT MY SON! GIVE HIM TO ME NOW!" she continued to scream at the top of her lungs. By now she was causing a scene and had the neighbors were coming outside to see what was going on.

Now I'm pissed because these white folks don't play and would call the police faster than a New York minute. Ebony kept trying to push me out of the way from blocking the door and get inside of my house, and I kept pushing her ass back. I was just about to lay my hands on her when the front door suddenly swung open.

"What the fuck is you doing on my porch?" Rome growled at Ebony with a deep scowl etched on his handsome face.

"Rome!" Ebony's eyes lit up, and I could see the lust all in them. I whipped my head back to look at Rome. All he had on were his black basketball shorts and a pair of Jordan's. His skin had that light coat of sweat on it, not making the situation any better.

"Rome, I—," was all she was able to get out of her mouth before Rome wrapped his hand around her throat and pushed her back, making her stumble.

"Didn't I tell your hoe ass to never show up at my shit? You're bringing the property value down. Standing out here looking like you just left KOD," he spat heatedly. I could tell by the way he was holding her neck that he wasn't really choking her and only applying light pressure. Ebony looked like she was feeling real small, like a child being chastised by an adult.

"What the fuck is she doing here?" she asked him. It was like she didn't hear anything else that Rome had said to her and was only focused on me and why I was here.

The scowl on Rome's face deepened as his lips twisted up to the side. "The fuck you mean why is she here? That's my damn wife! She belongs here!" he yelled in her face.

I saw the tears welling up in Ebony's eyes and kind of felt bad for her. Besides the lust that was evident in her eyes ninety-five percent of the time, you could tell that the other five percent was the love that she had for Rome.

"Mommy what's going on?" I heard RJ say from behind me while at the same time trying to peek around me to see what all of the commotion was about. I looked behind me to see both RJ and Kamron standing there, trying to be nosey.

Rome must have heard his voice as well because he hurried and let go of Ebony's throat putting some space in between them.

Ebony used the palm of her hands and tried to wipe the tears from her eyes before they fell. She then stepped around Roman and made her way back up to the door.

"Hey, Jay baby," she said in a fake cheerful voice as if she was happy to see him. RJ stood behind me, holding tightly onto my leg.

"Come on, baby. Go get your stuff mommy has come to take you to play at Chuck E. Cheese's."

Just putting Chuck E. Cheese's and play in the same sentence would catch RJ's attention faster than anything. He loves going to Chuck E. Cheese's. That was his favorite spot.

"Really?" he asked her, barely able to contain his excitement. Ebony forced a smile and nodded her head to RJ's question, giving him all of the confirmation that he needed. RJ quickly spun on his heels and raced into the house.

Rome walked behind Ebony and grabbed her by the elbow, pulling her closer towards him. "I fucking hope that you are not taking my son to Chuck E. Cheese's dressed like you're trying to win the Thot of the Year Award," Rome growled.

Ebony rolled her eyes and snatched her arm out of his grasp. "No., I'm going to go home, take a shower, and change before I take him to Chuck E. Cheese's," she spat with an attitude.

"I'm ready!" RJ yelled out in excitement, running outside and holding tightly onto his Batman backpack.

"Damn little man, you gon' leave your Pops without giving him a hug?" Rome asked him, faking like he was sad. RJ laughed before running up to Rome and giving him a big hug. "Bye, Dad," he said squeezing him.

"What about me?" I asked, faking like I was sad as well. "I don't get a hug?" I asked again with my bottom lip poked out in a pout.

"Of course you do," Jay said to me letting go of Rome and running towards me with his arms spread wide open. I squatted so that I was to his level and held my arms open as well. RJ ran straight to them and wrapped his arms around my neck squeezing me tightly. Despite me not liking his mother, I loved RJ like I had birthed him. The love I had for this little boy was too real. Y'all couldn't tell me that this wasn't my baby.

"I don't want you to go," I pouted, holding tightly onto RJ, making him laugh.

"Don't worry mommy," he said to me while slowly pulling back away from me and staring into my eyes. "I'll be back tomorrow."

My eyes widened as I feigned excitement. "Really?" I exclaimed.

"Yes!" he exclaimed back.

"Promise?"

RJ grabbed my hand telling me to stick my pinky out. I did as I was told and stuck it out only for him to wrap his pinky around mine and touch my thumb with his. "Pinky promise."

My heart swelled up at the gesture. I swear RJ was too cute! I grabbed him one more time, hugging him tightly.

"Maaaa!" he sang out, laughing. "I can't breathe!" he exclaimed dramatically making me, Rome, and Kamron laugh.

I laughed before reluctantly pulling away. I had grown too attached to RJ and really didn't want him to go, but I had to. RJ kissed me on the cheek before running over to Kamron and bumping fists with him. I looked up just in time to see the hate dancing in Ebony's eyes. I know she was feeling some type of way about Jay calling me mommy. But, oh well. Fuck her feelings. She should've been on her motherly duties instead of wanting to party all the damn time.

I watched from my spot at the door, RJ running up to Ebony's beat up Civic and opening the back door, jumped inside with Rome strapping him in afterward. He whispered something into Ebony's ear, making her frown up and hurrying to jump in the driver's seat. She quickly started up the car and skidded out of the driveway.

ump in the driver's seat. She quickly started up the car and skidded out of the driveway.

"Thank you God that I don't have any baby mamas yet!" Kamron playfully joked, tossing his hands up to the sky in praise mode. Just that quick, the scowl that was placed on Rome's face was completely wiped off, replacing it with a smile.

"Nigga, shut your dumb ass up," he said, pushing Kamron in the shoulder.

"What I tell yo' bitch ass about putting your big ass hands on me, little nigga. Fuck that, nigga, square up." Kamron pulled his pants up and raised his dukes. Rome pulled his basketball shorts up and squared up right along with Kamron.

I sat there laughing and watching them run around the front yard slap boxing with each other for a little while, until I got enough of seeing it. I left their asses outside and went back into the kitchen to finish cleaning up my mess before I raced upstairs to the bedroom that I have been occupying since I 'moved in' with Roman. I made sure that my brother and Rome were still outside and that my door was shut before pulling out my favorite pastime and put it to work. Even after all the bullshit that had just happened outside not too long ago, I was still turned on. I had hella pent up sexual frustration that I needed to release before I end up in jail facing rape charges.

# Chapter Fifteen

**ROME**

I swear Ebony makes my ass itch with the shit that she does. I can't stand her ass. Why must she continue to try to make my life a living hell, I don't know. Her ass is like the baby mama from hell. She's always blowing my damn phone up. Constantly in my business. Always wanting to know what girl I'm talking to or who is holding my attention. Threatening to put me on child support when she doesn't get her way. Disappearing on me and taking my son with her for months at a time when I refuse to give her money that she could fuck around on, and so much other shit that I don't care to name at this moment.

Nothing makes her ass happy. If I'm not laying dick all up in her, then she's miserable and bitter as hell. I'm about a few pushes away from just washing my hands clean of her ass. But if I do that, then that means I have to wash my hands clean of Jay as well, and I just can't see myself doing that.

I know y'all are probably wondering what do I mean by that. Well, I will tell you. To put it in the simplest form, RJ does not belong to me. I'd gotten the blood results back around the same time Aris was put in the hospital, so I never really had a chance to open the envelope and read it. It just sat on my coffee table for the longest, collecting dust. To be honest, I had actually forgotten about the damn test because my attention was staying by Aris' side until she woke up from her coma.

I found the envelope when I was moving all of my shit out of my condo and moving into the five bedrooms, three baths mini-mansion that I bought to move Aris into. By the time I did open up the envelope and read the results, months had passed, and my attachment to Jay was too strong. We had an unbreakable bond that only a father and son could have.

I ain't even gonna lie and say that shit didn't hurt, because it did. I was just getting used to being called dad and then to read that shit had me crushed. On the low, I was praying that Jay was mine, but as you can see God had other plans. After reading those results, I said fuck it. RJ was going to be my son regardless of the bloodwork. Blood couldn't make us any closer. He needed a father figure in his life, and I was going to make sure that I'm the only father figure he has. I even went as far as signing Jay's birth certificate. Nobody knows about me not being RJ's biological dad. Hell, they didn't need to ask. With each passing day, month, and year, it showed in his features.

Pushing Ebony and her bullshit to the back of my mind, I started to prepare for my day. Even her bitter ass wasn't enough to stop my shine. Today Kamron's people would be flying out to Miami and joining us for a night full of relaxation. It was my nigga AJ's thirty-second birthday. Him, Kasey, and my nigga Khyree were coming down to Miami to turn the fuck up. Kamron and I are throwing him a big ass birthday party at Club Secrets. I had to run a few errands and then I had plans to take Aris to the mall so  we could pick up this dress that I had custom tailor-made for her.

After kicking Kam's ass two more times in basketball, I went upstairs to shower. Today was the first. You know what that means, right? Today was collection day and since Quamir's bitch ass up and disappeared, I went ahead and took over that job as well. I can't wait until I see that bitch ass nigga again. I swear I got two hot ones ready for his ass as soon as I see him. It was real fucked up how the nigga had just disappeared while his "girlfriend" was left for dead in the hospital, fighting for her life. On some real nigga shit, that was just a straight up bitch move. Dude lost all fucking cool points for that pussy ass shit.

Landon and Kamron were running all over Miami stressing and trying to find out where the fuck ass nigga ran off to. Meanwhile, my ass was happier than a fat kid getting a free happy meal from McDonald's. I was glad that nigga disappeared. Good riddance.

I couldn't give two fucks about what happened to dude, even if my own momma begged and pleaded to me to give a shit I wouldn't. Fuck Quamir's bitch ass and I ain't never been scared to say the shit to his face. I'm glad his ass is gone. I never liked his ass any fucking way, and I let the shit be known each and every muthafuckin' chance that I got. I had always said that there was something about dude that I just don't like and the feeling only intensified when the nigga just disappeared. Call me paranoid, but I always listen to my gut. It never leads me wrong. Something ain't right about dude.

The whole time Aris was in the hospital, I spent every day sitting by her side, refusing to leave her unattended. I hate hospitals and never trusted them. The only time I left Aris' side was to go home and take a shower. Once my balls were squeaky cleaned and I had on fresh clothes, I would find my way back to the hospital.

I was so focused on Ari that I couldn't tell you the last time I had a decent sleep or the last time that I actually ate a decent meal that didn't consist of something out of the vending machine. Sometimes Kamron had to force me to eat. I was happy as fuck when I woke up after falling asleep in that hard chair to Aris' gray eyes staring down into mine.

I was ecstatic, but nothing could have prepared me for the shit that followed after her being released from the hospital. Shit was like running through hell and back in gasoline draws. I had to literally drag her by her bald ass head through everything. Most niggas would've run off a long time ago, but then again I'm not like most niggas. I'm a real ass nigga, and real niggas do real shit, no matter how difficult the circumstances are. I'm the last of a dying breed.

I faithfully stuck by Aris' side through the depression, the drug addiction, the suicide attempts and was there for her while she received the psychiatric help she needed. I refused to sit back like everybody else did and wait until Aris decided to come out of her funk. I fought one hell of a battle but at the end of it all, it was well worth it. Aris was almost back to her normal self, and I couldn't be prouder.

What still fucks with my mental even to this day was the way she had reacted after she woke up from her coma. A whole lot of shit threw up red flags and had me questioning what was really going on. First off, she didn't want to tell anyone who did that shit to her. Not me, her Pops, Kamron, or even the girls. Her lips stayed sealed. Then there was the dark and soulless look she had in her eyes. I had never seen Aris' eyes turn that damn dark before. The shit was creepy as hell to me. And finally, the way she acted when Kamron told her about Quamir disappearing. She acted all nonchalant and had that 'I don't give a fuck attitude'. That shit really threw me for a loop. I was like damn, my baby fall back game ain't no fucking joke. She still walks around, to this day, acting like the nigga and what she had never even existed.

Standing in the mirror, I gave myself one last look before nodding my head in approval. I'm not a pretty ass nigga that only cares about his looks, but I do like to make myself look presentable wherever I go. I liked to keep shit simple. Simple and clean is the best route to go. But I must admit that I looked fly as hell in my white Givenchy Cuban-fit straight leg jeans, white Ralph Lauren Polo t-shirt, and my white and tan Jordan Retro 13's. I topped my look off with diamond studded earrings, gold herringbone chain, and custom-made golden Gladiator diamond studded watch. Although my fit was simple, I was on my GQ fly shit. I sprayed myself down with my Clive Christian No. 1 cologne, grabbed my phone, and keys to the Maserati.

Before leaving, I was going to check on Aris and let her know I was leaving, but that shit immediately went flying out of the window the moment I pushed her bedroom door open. Aris was lying on her back naked, in the middle of her bed, with her hand in between her legs, playing with herself. Her eyes were closed tight, and her back was arched. I could tell by how hard her breathing became and how hard her legs started to shake that she was close to releasing a powerful orgasm. My dick instantly rocked up at the sight.

"Ah…sh…shit! Mmm… Rome baby. It's cumming," she moaned biting sexily into her bottom lip.

"Let that shit go then and show daddy what his pussy can do," I slightly growled, my deep voice startling Aris.

Aris' eyes snapped open wide, and her face turned beet red from embarrassment. "Oh my God, Rome! What are you doing in here?! Get out!" she screamed out hysterically while trying to pull the covers over her naked body. I couldn't do anything but laugh. She reminded me of a little kid hiding underneath the sheets from the boogeyman. It was hella hilarious and cute at the same time.

I smirked as I folded my arms across my chest and leaned back against her bedroom door frame. "You act like I ain't never seen you naked before. You might as well pull the covers back and let me see some more. It's been five years since the last time I've seen that thang squirt," I said licking my lips.

"Eww! You are such a pervert! Get out, you creep! Get out!" she screamed picking a pillow up and throwing it at me. I laughed when the pillow landed at the foot of the bed.

"Aww… is the poor baby embarrassed that she got caught playing with herself?" I cooed in a grown man trying to speak baby language voice. I was teasing her, and she knew it. "It's ok. I won't tell nobody. It could be our little secret."

"Oh my God! Rome! If you don't get your ass out of my room! I'm gonna to–,"

"You ain't gone do shit but bend over and take this dick," I said in a no bullshit tone. "You can walk yo' little ass over here if you want to and I promise you that you'll be getting fucked today."

Aris' face flushed red as hell she was blushing so damn hard. I saw from out the corner of my eye her squirming underneath those covers. I don't know why she keeps playing with me and acting like she just ain't into a nigga anymore. She knows damn well she has a leakage in between her thighs that only I can fix.

"I swear you are the biggest perverted creep that I have ever known!" she yelled at me and at the same time tossing the covers from around her body and taking flight to the bathroom. Aris slammed the door shut and locked it.

I was laughing hard as hell. You would've thought that bed had suddenly caught on fire how fast she jumped up from the muthafucka and flew into the bathroom. I walked over to the bathroom and knocked twice on the door with my knuckles.

"Aye," I called through the door.

"Get away from the door, Roman! I'm not playing with yo ass!" she screamed making me laugh harder.

"I'm about to leave damn. I was just trying to tell yo' nasty ass that I'm about to leave."

"You could've texted me that shit!" she spat heatedly.

"Good thing I didn't. I walked in and had front row seats to an amazing, spectacular show. You really outdid yourself, this time, Ari. The only compliant that I have is you walking off the stage without finishing the performance. Talk about a cliffhanger."

*BAM!*

Aris' palm came banging on the door. "GET THE FUCK OUT! OR I'M GONNA CALL MY DADDY AND TELL HIM THAT YOU ARE BULLYING ME!"

I laughed while throwing my hands up in mock surrender. "Ok, ok. I'm leaving for real now."

Just like a spoiled daddy's girl to throw that card in. She knew damn well that I was afraid of Kaseem's crazy ass. My jaw still hurt from the last time I saw that nigga. It was the day after Aris was admitted into the hospital for that bullshit. Killa Mills and my old head quickly hopped on the first thing smoking back to the United States. I told y'all them niggas didn't give a fuck. Knowing damn well their asses are wanted in all fifty states, they still snuck back into the country after they heard what happened.

Killa came in on one. Beat mine and Kamron's asses all over that damn hospital. It took my Pops, three doctors, and two fake rent-a-cop ass niggas to get Killa off of us. That nigga was like the Incredible Hulk on energy drinks. By the time he was finally finished with our asses, Kamron and I both had matching black eyes, busted noses, and swollen jaws. Killa did not play when it came to his only princess. Hell, Landon would have gotten it too, if the nigga didn't run out like a little bitch.

"I'm about to run out and check up on a couple spots real quick. Put something on and be ready by the time I come back. I'll be back in a two hours."

"Why?"

"Did you forget that tonight is AJ's birthday, and your brother is throwing him a birthday party at Secrets tonight?"

"Shit. I forgot."

"Good thing I reminded you, huh?" I replied smartly.

"Suck an ass, smart ass," Aris spat heatedly. I could tell that she was annoyed with me by now, and the shit was funny.

"Open the door and let me come in there so that I can eat the booty like I'm at an all you can eat buffet."

"Nigga, fuck you!" she spat.

"Ask and I shall give."

"Ugh! I can't stand you! I swear I'm moving back in with my brother."

I scoffed. "Yea. Aight. Do that and see where yo' ass would end up back at."

"Just do what I said. Come out and chill with me while RJ is with his mom."

"Yes, father!" she said sarcastically.

"Aye?" I called out to her again.

I heard Aris sighed out loud as if I was irritating her or some shit. "What now, dad?"

I laughed. "Dad is the nigga that helped make you. Daddy is for the nigga that's going to be rearranging your insides sooner rather than later."

Aris sucked her teeth and me knowing her like I do, I just knew she was in the rolling her eyes. "What. Do You. Want?" she asked me through gritted teeth.

I chuckled while leaning in closer towards the door. "While you're in there, make her purr one last time for me and scream my name out when you do. I like that shit. That shit had me harder than a muthafucka."

*BAM!*

"GET OUT YOU FUCKING PERVERT!" she screamed out again.

I doubled over laughing again, getting seven or eight chuckles out before finally leaving her alone. Right before I exited of her bedroom, I reached in my back pocket for my wallet and left my black card on the dresser just as I said I was going to do. I made sure that I had everything I needed before leaving the bedroom and officially started my day.

***

After I finished my rounds and dropped the money off at the warehouse so that it could be counted up, I stopped by Secrets to make sure that everything was going as planned. As I pulled up into the parking lot, I noticed that Kam's candy red 2016 Camaro SS was there, meaning that he was already inside and that we were both on the same page.

Entering the club, I saw Landon and Kamron occupying the bar with the chef sampling tonight's dishes which was a mixture of American, Columbian, and seafood. Seeing Landon there as well meant that he rode with Kamron because I didn't see his car outside.

"Damn, y'all just going to start without me, huh? Where is the love and loyalty?" I joked as I dapped Landon up first, and then Kamron.

"Bruh, ain't nobody about to be waiting on yo' pretty boy ass, and we got shit to do," Kamron joked, laughing.

I playfully pushed his ass on the shoulder laughing as well.

"I know yo' ass ain't talking?" Landon said to Kamron with his eyebrow raised. "You take just as much time as a female does."

"Man, shut yo' black ass up. Wasn't nobody talking to you," Kamron said, mean mugging Landon.

"I don't need an invitation to put my two sentences in," Lay retorted.

"Hola amigo, Rome," Juan greeted me as he was giving me dap. I reached across the bar and met his fist halfway bumping it with mine.

"Wassup Juan. What's on the menu?" I asked him, tuning out the back and forth bickering that Kamron and Lay were doing. I picked up a fresh plastic spoon and dipped it in the mini sample bowl of clam chowder soup tasting it. I nodded my head in approval as I slowly chewed to savor the taste. That shit was fire.

"Well, for the appetizers I prepared clam chowder, crab cakes, cheese stuffed meatballs, creamy spinach roll ups, and bacon wrapped grilled shrimp. I mixed it up with American, Columbian, and a couple of seafood dishes. For the main course, I've made lobster tails, baked scallops, Cajun seafood pasta, garlic shrimp scampi, Colombian beef stew, roasted chicken legs served on a large bed of rice and avocado, grilled pork Fajita's, chicken burritos, filet mignon, honey glazed chicken strips, lemon pepper, tangy BBQ hot wings, oxtail soup, jerk chicken, and red beans and rice."

"My muthafuckin nigga!" I exclaimed reaching across the bar and slapping hands with him. "All of that shit sounds good as fuck! You really outdid yourself with this one, and if everything tastes just as good as this chowder, then I know everything is going to be dope as fuck. What about dessert?" I asked taking another bite of clam chowder.

"For dessert, I made Crème Brule and a triple chocolate cheesecake."

I nodded my head in approval and took one more bite of chowder when Kamron slapped me on the hand and yank the sample bowl out of my reach.

"Damn nigga, we didn't get a chance to sample this shit and yo' greedy ass damn near ate it all up," Landon spat heatedly looking back and forth between me and the damn near gone chowder.

I covered my mouth with the back of my hand and started laughing at the expression on his face. If looks could kill, then my ass would've been dead right where I was standing. This nigga and Kamron's ass really looked like they were about to box my ass.

"My bad, bruh. I ain't trying to eat it all up. The shit was just too good to stop at one bite," I managed to say through my laughter.

"If yo' ass wasn't playing so much then we could've been watching this nigga. You know that big ass nigga could eat the whole fucking farm up by himself," Kamron turned to say to Landon.

"Don't blame that shit on me. That was your big kid ass," Landon retorted back with a deep frown etched on his face.

"Fellas, fellas, amigos," Juan intervened causing both Kam and Lay to shoot daggers at him. "Don't argue I have more," he said sitting another bowl of chowder down in front of them. Kamron and Landon didn't say nothing else. They dove in like they ain't ate since the Stone Ages.

I couldn't do nothing but laugh and shake my head at them. I swear they were like some big ass kids sometimes. Always throwing tantrums when shit doesn't go their way.

"I'm going to leave y'all here and check on my kitchen. I will see you tonight Senor Rome."

"Aight."

Juan turned and went back to the kitchen leaving us at the bar. I took a seat next to Landon and ordered a bottle of Hennessey. I reached into my pocket for my weed stash and sat it out on the counter top. "How long y'all punk asses been up here?" I asked as I started breaking up the weed to put in my grape Cigarillo.

"We just got here thirty minutes before you did," Landon said taking one more bite of the chowder and pushing the empty bowl to the side.

"How did the pickup go? Shit was straight? No bullshit?" Kamron asked me while pouring himself a shot.

"Shit man, everything been good. Besides having to get into Demarious' ass, everything was straight. I can't really complain. Niggas had the money ready as soon as I pulled up making my job much easier and much faster," I said as I put the weed inside of the blunt, rolled it up real tight, and licked the sides down really good, making sure that none of the weed would seep out. Reaching inside of my pocket for my light, I ran it along the length of it and lit it. I slowly took a deep pull on it, holding the smoke in my lungs for a little minute, before letting it out slowly through my nose and passing it to Lay.

I saw the irritated and frustrated look on Kamron's face. He looked pissed. "What did Dee's ass do now?" he asked me while taking the blunt out of Lay's hand and took a long puff.

"Stupid ass nigga was sitting on the porch in broad daylight, smoking weed, and flirting with them young ass, fast ass girls over there. Had the spot looking like a straight up hoe house. Those girls could be his daughters, that's how young they were. I had to burst him upside his shit with my gun because that nigga is old enough to know better than letting them or anyone else hang around the spot like it was a clubhouse or some shit. I had to let that stupid muthafucka know that I didn't give a fuck what he did when he was at his own crib, but not to ever in his fucking life again bring that shit back over to the spot. Y'all know I don't give out warnings, I'm straight murdering me a hardheaded muthafucka, but just off the strength that he used to run with Pops and them, I let his ass off."

"This muthafucka," Kamron mumbled through gritted teeth. His grayish blue eyes darkening.

"Yo, I think we should let that muthafucka go," Lay said, after passing the blunt off to me.

I grabbed it and took a deep hard pull from it, agreeing with what Lay had just said. I'd been said that shit, but never out loud.

"Ever since you downgraded him, he's been acting real salty lately. Instead of trying to work to get his position back like you told him to, the nigga just sitting there collecting dust with a mean mug on his face. Cario has even said that he's losing all of his normal customers because the muthafucka always having an attitude with somebody. He had to put the nigga on kitchen duty."

"I think that's what the fuck I'm going to end up doing. The nigga ain't making no type of noise and is getting too flamboyant for my liking. Always starting shit with them Haitians over in Little Haiti. Shit between us and them Haitians have been peaceful until he took his dusty ass over there, starting shit like we need a fucking war to happen right now. I swear I'm going to end up killing his ass."

"I say do what you need to do. It's better to kill the weed before it spreads and becomes a bigger problem later on down the line."

Instead of responding, Kamron had just nodded his head in agreement. He had that far-off glazed look in his eyes that said that he was lost deep inside of his own thoughts. After taking one pull from the blunt, I handed it to Lay who finished it off.

"Wassup with you and sis?" I asked Landon pouring me a cup full of liquor.

"Who? Monae?" he asked me, sounding stupid as hell with his response.

I looked at him with my head cocked to the side and a duh expression on my face. "Nah, nigga Monae," I answered him sarcastically. "What other sis do I have?" I asked him rhetorically, throwing my shot back.

Landon started laughing like what I said was funny. "Mo and I are cool."

"That's not what I'm asking. What I'm asking is are y'all fucking?" I just came out and said it. When it came to getting the answers that I so desperately wanted to know, I didn't believe in beating around the bush and playing games. Regardless if I come off blunt, straightforward or just rude, if I want answers I'm going to get them.

Landon chuckled. "Nah, bruh. Ain't shit going on between Mo and me. We're just friends."

"Don't you believe that shit," Kamron intervened looking over Lay and at me. "You and Ari used to say that shit all of the time and look at what everybody found out years later. Don't believe that 'we're just friends' bullshit. That's a cover up. Muthafuckas only use that excuse because they just can't come out and just say 'yes, we're fuckin'."

"Nigga, shut your bugging ass up, " Lay said, mushing Kam in the head. "Wasn't nobody talking to your ass," he said in an irritated tone.

Kamron looked at Landon and smirked arrogantly at him. "I don't need an invitation to put my two cents in."

I fell over laughing because Landon had just used that same line with Kamron not even thirty minutes ago. Landon sucked his teeth after mushing Kamron in the head one last time making Kamron laugh. "Ain't no fun when the rabbit got the gun huh?" he asked teasingly.

Landon had just turned his back to Kamron giving me his undivided attention. "Back to what I was saying before this mentally retarded muthafucka butted in our conversation." I looked at Kamron standing behind Landon trying to do his version of sign language and mouthing to me not to trust shit that he was saying. Landon stopped talking to turn around and push Kam back into his seat. "Nigga, get your lava breath ass off the back of my neck. Fuck around and gonna melt my lining away!" Landon yelled heatedly. You could tell just by from his tone that he was getting both agitated and irritated with Kamron's ass. Which was one of his specialties if you haven't noticed.

"Don't blame your fucked up lining on me! You better blame that shit on the muthafucka who you let cut your head with a blindfold on," Kamron retorted back.

I tried to keep myself from laughing but failed to hold it in. Kamron and Landon were like the male versions of Mona and Kelly. One minute, they were cool as fuck and the next, they're bickering. I'm telling you it's like babysitting some overgrown ass kids. "Alright now. I heard enough arguing for the day," I said and then chuckled as I sipped on my brown liquor.

"Anyway. If there was something going on with Mo and me, then you know that I would've stepped up to you like the real nigga that I am and told you what the deal is. Although I can be quiet at times, I don't like sugar coating shit. I keep everything a hunnid and expect the same in return."

I couldn't do shit but nod my head in agreement. Lay was a man of so many words. If he didn't speak then, you never would have known he was standing there. When he does speak, he speaks nothing but real shit. Shit that would have you really thinking. Lay was a tall muthafucka, standing at six-foot-five, dark-skinned, distinctive features, onyx-colored eyes and weighed two hundred sixty pounds of pure muscle. Looking at him you would've never guessed that he was the deadliest out of us all. The nigga was a straight beast in the streets. He was a quiet killer and a quiet killer always moved in silence. He was keeping it real two hundred percent of the time and being just a stand-up kind of guy is why I respect him the way that I do.

"But I'm not even gon' sit up here and lie to you and say that I don't have feelings for Mo either," I heard him say. I swear I whipped my head in his direction so fast that I thought that I had whiplash. Now I was not expecting that nigga to say no shit like that. So you could bet your ass that had my attention.

"I told yo' ass!" Kamron said from his spot behind Landon.

Ignoring Kamron's ignorant ass, I kept my eyes and attention on Landon. No lie, I felt the overprotective big brother in me starting to kick in. It was taking everything in me to stop myself from wrapping my hands around his thick ass throat and snap that muthafucka. Just imagining my right-hand man and my baby sister fucking behind my back had me oven hot. Hell, I'm still looking for the little nigga that knocked my baby sis up. I got a bullet and a closed casket just waiting on his ass. I was pissed, but you couldn't tell by the emotionless expression on my face.

"So you have feelings for her, huh?" I asked calmly as I took a small sip from my liquor.

"Yes, I do. There was an actual time where I thought I loved her," he answered me honestly. His facial expression never changed.

My eyebrows deepened in confusion. "What the fuck you mean by you thought? Nigga are you in love with her or nah?" I spat impatiently.

"Just like I said I thought I was in love with her, but as time went by the more I came to realize that the type of affection that I had for Moe was the same kind of affection that an older brother would have for his younger sister. There is nothing going on between Mo and I. After you went to jail I stepped up and took the role of a big brother. Mo is like the little sister that I never had, and Levi is my godson. I can assure that there is nothing going on between us. If there was then, I am man enough to come to you and tell you what the deal was," he replied.

For a minute, I just sat there staring at him with a blank facial expression on my face. I was looking for any sign of him lying just so that I had a reason to fire off on him, but I knew that he was telling the truth. Lay just didn't have a lying bone in his body. With the type of character that he is, Landon would have pulled me to the side and told me how he was feeling.

"Because you are a nigga that I got mad respect for I'mma take you word and run with it."

"You got my word. There isn't anything going on between us."

We talked shit, sipped and smoked so many damn blunts that before I knew it time flew, and it was already going on four in the afternoon. I was higher than a Tyrannosaurus Rex's pussy. After handling my business, I headed home, ready to see my baby.

Pulling up to the house, I put the car into park and took my time climbing out and going inside. Knowing Aris, her ass probably still wasn't ready. Entering the house, I deactivated the alarm and stood at the end of the stairs.

"Aris? Come on girl bring your ass on!" I yelled up the stairs.

"Nigga, here I come! Don't be rushing me!" she yelled back at me.

I felt my phone vibrating in my pocket. I unlocked the screen and I saw that is was only Ebony's ass sending me a text message. Thinking that it had something to do with my son I didn't hesitate to click on the message icon. I wished that I didn't do that shit. It was a picture of Ebony butt asshole naked laying on her back with her legs spread opened wide using her index and middle finger to spread open her labia lips.

**EBONY: I was in the shower just thinking of you. See what you did?**

I shook my head in disgust while deleting the text message altogether. To me a woman sending her a picture of her shit to a man that didn't want any fucking thing to do with her was just desperate. I don't know how many times I have to tell her that I don't want her. Her ass just won't listen. The sound of heels clicking against the marble stairs caused me to glance up from my phone and watch her coming down the stairs as if she was about to hit the runway.

Aris was dressed simple, just like I was. But the sight of her in a pair of Miss Me acid wash denim super skinny jeans, a plain white V-neck t-shirt, YSL leather satchel and a pair of nude pointy toe Christian Louboutin red bottom pumps had my dick hardening against my leg. She had her short hair flat ironed bone straight and flipped to frame her pretty face. Her bangs were pulled back and pinned down with a hair pin. She also wore a light layer of nude makeup with a wingtip eyeliner, mascara and a nude and pink lipstick with a light coat of lip gloss to give her lips that extra pop. I could smell her Dior perfume a mile away.

Aris was smiling so big it looked like her cheeks were starting to hurt.

"Damn," I tried mumbling to myself. I was staring Aris up and down while biting on my bottom lip. Giving her that lustful 'C'mere look' that always seemed to have her blushing. I was ready right then and there to bend her ass over and give her soul shaking strokes.

"I see yo' ass trying to steal my swag," I said laughing meeting her at the bottom of the stairs.

Aris looked back and forth between our outfits and giggled before flipping her clear stiletto designed fingernail at me. "Nigga you wish. That's yo' ass always trying to steal my swag," she said with a playful roll of my eyes.

I just gave her my infamous crooked grin. "C'mere." I beckoned with a head nod.

"What?" she said nervously now standing in front of me at the second to last stair.

I wrapped my arms around her waist cuffing her ridiculously big ass into my large hands and lifted her up. A loud surprised scream escaped from the back of her throat as she grabbed onto my shoulders for extra support. "Roman, you better not drop me, or I swear I'm gonna hurt you if you do."

"Oh shut up and wrap your legs around my waist," I said in a calm yet demanding deep voice.

Aris just smiled and did what I asked her to wrap her legs around my waist and running her fingers through my soft curly hair. I had to hold her by the ass and jump shifting her body in my arms to keep her from falling. The whole time I was staring her deeply into her eyes. Aris continued running her fingers through my hair massaging my scalp while staring deeply into her eyes. Her fingers felt good as shit, and a moan almost slipped out of my mouth.

"You know you the syrup to my Sprite... the grape flavor to my plain ass Cigarillo… the weed to my lungs... ma fucking cinnamon apple cereal for when it's late night and a nigga got the munchies," I said to her jokingly.

"Nigga…what?" she asked me in disbelief; her smile widening. "Nigga, did you just say that I'm yo' apple cinnamon cereal for when you get the munchies?" she asked me again for clarification. When I didn't bother to say anything to correct what she heard she fell out laughing hard as hell. That shit that I said came out of nowhere, and it had her ass crying.

I gripped my ass harder and grinned up at her. "So you really just gonna sit up in my face and laugh while I'm trying to be romantic and shit huh?"

"You call that being romantic?" she asked through my laughter. "Boy please!" she exclaimed laughing harder. Just hearing her laugh caused me to chuckle as well.

"Oh, girl hush. You know that shit made your heart skip a beat quit frontin'."

Me saying that made her laugh even harder. "I'm not about to entertain yo' crazy ass today," she said still laughing and fanning herself with her hand so that she doesn't ruin her mascara. "You had to fuck up the moment with that corny ass joke, huh?"

I smacked my teeth and playfully rolled my eyes at her. "See a nigga can't even get romantic with yo' ass. My heart and soul were in that shit," I said faking an attitude.

"Aww… is my baby upset?" she cooed pinching my cheeks.

I yanked my head out of her grasp and glared at her through tiny splits still faking my attitude.

"Aww, boo bear. That was the most romantic shit anybody has ever said to me. I only laughed to keep myself from crying. I was so… touched," she said, putting a hand over her heart and wiping a fake tear away for dramatic effects. This caused me to stop glaring at her and laugh hard as hell.

"You are so full of shit I'm surprised flies ain't been flocking to yo' ass."

She laughed while playfully mushing the side of my head. "Whatever!"

"Are we going to continue standing here cracking jokes and shit or are we leaving? Your hands are getting a little too frisky down there," she asked me. I couldn't help it, though. Her ass was feeling too loose in them jeans. I was checking to see if she had any panties on. Once I was able to finally locate them, I stopped squeezing her ass.

"We'll leave once you give me a kiss."

Aris smacked her teeth and rolled her eyes. "Begging ass nigga," she mumbled before kissing me two quick times on the lips then pulled away. I looked at her through tiny eyes before pinning her body against the nearest wall and pinning her arms above her head.

"Wha… what are you do—," She started to ask me but my mouth coming down on hers shut her ass up and had her body stiffening at the same time. Moaning softly into my mouth she closed her eyes and kissed me back. I took turns sucking and nipping at her bottom and top lip before sucking them into my mouth. Aris continued moaning into my mouth while I intertwined my fingers with hers just as her legs around my waist wrapped tighter around me. My dick was hard as shit, and I wanted her ass to feel it. Her nails dug into the nap of my neck as I slid my tongue in and out of her mouth deepening our kiss. I could feel the heat from her pussy through the material of her jeans as she ground her hips against my hard on. In my head, I was screaming fuck the mall. All I wanted to do was take her ass upstairs and fuck her ass to sleep. The whole seat of her panties was soaked with her juices. Her hips winded faster against me and judging by how heavy and fast her breathing had just gotten she was so close to cumming. She just needed a few more minutes, and she would be telling Vickie's Secret.

Humming softly into her mouth, I kissed her once more as I gave her ass a squeeze then a hard slap before letting go and pulling back. "Aight let's go. We already spent too much time bullshitting around. We still gotta get to the mall before it closes and get our outfits for tonight," I said gently putting her down and putting distance in between us. I reached down to readjust the hard on in my jeans. My shit was straight throbbing. As bad as I wanted to I knew that it was too soon for us to even take it there.

Aris stood there looking at me with her mouth agape in shock as her brain tried to process what the hell just happened. I couldn't help the sneaky grin crossing my face. I got a kick out of teasing Aris. I would always play with her kissing all of her passionate spots to get her hot and ready for me and then stop. She hated that shit and each time that I did it she would look at me with a deathly look.

Looking at me, she poked her lips out while rolling her eyes with an attitude. Not saying anything else to me, she walked right past me and out the front door; bumping me hard as hell on the way out.

I chuckled as I shut the door and locked it behind us. I walked her over to the passenger side of my Maserati and opened the door for her. I waited until she climbed inside and fastened up her seatbelt before closing the door. As I walked over to the driver's side, Aris reached over and opened the door for me. The gestured had me smiling hard as hell.

"Oh shit! So she does have manners?" I said jokingly making her laugh.

"Kiss ape ass" she cracked back.

As soon as the car started up, T.I.'s I'm Back, starting booming through the speakers. Aris cocked her head to the side and looked at me through slanted eyes with the sides of her lips curling up into a smile. Anybody that knows Ari knows that she loves her some Tip. I smiled and lowered the windows with my head nodding up and down to the music. Aris turned the radio up some more as I put the car into reverse backing out of the driveway and pulling off. She got comfortable and continued rapping along with Tip.

***

"Man, if she doesn't take that big ass cereal bowl off the top of her head! The hell is wrong with these girls these days?" I asked as I rubbed my hand through my curly hair while glancing behind myself at the girl I was just talking about who's bun was bigger than her head and her friend's that was with her.

We have been shopping for outfits at Dolphin Mall for two hours, and I was ready to go. We had gotten so much shit for ourselves and RJ as well that I and a few security guards had to make two trips to the car. We were just leaving from Haagen-Dazs ice cream shop when all of a sudden the girl with the big ass bowl on top of her head caught my attention. Aris fell back laughing hard as hell before shaking her head at me. She was laughing while I was looking at ole girl with wide eyes. This was my first time seeing some shit like that. Like, I've seen bitches walk around looking like NASA's lost experiments but not no shit like that.

"Bruh," I exclaimed animatedly while nudging Aris in the shoulder almost making her drop her ice cream cone. "Check out her friend! Her head is brighter than my future!" I leaned over and whispered in her ear while pointing to the girl who tried to rock the Amber Rose cut only for her barber to fuck her shit up. Like a dumbass Aris just had to entertain my nonsense and look back and doubled over laughing. That had me laughing hard as well. Baby girl's head looked as if somebody had spilled a whole bottle of Johnson & Johnson baby oil over her shit.

"Look! If you stare too long at it, you could see your future," I said to while pointing the girl out.

"Stop it!" Aris said laughing while slapping my hand down. "It's bad to point at people."

"Hell, it's bad for people to come out of the house looking like that!" I retorted back shaking my head. I reached out and gently grabbed Aris by the elbow pulling her into my chest. "Don't move."

"Huh? Why?" she asked looking up at me with a look of confusion on her face. She tried to take a step back, but I grabbed her by the hips holding her in place.

"Just don't move aight?" I said leaning down and licking her ice cream. Aris looked up at me through tiny, menacing eyes before punching me in the chest. "Don't be licking my shit! I don't know where yo' tongue been at," her lips pressed together feigning an attitude.

My shoulders shook slightly as I let out a low laugh. "Down your throat a few hours ago, " I said arrogantly with that crooked ass smirk of mine that she loves and hates at the same damn time.

"Man, shut up," she said laughing while playfully mushing me in the side of my head.

My laughter immediately came to a screeching halt as my head snapped up to look at whatever was behind her. "Damn!"

"What?" she asked me turning around to see what had my attention all of a sudden. While she was too busy being nosey, I snatched her ice cream cone out of her hand. Aris turned around to cuss my ass out about taking her shit. "Muthafucka no you did not just—," She started to go off, but her sentence was cut off by me taking her ice cream cone and mashing it in her face. Aris gasped as she quickly jumped back to avoid any ice cream staining her clothes.

"Oh my, God! Why did you do that Roman! You got it on my nose you ugly, dirty bastard!" she yelled at me while punching me in the chest. Her sudden outburst gathering the attention of other shoppers. I laughed grabbing her arms and pinning them down at her sides. I wrapped my arms around her waist and held the back of her thighs so that she couldn't move.

"Let. Me. Go," she said through clenched teeth. The attitude in her voice didn't go unnoticed. Laughing, my grip tightened even more around her.

"Aww, does the po' baby got an attitude now?" I cooed teasingly.

Aris tried fighting out of my embrace, but her resistance only made me hold onto her even tighter.

She let an irritated sigh escaped from the back of her throat. I could tell that she was getting very aggravated with me. The more the ice cream melted and slowly dripped down her face the more pissed off she had become. “So, you really not going to let me go?” she calmly asked me. I looked at her and smirked. She nodded. “Ok. If that’s how you want to do it,” She said softly.

She leaned forward and tried to wipe her face off using my shirt, but I had already caught on and pushed her back; releasing my hold on her.

“Man, go on somewhere with that bullshit. I quit,” I said laughing throwing my hands up in mock surrender.

Now it was her turn to grin. “Nah, don’t try to quit now. The game just started,” she took a step forward, and I took two steps back.

“Why you running? I know you ain’t scared of little ol’ me?” she asked laughing.

“C’mon Ari man. Quit playing. You got these white people looking at us like we crazy and shit.”

“Fuck them!” she exclaimed taking more steps closer towards me. “Stop running and bring that ass here boy!” she yelled before taking off running up on me. When she was at arm’s length, she tried grabbing the end of my shirt and wipe her face clean with it.

“For real, Ari, I quit man. You play too much!” I exclaimed, panic evident in my tone, as I quickly snatched my shirt out of her hand and jump backward putting more space between us.

Aris stopped advancing towards me and fell over laughing. She was bending over with her hands on her knees laughing even harder now.

“Ok! Ok! I quit!” she said laughing and tossing her hands up in mock surrender. Although she said that she quit playing, I still wasn’t going anywhere near her ass until she wiped her face. Aris must have known what I thought because she reached in her back pocket for a napkin and wiped her face off with it. “There. Happy?” she asked me after disposing of the soiled napkin.

“I was just about to two piece yo’ ass if you had succeeded and wiped your face off with my shirt,” I said jokingly but also with some seriousness behind my statement.

Aris laughed while wrapping her arms around my neck and pressing her chest into mine. "Negro, please. You don't want those kinds of problems homie. I would really fuck your ass up in this mall."

"In yo' dreams lil' shawty," I said after mushing her in the head. "I taught you everything you know. You already know that is a battle that you will not win."

"Whatever nigga. Gimme a kiss," she said closing her eyes with her lips poked out. I laughed pushing her away. "Are you ready to go?" I asked, leaving her lips poked out, looking crazy ass hell.

Aris playfully rolled her eyes and sucked her teeth. "I been ready. That's your ass wanting to sit here and play in the mall like we five or some shit," she tossed her hair over her shoulder and walked around me with her nose high in the air putting an extra pep in her step.

"Damn girl. What's that sitting high up in those jeans? Let me see if it's real," I joked, slapping and cuffing one of her ass cheeks in my hand. "Damn, it is." Aris quickly spun around on her heels pushing me in the chest.

"Damn pervert!" she yelled before turning back on her heels and stomping out of the mall. I ran up behind her and wrapped my arms around her waist with her ass sitting directly on my hard member. She went to say something but was stopped by me nibbling on the back of her earlobe. "Shut your ass up and keep walking," I demanded, sinking my teeth into the flesh. She went to say something smart but was hushed once again. "Say one more thing smart to me and I promise you when we get home I'm gonna fuck the lining out of your pussy. I'mma fuck you so good your ass would need crutches to walk for the next two weeks. I'm telling your ass now keep your smart remarks to yourself."

Aris' mouth quickly snapped closed, and her pace speeded up. She was hauling ass out of that mall trying to get away from me. I just started laughing because I know she was fighting hard against the temptation. I ain't even gon' lie and say that I wasn't fighting hard as well because I was. I tried respecting Aris by giving her the time she needed to bounce back from the bullshit that happened to her. But, I don't know how much longer I'll be able to put up with this shit. Temptation was a bitch.

# Chapter Sixteen

**ARIS**

"Damn Ari! Your cousins are fine as hell!" Kelly yelled in my ear so that she could be heard over the loud music.

"Man, who are you telling?" Mona said co-signing with Kelly's retarded ass while fanning herself at the same time. I started grinning at them watching as they stalked my people sitting in the VIP section from the bar before bursting out laughing. Just thinking about how true that statement was, I felt some sort of pride swelling up in my chest. Not that I'm trying to brag or anything, but my whole family on my mom's side were drop dead gorgeous. Some of God's best creations. Them sapphire icy blue eyes that run heavy on that side of the family would have your ass doing all kinds of retarded shit. If they told you to bend over and touch your feet while hopping around on one leg, you would've done it with no questions asked.

It was twelve when we finally reached the club. It took another thirty minutes just to make it to the VIP section upstairs because of everybody who knew my brother's crew was stopping us to show some love. Women were breaking their necks trying to catch their attention, but when they took one look at my girls and me, their faces dropped with hate, envy, and disappointment.

All of the men went straight to VIP while the girls and I branched off and found ourselves at the bar knocking Patron shots back. "Yo, you better chill that shit out. Let your boo find out that you are over here lusting after his cousin, and he's gonna kick yo' ass," I said laughing.

"You right," she laughed.

"Come on! Let's hit this dance floor before the boys come over here and try to ruin our fun!" Mona yelled over the music while pulling

Kells by the hand in the direction of the packed dance floor. Kells grabbed my hand and pulled me up as well. As soon as we got to the middle of the dance floor, the DJ switched songs and played Rihanna's Work. The club was straight going crazy!

"Aww, shit!" Kelly yelled excitedly over the music grabbing Mona by the hips and turning her around. "Bitch you better work work, work,work work," she sung while moving her hips along to the beat. I closed my eyes and let the lyrics to the song hypnotize me. Rihanna's smooth voice and Drake's sexy ass was doing something to me. As the song played my hips began to move unconsciously carefully following the beat. Glancing up at the VIP section I spotted Rome staring at me with lust-filled eyes. Locking eyes, we stared at each other while I started mumbling the lyrics to the song. I let my hands seductively roam over my curves imagining they were Rome's hands instead all the while never breaking my stare. Before I knew it, I was pop locking and dropping it while seductively rolling my hips. I could tell that Rome was enjoying the show because he started biting on his bottom lip and giving me that look.

Still biting on his lip, Rome gave me the signal to come back up to the VIP section. "C'mon, the boys want us back in the VIP section," I whispered in Kelly's ear so that she could hear me over the music.

Kelly sighed irritably and rolled her eyes. "I swear I can't never have fun with your brother around. Let's go," She said before taking another sip of the drink she had in her hand. As we turned and headed back into the direction of the VIP section, someone had bumped into me hard as hell damn near making me fall in my five-inch YSL stilettoes. I turned around getting ready to cuss somebody clean the hell out when I noticed that the person who bumped into me was no one other than Slim herself. My eyes lit up like a Christmas tree. I was so happy to see her.

"Oh my God, Slim!" I yelled excitedly over the music as I pulled her into my embrace and hugged her.

"Aris? Is that you? I didn't recognize you with your hair cut like that," she said as she squeezed me. She was just equally surprised to see me as I was to see her. We kind of lost contact with each other after Quamir broke my last phone. I hugged Slim for a little while longer before finally releasing her from my clutches. I was genuinely happy to see her and judging from how hard she was smiling she was as well.

"Damn girl. What are you doing on my side of the town? You're a long way from home aren't you?" I asked her jokingly while stepping back to get a good look out of her.

"You know. Just came into town yesterday to check up on the Spa. One of the girls invited me out for tonight to show me a good time before I head back up north tomorrow," she replied.

I nodded to show her that I was listening, but I was too busy admiring the dress that she was rocking. It was to die for! Slim was wearing a backless blush pink ruffled wrap dress. It had a deep V in the front showing much cleavage with her high slit in the middle, a thin layer of sheer and her sides were exposed. Her long pretty hair was styled in Bahamian curls going down her back and over her shoulder, and she had on a pair blush pink open toed caged pumps with a gold strap going across the ankle.

"You looking good. I'm secretly loving that dress you wearing. Where did you get it?"

"A friend of mine made it," she beamed.

I nodded in approval as I gave her dress the once over one more time. It was just that pretty. I felt eyes burning the back of my head and just knew that it was Mona and Kelly wanting to know who Slim was.

"Ah, I'm sorry I want you to meet my best friends Mona and Kelly. Kells, Mo, this is Slim. She's the girl I was telling you guys about. The one I wanted y'all to meet. She owns Beautify My Beauty." Surprisingly, Mo, Kells, and Slim all got along. Which surprised the hell out of me because Kelly and Mona were some mean muthafuckas when it came to meeting new people. Especially when it came to females. I guess you can say it was because they all clicked and saw that they had in common. On the low, I was kind of jealous because they got along so well. For years it's only been the three of us. The VIP was straight popping when we got up there. The crew was having the time of their life. There were expensive champagne bottles being popped, top grade trees and countless bottles of Hennessey being passed around. AJ was seated in the middle like he was the damn king surrounded by a variety of different breeds of women with a big ass plate of food sitting in his lap. Nigga is straight in his thirties and still living that single life. He was going ham on the chicken wings and blue cheese ranch.

Khyree was sitting not too far from his older brother with his fiancé/baby momma sitting in his lap clenching onto him tightly and mean-mugging every girl that tried looking his way. I don't know why he even brought her ass knowing that I can't stand her. Especially since the bitch was pregnant and looked like she was ready to pop any day now. Like who in the hell comes to the club pregnant? I swear I hated her bougie acting ass. Ever since we went down to Columbia a few years back for Christmas and she tried to go off on me because she thought that I wanted her man. I was like 'bitch, that's my fucking blood cousin stupid ass hoe'. I damn near killed her ass at that dinner table because she really tried to take me there in front of my family. To be honest, I hated how Khyree acted like she was the best damn thing God had put on earth. He straight worshiped the ground t she walked on and treated her like she was a Queen when she is a low key gold digging hoe. My cousin was too good for her skank ass.

I caught Khyree staring at Slim a couple times throughout the night. Ever since she walked into the VIP section, she had everybody's attention. Niggas were trying to break their necks to get a glimpse of her. It was comical to me because he couldn't keep his eyes off of her even if he tried. The only time he wouldn't look her way was if his fiancé was staring at him clocking his every move. You could see the infatuation in his eyes. I don't blame big cuz because Slim was gorgeous. A lot of men was trying to approach her that night but were immediately turned down with that mean ass scowl on her face. Nobody could approach her without getting bit by her vicious bark.

Kasey was branched off to the left with Landon both in their own little world with a fifth of Hennessey. The girls and I were bugging the fuck out when he pushed this scantily clad , big fake booty bitch on the floor after she tried to sit in his lap. I mean she didn't even ask she just went ahead and tried it. He was cussing her ass clean the hell out in Spanish. Everybody in VIP was cracking up. Now her ass sitting on the floor with all of her goodies exposed looking embarrassed as fuck.

I was sitting in Rome's lap with my arms wrapped around his neck and my legs around his waist nibbling on the side of his neck and grinding my hips to Beyoncé's Drunk in Love. Rome had his hands wrapped around me cuffing my ass.

"I've been drinking... I've been drinking," I sang into his ear in a low sultry voice while grinding my womanhood against his hardening member. "I get filthy when that liquor gets into me. I've been thinking... I've been thinking. Why can't I keep my fingers off you baby? I want you. Na Na," I continued to sing as I licked from his earlobe to the outline of his jaw structure. My hips continued to wind and grind against him.

"You're drunk," Rome said then chuckled as he took a sip of his brown liquor.

I giggled as I leaned in and licked his bottom lip. "I'm drunk, and I'm in love. What else can I say?"

"So you're in love with a nigga, huh?" Rome asked me with a wide sexy ass grin on his face.

For a second, I just sat still asking myself that same question over and over again. Was I still in love with Rome? Hell, yeah. My love for him never went away even after all of these years that we let get by all because of some bullshit and that's my fault. I was too hurt and instead of trying to hear him out I tried moving on and replacing his love with a fake one. That was the biggest mistake and the biggest regret that I have ever made in my life. My heart swelled with all of the love that I still had for this man.

A year ago I didn't want shit to do with Rome. All I wanted to do was move on from the past and be happy just like how I was back in my younger teenage years. Now I can't see myself living without Roman ever again. Although I had yet came clean to him and told him how I feel this man still has my heart. He's my rib. My rock. My very existence. I don't know when or how he did it, but he was able to sneak back into my heart and like a thief in the night, he had once again stolen it from me. This past year, Rome hasn't done anything but reminded me just how crazy in love and gone in the head I was about his ass.

Instead of answering him I just nodded my head finally coming clean about my feelings. Rome grabbed me by my face and tilted my head back before planting a kiss so deep and so passionate that it literally took my breath away.

After what seemed like minutes of us just kissing Rome finally pulled back letting me breathe. "Took yo' ass long enough," he said making me laugh.

"Do you still love me?" I asked. I already knew his answer, but still, I wanted to hear him say it. It's been six years since the last time I heard him say those three words.

Rome stared deeply into my eyes with such intensity that it made my stomach flutter, and my heart beat faster. "I never stopped loving you ma," he responded genuinely. The raw emotion that I saw in his eyes when he spoke those words to me had me wanting to cry. I went to drop my chin in my chest because I didn't want him to see the tears in my eyes. But before I could do it Rome grasped my chin in his hand forcing me to look into his light brown eyes.

"I love you so much girl sometimes it hurts. Even when I was locked away like a caged animal, my feelings never wavered. Losing you was like someone ripping my beating heart from out of my chest and burying it somewhere. My whole fucking world came crashing down when you left. I thought I was going to die without you. I could hardly catch my breath, and I stayed on go mode. To be honest, I still don't see how I was able to survive four and a half year in jail without you being there keeping a nigga's head above water. I was literally going insane without you in my life. You are my heart, and I will give up everything just to keep you by my side." By the time he was finished confessing his feelings for me, I let the waterworks go. Rome wiped them away with his thumbs then kissed me.

"Shhh… don't cry ma. You so ugly when you do," he said jokingly.

I started laughing through my tears as I playfully punched him in the chest. "So not funny."

Rome laughed wrapping his arms back around my waist. "Yo, you just went from being the baddest in the club to ugly as hell. I think it's the Hennessey finally getting to my ass," he cracked laughing harder at his own joke.

"Ugh! I can't stand you!" I exclaimed with a laugh as I wiped my eyes with the palms of my hands.

Rome leaned forward and gently sunk his teeth into my hard nipple that was poking out through the thin material of my dress causing my back to arch and a moan to slip from my lips. "Can I sleep in between your legs tonight?" he asked me before switching to the other side and doing the same thing to my other nipple.

"I–,"

*Rat-Tat-Tat-Tat! Blow! Blow! Pow! Pow!*

"Everybody get down!" Rome yelled as he pushed me down onto the floor and climbed on top of me. Pandemonium erupted throughout the club as innocent bystanders screamed and all fought to get out the door without becoming a victim. Knocking others over then stomping on them. With paralyzing fear, I sat still with wide wet eyes as I began my search for my best friends. My hands were shaking, and my heart was beating so hard I was scared that I thought it was going to stop. I ain't never been in no shit like this so I was deathly afraid. This shit was like what you see in the Wild Wild West. Kamron and Landon had Mona and Kells hiding underneath the table with their weapons out shooting back. All of my people and brother's crew had their guns out shooting back. My cousin Khyree was the only person out of the crew who wasn't shooting, and that was because he was too busy trying to protect his pregnant fiancé.

Because the club was so dark, I couldn't tell how many men were shooting at us. With only half of his body covering mines, Rome reached into his waist and pulled out his Desert Eagles bussing right along with everyone else. I saw that Roman had hit one of the masked gunmen dead in the center of his forehead.

What surprised me the most was Slim. She was crouched down low on the floor looking like a lioness on a hunt. She reached for the mini holster that was strapped to her inner thigh and pulled out a shiny .9mm. She cocked her gun back placing one in the chamber before taking her spot beside of Kasey and Landon. Both of them stopped shooting and looked at her with wide eyes just as she landed a perfectly clean shot right in the middle of somebody's head followed by a couple more.

"Damn," Kasey exclaimed in amazement.

*Rrrraatt Tat Tat Tat Tat! Boom! Boom!*

I covered my ears with my hands as if that helped with the noise. I wanted to close my eyes but was too scared. By now the club was empty, and all that could be heard was bullets leaving their chambers.

"Watch out!" Slim yelled as she practically dived on top of Khyree and his fiancé pushing them out of the way just as a bullet whipped right passed them. I watched her as she bit down on her bottom lip and her face frowning up in discomfort. When the masked man came closer towards Slim, he shot at her but missed. Slim moved her head to the side dodging the bullet at the last minute and at the same time releasing one from her chamber. The bullet entered right on the side of his neck causing his body to drop hard like a sack of potatoes. Even through all of the gunfire, I could hear him choking on his blood and gasping for air. Slim slowly climbed to her feet. Before I could blink, Slim shot him in the head ending his suffering and killing the last gunman that was left standing.

Once all gunfire ceased, Kamron jumped up from his spot near the table where Mo and Kells were hidden under of and jogged over to the dead man that Slim killed. He leaned down and pulled off of his mask. "The fuck?" I heard him spat in confusion.

"Who is it?" Landon asked him.

"Fuck if I know," was his response as he inspected his body some more.

"Yo, get the girls out of here and let's go before the police arrive," Rome said as he helped me from underneath the table and grabbed my arm. You could hear the police sirens blaring as they neared us.

"Somebody grab the tapes," Landon yelled while picking up a clearly spooked Mona and putting her on his back.

"Got that shit," AJ said showing everybody the video cassette.

"Let's go!"

Rome held me by the elbow as everybody followed him out of the back door and down the alley where the limousine was waiting for us a few blocks over. Kamron made a left and trotted down the alley in a mild/fast pace. I was trying to keep up, but I was still so shaken my legs were giving out on me. Rome had to pretty much carry me. We continued running down the long dark alleyway and even cut a few corners putting enough distance between us and the crime scene. Finally making it to the limousine everybody jumped in and our driver Lance pulled off going in the opposite direction from the police.

Although it was over, I was still shaken up and scared inside. My heart was still beating fast, palms were still sweaty, and I was aware of everything around me. I thought I was going to lose my life tonight. Rome must have sensed that I was because he wrapped his arms around me and pulled me into his chest. Being wrapped in his strong arms calmed me down a lot, and I was finally able to breathe again. After my breathing returned to normal, I finally looked around just to make sure everybody was ok. That was when I noticed that Slim had disappeared.

## Chapter Seventeen

**QUAMIR**

"Fuck! Fuck! Fuck! Fuck! Fuck!" I spat heatedly as I took my frustrations out on the steering wheel. I was sitting outside of Club Secrets fuming while watching the police block off the crime scene with yellow tape.

I can't believe I was so fucking close to ending that bitch ass nigga's Rome life and still ended up failing. I had the fucking opportunity to end that nigga's life and fucking ruined it. Fuck! He was so fucking busy shoving his tongue down my bitch's throat that he wasn't aware of the red dot sitting in the middle of his forehead. I had a perfect shot, but because Aris was sitting in this nigga's lap, I couldn't force myself to pull the trigger and chance it to end up hitting her.

I swear that bitch had my head gone. I wasn't supposed to fall in love with Aris because I was still in love with my wife Monica, but I did. My original plans were to come to Miami and get close to her brother, gaining his trust, figuring out how he ran his operation before giving his ass a permanent dirt nap. But meeting Aris caused me to change it up a little and just be content with being her brother's right-hand man. I was fucking content until that bitch ass nigga Rome came home from jail and everybody started acting brand fucking new. Including her hoe ass. I knew there was some shit going on between them, but she swore up and down there was nothing going on. Now look at this shit here. This bitch living life and acting like what we had didn't even exist.

For a while, I sat in VIP watching them. I was so fucking pissed watching her kissing all over him that I was really contemplating whether or not I should kill her ass too. I had to bite the inside of my cheek to keep myself from exploding and going over there blowing my cover. So far nobody knows that I am back and I want to keep it that way.

Speaking of that bitch, I can't believe her ass is still alive. I could have sworn after I got through splitting her asshole open the bitch was barely hanging onto life. Her ass should have died for sure, but seeing her ass kissing all on this nigga let me know that she was touched by an angel. I don't see how I hate her, but love her at the same damn time. At first, I wanted to kill her ass right along with her nigga, but now all I wanted to do is kiss her, hold her, smell her and lie in between those thick ass thighs of hers.

Just thinking about that night, I almost killed her had me feeling guilty as fuck. I swear I didn't mean to do that shit to her. My intention was to go over there and get her to listen to a nigga, but as you can see that shit didn't go as planned. I can sit up here and try to blame it on the few lines of coke I had snorted right before going to her house, but then that would just be the coward's way out. When she told my ass it was over, I snapped. All I could think at that moment was another nigga having what's supposed to be forever mine. In my head, all I was thinking of is if I couldn't have her then no one can. I blacked out.

By the time I finally came to and started thinking logically; Aris was hardly breathing. I panicked and ran out of there. I didn't know what to do. All I knew was to get as much money as possible and get ghost. So a few partnas of mine and I hit up one of Kamron's main spots, took the drugs, and the money split the money in three ways, and I got the fuck out of Dodge. Yeah, that's right I actually got a few people that were inside of Kamron's camp to turn on his ass with high hopes and fairy tale dreams. Fake ass pretty boy so far stuck up inside of Kelly's hoe ass that he wasn't even aware of that the whole time I was working for him; I was robbing his ass blind. He trusted my ass so much that he would never recount the money after I counted it. Dumb ass nigga.

The fact that Aris had lived and told her brother that it was me behind her attack kept my ass out and away from Miami as long as I was. Don't get me wrong. I'm nowhere near scared of Kamron. It's her father that puts fear into my heart. I heard through the grapevine how thoroughbred the nigga really is. I heard that he will kill yo' ass, bring you back to life, only to kill yo' ass again, but very slow and painful. The muthafucka is a walking lunatic. If you ever cross him or his family, you are better off offing yourself. When Killa Mills is after that ass there is nowhere you can run or hide. That nigga got reach every fucking where.

I took my ass back home to Houston, Texas where I kept my family hidden away. For one year straight I struggled to get back up on my feet. I took the money that I stole from Kamron and tried getting work elsewhere, but it was easier said than done. For some reason, nobody wanted to fuck with me on that type of level. It wasn't until I ran into one of my homeboys from back in the day that I finally hooked up with this cat by the name of B. Smooth and tried working under him for a little while. I was having a harder time stacking my dough up here in Dallas than I did in Miami. In Miami, I was sitting on a fucking gold mine!

Between the bullshit ass drugs that Smooth had everybody moving and Monica's expensive spending habits damn near all of my savings were gone. The shit Smooth had everybody selling was straight up baking soda. Shit couldn't even get you high. His shit was so whack that most of his workers were leaving his ass and working for his competition. It was hard convincing some of Smooth's soldiers to switch sides and work with me to take down Miami's biggest drug kingpin. I recruited ten of his most loyal and trusted workers and brought them with me to kill Kamron. Our first attempt on his life tonight resulted in six men of the ten in being killed. I was beyond pissed. My hatred for Kamron, Rome, and even Landon who…at one point in time I consider to be my brother had only quadrupled. I wanted them all dead!

"Bitch ass muthafucka!" I yelled out in frustrations as I slapped the steering wheel one more time. "Fuck!"

"Don't know why the fuck you so pissed off. You had the perfect shot and yo' ass hesitated all because of a bitch being in the way," my cousin Tron spat from his seat on the passenger side. I cocked my head to the side and looked at him like he had suddenly grown two heads.

"First, off lil' nigga don't be fucking disrespecting my girl like that by calling her out her name. I will straight kill yo' ass where you sit. You understand me?" I spat heatedly through clenched teeth.

Tron started chuckling like what the fuck I said was funny. I continued glaring at him watching him as he nonchalantly lit the end to his blunt and took a deep hard pull from it. I wanted to swing and hit this nigga dead in his shit but already knew that wasn't a fight that I was going to win. Clenching my teeth in anger, I turned back in my seat and focused on the police walking around asking questions and taking statements. I don't know why because ain't one muthafucka going to speak up. People around here already knew not to talk unless they wanted their whole bloodline to cease existence. I was deep in my own little thoughts thinking about the day I would finally catch up with Kamron and them when all of a sudden I was struck so hard that my head went bouncing off of the window and the whole right side of my face was throbbing in pain.

Shocked as fuck, I turned in my seat and stared at Tron, who was just continued smoking his blunt like he did not just snake my ass when I wasn't looking.

With his eyes straight forward he said to me in a dark, deadly tone, "I don't know who the fuck you think I am but I ain't yo' one of your fucking friends. You got one more time to threaten me, and I promise you, cousin, or not, the next time you try to threaten me you'll be eating lead for dinner. Now do you understand me?" His tone was so cold and menacing that even I knew not to say shit back. As bad as I didn't want to I just had to chuck that sneaky ass move he pulled as an L. There isn't one man on this earth that I fear. I don't fear nobody but God. As bad as I didn't want to admit it… I needed Tron. That nigga was a beast in the streets back in the Houston. Niggas knew to stay far the fuck away from him and out of his path. The dude was a psychotic ass muthafucka and was extremely sick in the head. Tron was known for killing muthafuckas with just his bare hands choking them until their neck snaps in half. Tron was just who I needed to kill Kamron. I had to bit my inner cheek to control myself from wanting to reach across the console and fuck Tron's bitch ass up but knew that us going at each other's necks right now would only distract us from our main focus.

Focusing my eyes back onto the screen in front of me, I reached into my pocket and pulled out my cell phone, dialing my homeboy's number up. The phone rang twice before he answered breathing heavy as fuck. I didn't even get his ass time to say hello before I chewed into his ass.

"You bitch-made ass muthafucka! You told me that if I distracted Kamron and his crew that you would be able to put a bullet in his fucking skull! Why is that muthafucka still breathing!" I barked heatedly into the phone. The vein in my temple throbbing hard in anger.

"Man, I tried and was almost successful in killing that nigga, but he had some bitch that I ain't never seen before busting niggas down from left to right. While nobody was looking, I was getting ready to put one off in his head, but the bitch must've seen me from out the corner of her eye because she turned around and shot me in the leg! I had to play it off like I was aiming at the enemy just so that I wouldn't be exposed and blow my cover!" he responded back to me; equally pissed off.

I bit down on my back teeth and gritted them in anger. It seems like every time I think I'm three steps ahead I get thrown ten steps back.

Kamron must've been a saint in his past life because that muthafucka got a fucking angel watching over him. "I'm getting real sick and tired of this nigga breathing the same air that I'm breathing. I want his ass dead like yesterday! I don't care what the fuck you do… you better kill him or else!" I yelled before hanging up.

Tron snickering had me whipping my head in his direction to see what the fuck was so funny. "Did I say something funny?" I asked him through gritted teeth.

Tron shook his head no. "Nah, cuz. It wasn't you. I was thinking of some shit and it tickled my sides."

I looked at Tron shaking his head and snickering under his breath and automatically knew his ass was lying. I wanted to speak on it but decided to keep my mouth closed instead. Cussing his ass out under my breath, I started my car up and quietly pulled out from in front of the crime scene and drove off. If I wanted Rome and them dead, then I will need Tron's help regardless of how I'm feeling. I know one thing is for certain, and two things are for sure, though. As soon as I handle Roman and them I'm handling Tron's bitch ass as well. I don't give a fuck. When it comes to being bluntly disrespected and feeling threatened all bets are off the table. Blood or not that nigga had to go.

# Chapter Eighteen

**ROME**

Turning the door knob to Aris' bedroom, I quietly pushed the door open to see how she and the girls were feeling. Aris, Kells, and Mona were all laying in Ari's bed cuddling and tightly holding onto each other in their sleep. When we finally made it back to my crib after the shootout at the club, the girls were still pretty shaken up. Every little sound scared them. Kamron saw this and made them all go lay down for the night. Surprisingly, none of the girl's objected and did what they were told. I walked up to Aris' side of the bed and planted a gentle kiss on all three of their foreheads before walking out of the bedroom and quietly closing the door behind me.

After checking up on the women, I made my way down to the basement to my man cave with the rest of the men. I guess we all had the same idea and felt the need to release some stress by burning some trees. There was weed smoke everywhere. Each man had a cup of Hennessey in their hand and smoking their own blunt. Kamron and Landon were sitting on the couch. Khyree was at the bar, and Kasey was sitting in my recliner chair with his feet kicked up with a nonchalant expression blowing smoke rings in the air. That nigga was too comfortable. I sighed as I went straight to my bar area and poured myself a glass of Henney.

"What are the girl's doing?" Kamron asked me. I looked at him briefly before taking a small, moderate sip from my glass.

"Finally took their asses to sleep," I responded taking a seat next to Khyree at the bar.

A low sighed escaped from Kamron's throat as he ran his hands over his low waves and down his face. I could tell by the way his face was etched in worry and concern about the girls. Just like me, Kamron never wanted to expose this type of life to the girls. Being that both Aris and Mona are daughters to Miami's biggest kingpins they know what to expect when it comes to the life we lead, but they were never exposed like this. Back when Kamron and my Pops were in the drug game they kept their personal and street lives separate; never bringing any dirt back to their doorsteps and only telling our mothers what they wanted to tell them. That way if the Feds ever came in questioning them they wouldn't know anything incriminating. Kamron and I did one hell of a job following our Pops footsteps and keeping the girls safe from these grimy streets. Tonight fucked everything up.

"Any idea on who it is that's after y'all asses?" Khyree asked us in his slightly heavy accent as he looked back and forth between Kamron, Landon, and finally me.

I shook my head no, and Landon shrugged his shoulders in response.

"I honestly don't have one fucking clue who it could be," Kamron said in frustration.

"Could it have been those Haitians?" AJ suddenly asked. "I did hear from the streets that when y'all took over Little Haiti they were feeling some type of way about it. They didn't like the fact that y'all just came in and took over their territory making them pay a monthly fee to do business."

"If they were feeling some type of way then it could have been the Haitians finally getting tired of y'all asses and made that move at the club. Or it could have been the Jamaican's that used to run Opa Locka. Them and those Haitians could have joined forces and put a mark out on y'all heads," Kasey said before he took a long pull from his blunt and slowly exhaled the smoke out through his nose.

"Either could be a possible threat," AJ added.

"Nah. Back when we took over our Pops operation; us, the Haitians and the Jamaicans all came to a mutual agreement. Either jump ship or drown. If they chose to drown there was only one lifeline being thrown out. It's either jump on board for our team or rent the blocks out. That was the only lifeline that was being thrown out. Either way, we still eating," I said while slowly sipping on my drink.

"I agree with Rome," Landon said crossing his legs at the feet and folding his hands behind his head. "They already know how we get down. Neither wants that kind of problems. Especially when they know that we have connections to the Rivera Familia. Everybody knows that Kamron and Aris is a part of y'all crazy ass bloodline. Going up against the Rivera Familia is something no man in his right mind wants to do. You muthafuckas got a ruthless ass reputation."

"I don't give a fuck if it was the Haitians or if it was the fucking Jamaicans! I swea' I'ma find out who the fuck was bold enough to shoot at us and when I do I promise you, on my momma's soul, I'm wiping niggas clean from off the face of this earth!" Kamron spat vehemently through gritted teeth as he jumped up from his spot on the couch and began pacing the floor with his hands in his front pockets. "I play no games when it comes to my baby sis' life and when it comes to my fucking money. Niggas crossed the mutha fuckin line when they shot at me, and my sister was sitting right there! I'm tired letting niggas think its oh muthafuckin' kay to fuck with either one. It's about time I let Beast come out and play and remind these stupid muthafuckas why they should not cross Kamron Caseem Miller!" Kamron yelled as he began to pace the floor while gritting his teeth in anger.

His grayish blue eyes immediately went dark, and his face turned bright red from the anger that was boiling in the pits of his stomach. That nigga was pissed and I can't say that I blame him because I'm was just as pissed as he was. Anything could've happened to my sister, Kells, who is like another sis to Aris and me. If anything happened to either of them, Miami was sure going to rain blood because I'm killing muthafuckas just for breathing wrong.

Niggas are really trying to sleep on Kamron. They think that just because he is a pretty ass nigga that he's too good to get dirty. WRONG! They will learn though when they meet Beast as Kamron calls him. Beast was Kamron's alter ego. Just like the meaning of his name Beast is a muthafuckin' monster that everybody should fear. It's been a while since the last time I've seen Beast in action and let me be the one to tell you now that Beast is not the muthafucka you want to meet. When Kamron turns into Beast, there is no bringing him back unless Beast is satisfied and the only thing that can satisfy Beast is bloodshed. When Beast is free, there will be so much bloodshed the blood bank ain't going to know where to put everything.

Kamron created Beast back in our early pre-teen years after some punk ass jack boys ran up on us and robbed us. I ain't even gonna lie and say that they didn't beat our ass because they did. And that's because it was only two of us against six. Instead of going back and telling our Pops what the hell happened Kamron went on a killing spree. That was around the time Kamron, and I caught our first bodies and around the same time Beast was created. No one… not even our dads knew about Kamron's alter ego Beast. Our cousins and Landon have heard about Beast, but they never saw him in action. Back then Kamron was murking niggas just for the fun of it and adopted it as a hobby. He was bloodthirsty then and was like a reckless ticking bomb just waiting to explode. I mean he still acts the same way he did when he was younger, but now he's much calmer and tamed. As he got older the more he was able to control Beast's blood thirst desire.

"Aww shit! Kamron is about to bring that nigga Beast out to play. Niggas done fucked up now! Bruh, I gotta be here to see this shit when it happens. I'mma have front row seats with Kermit the Frog on my left sipping his tea and Michael Jackson back when he was black and rocking the Jheri Curl eating his popcorn on my right while I sit in the middle sipping on my cup of lean," AJ's dumb ass cracked making everybody burst out laughing. His joke was so random and so stupid that it lightening the tension in the air and made Kamron sit back down.

"This nigga here," Khyree chuckled as he sipped his Hennessey.

"I don't mean to change subjects but this I gotta know. Who was that chick that came into the VIP with Aris and them?" Kasey asked leaning up in his seat with animated eyes.

"You talking about that baddie with the exotic green eyes and beauty mark underneath her left eye?" AJ asked him.

"Yea bruh, her!"

"I know who you talking about!" Kamron yelled out in excitement as well.

"What's her name then lil' nigga?" Kasey impatient ass quipped.

Kamron's eyebrow dipped downwards as he snapped his fingers repeatedly while trying to remember her name. "Shit! It's right on the tip of my tongue. Fuck! What is her name?"

"Y'all talking about Slim?" I asked them for clarification.

Kasey's sapphire blue eyes instantly lit up at the sound of her name rolling off my tongue as a smile a mile-long tugged at the corners of his lips. "That's it!" he and Kamron shouted at the same time.

Kasey was now hanging off the edge of his seat wearing a satisfied lazy smirk. "Man, I don't how cuzo know her, but damn lil' ma was bad as fuck with the nine. Did you see how she was knocking niggas down? Straight head shots!" he exclaimed again all animatedly.

"I saw that shit!" Landon replied just as animated as Kasey was. "I was so surprised I stopped shooting and was looking at shawty like…"

"…daaaaaaaammmmmmnnnnnn," Landon and Kasey yelled out in unison leaning back in their seats with their hand planted firmly in the center of their chest imitating Smokey and Craig from Friday. The shit had me bugging the fuck out, Kamron spitting his drink out and Khyree choking on the smoke he inhaled from his blunt from laughing so hard.

"Lil' momma was straight going harder than most of these niggas," Lay said.

Kasey lets out a lazy shaky sigh . With a goofy smile on his face he looked at us and said, "Man, I think I'm in love!" he said jokingly. "Khyree, let Ma know that I'm ready to settle down and that she's about to be a grandmother! I'm about to go find shawty and get down on one knee and marry her ass. I don't care that we don't know nothing about each other. We can learn that shit on the way to our honeymoon. Love has no time frame."

By now I was doubled over laughing holding my side and had tears running down my face. Everybody in the room was dying laughing that nigga was stupid as shit for saying that. Over the next hour and a half the men smoked and drank while planning our next move. Our top priority was to find out who the fuck was behind the attempt on all of our lives. Khyree had offered his assistance to us, but I immediately disregarded it. I appreciated the offer but wanted to find out who these muthafuckas were and kill them on my own without any help from them. Khyree understood where I was coming from and told me he respected that. Khyree understood where I was coming from and told me he respected my wishes and if I needed anything just call him. Which I'm pretty confident that that would never happen. After everybody had left and taken their women with them; I locked the house and set the alarm.

I was walking down the hallway when I stopped in front of Aris' bedroom. I turned to walk to my room, but a sudden urge to open the door and go inside had taken over me. I turned the knob and push the door open just to peek inside.

Aris was asleep lying on the bed on her stomach with one of my silk shirts that she must have stolen out of my room on that had her ass cheeks were playing hide and seek with the material. The site alone had me ready to break through the material of my sweatpants. That shit was so damn sexy. A nigga was harder than a muthafuckin' brick house. I quietly stepped inside, closed the door and climbed in the bed with her.

"Baby…you sleep?" I whispered in her ear while placing feathery light kisses along the side of her neck.

Pressing the front of my body against her back, I continued placing wet kisses on the side of her neck paying extra close attention to the spot behind her ear. I licked and lightly sucked the spot until it turned into a hickey.

Gently, I rolled her over onto her back careful enough not to wake her up and climbed on top of her.

"Baby…" I mumbled into the side of her neck while easing up my t-shirt over her bare breast.

I placed light kisses down from her neck to her right breast, capturing her semi-hard nipple with my warm wet mouth. The feeling of me biting and teasing her erect nipples with slow, tentative licks caused Aris' lust-filled eyes to open up.

"Mooovveee Roman," she mumbled breathlessly while attempting to shoo me away.

"You want me to stop?" I asked, while pressing both of her breasts together and sucking on both stubs at the same time. I knew that when Aris' breath got caught in her throat for a few seconds that I had her little ass right then and there. She wanted me to stop, but the way her body was responding to me said otherwise. Her breathing was hard, and her chest heaved up and down.

Moving from her breast, I licked down her stomach, skipped her panties and placed feather kisses on her inner thighs. I haven't even done anything, and she was dripping wet. Going back up to her panties, I leaned forward and inhaled her sweet intoxicating scent. I'm not even going to lie and say that a nigga wasn't anticipating this shit. It's been six years since the last time I was in between her wet centerfolds. Just thinking about sliding inside of her and stroking her insides had my dick was harder than a brick and already pulsating. As bad as I wanted to find my place deep in between her thighs I had enough self-restraint to control my urges. All I wanted to do was taste her, make her cum a few times and send her ass back to sleep.

I glanced up, and she was leaning on her elbows anticipating my next move. "Uh huh. I want you on your back," I said as I laid her back down and at the same time ripping her panties off. I looked up in just enough time to see her narrow her eyes at me. It's a known fact that women hate their panties to be ripped off.

Aris' mouth opened she was about to start complaining, but it was kind of hard to do so with my tongue down her throat. Moaning softly into my mouth she took turns nibbling on my upper and bottom lip before shoving her tongue down my throat. I opened my mouth, and we took turns wrestling with each other's tongue. She then wrapped her arms around my neck and deepened the kiss.

I let my hands travel down to my favorite sacred place and rubbed my finger all in her juices. I watched in amusement as Aris' eyes rolled to the back of her head in pure satisfaction as I slid two fingers in between her wet centerfolds. A cocky chuckle escaped my lips as I leaned forward and blew on her hardening pearl. "What happen to you wanting me to stop?" I asked as I thrust my fingers inside of her wet folds and used my thumb to massage her clit.

She decided to keep quiet and answer me by squeezing her muscles around my fingers. A familiar groan sounded off in the back of my throat. I raised her legs up higher until her ass was lifted off of the bottom of the bed. My thumb continued rotating against her clit while my fingers massaged her inner walls until her juices flooded out into the palm of my hand.

"Mmmmm…. Roman baby! Ah, shit!" she yelled out in ecstasy as her legs began shaking signaling her release.

My fingers dipped low looking for that soft, gushy spot inside of her. It didn't take long before I was able to find it and when I did, I curled my fingers into a "come here" motion and thrust them even faster inside of her. Aris' mouth formed an "O" as she tossed her head back in pure satisfaction.

"Ooooh, shit baby! I'm cumming! Shit!" she screamed. Two thrusts later and her clit was jumping as a clear liquid shot out of her.

"Mmm…mmm…mmm. Look at this shit here! Damn girl!" I groaned in a deep voice. Slowly I pulled my fingers out of her and sucked her sweet juices off of them. Aris' chest heaved in and out as she panted heavily trying to catch her breath. I looked up with an intense grin flashing her a wicked smile. She should have known by now that this was just the beginning. There was no way in hell was I was done with her.

Smiling, I moved down to her pussy, kissing her second pair of lips while sliding two fingers back inside of her.

My fingers moved expertly in and out of her, massaging her inner walls and playing hide and seek with her g-spot while drumming my tongue against my clit. The combination of both had her eyes pop opened and her mouth opening and closing; looking like a fish out of water. Her legs were shaking already, and another orgasm crept up.

A nigga straight turned into a beast and got sloppy with it. I was eating that shit as if my ass has been starving these past two months. I greedily sucked onto her throbbing pearl placing sloppy kisses all over her second lips. I used my tongue to lap up all of her fallen juices and tried to stuff them back inside of her. I was mixing shit up by drumming my tongue against her sensitive stud, stop and give teasing licks from her clit all the way to the crack of her ass. Out of instinct, she grabbed the back of my head and pushed me deeper inside of her water.

"Ahh! Ooh! Fuck! Ahh, Rome!" she screamed out as her thighs shook violently.

"Damn, ma, you taste damn good," I groaned taking a break from her sensitive clit now teasing the opening.

"Oh my fucking God!" her hips bucked as my fingers moved in and out of her deeply while I sucked even harder. "Rome, please!"

"Please, what?" I mumbled into the inner thigh placing a kiss there then sucking on it until it turned purple. "Answer me Ari. You want me to stop?"

"No, don't stop!" she almost screamed.

"Make me cum!" she screamed while breathing heavy.

On command, I went straight into beast mode. Licking, sucking and slurping while finger fucking her hard and deep. Aris' back arched and her legs began to shake out of control. They shook for a minute then her body stiffened as she released all of her fluids down my throat. I swallowed her sweet juices and kept nibbling at her sensitive clit until she began to try to run from me. Grasping her thighs, I pulled her back and held them down as I continued to wreak havoc. I licked and slurped on her pussy until she came in my mouth for the third time.

"Mmmm…" I moaned softly into her sending vibrations throughout her body as I sucked her completely dry. I gently licked her sensitive clit, making her body shudder with pleasure then kissed her lower lips before making my way back up her amazing body. Her lips touched mine, and I opened my mouth letting her taste her own juices on my tongue. Aris wrapped her arms around my neck turned her head and deepened our kiss. We both groaned at the same time as we kissed each other deeply and filled with a burning passion. As I was sucking and nibbling on Aris' bottom lip, I let my hands traveled up her beautiful body and cuff her shapely breasts into my hands. Aris' hands began their own journey and roamed across my body going straight for the hem of my shirt. We continued to savagely kissing each other only stopping and breaking our heated kiss so that Aris could pull my shirt over my head and throw it across the room. I watched as she seductively sinks her top teeth into her bottom lip as she attentively caressed my hard pecs. Using two of my fingers, I gently grabbed her chin and lifted her head up before pulling her back into a heated kiss. I felt Aris' small soft, delicate hand reached down into my sweats and wrap her hand around my hard dick. Slowly her hand ran up and down the length of my hard dick and gently caressing the head of it. She then gave it a squeeze, and it was enough to make my knees buckle.

Groaning, I broke our kiss first and pressed my forehead against hers staring her deeply into her beautiful gray eyes. Nothing was said as we both panted heavily and gazed upon one another with the love and lust that we both have for each other. Aris leaned in and placed a five-second kiss on my lips followed by three quick pecks.

"Pull it out bae. I want to feel you inside of me," She said softly almost in a whisper as she began to tug at my sweats. Before she was even able to get them over my hips, I reached down and grabbed her by the wrist stopping her advances.

"Are you sure that this is what you want?" I asked her just for confirmation. I needed to know if she was ready and actually willing to take it there with me before actually doing it. I don't want us to be fucking and in the heat of the moment she starts having flashbacks of her assault one year ago. I wanted to make sure that she was ready and genuinely wanted me just as bad as I wanted her and not be doing this because this is something that I wanted.

Aris leaned up on her elbows and with no more hesitation she kissed me on the lips. "Yes," she said in a tone so firm that I just knew that she was sure. Smirking, I quickly hopped up from the bed and got undressed. I was so fucking hard that my dick was in a full salute, and the veins were showing. I watched Aris' eyes widened and a look of terror crossed her face. I started to grin cockily. I was no longer that nigga I was six years ago. A nigga done grew up.

"Don't look so scared now," I said as I continued to stroke my dick as I neared the side of the bed. I didn't even give Aris a chance to even say anything as I grabbed her by the ankle and pulled her towards me. Grabbing her legs, I folded them into a pretzel holding her ankles in one hand and leaning down until I was face to face with her glazed pussy. I opened my mouth up as wide as it could go and gave her sweet essence one slow long lick; staring from the crack of her ass on up. That one little lick had her legs shaking and her eyes rolling to the back of her head. Latching onto her clit, I gently bit into it sucking and pulling on it hard while drumming my tongue against it. I licked and slurped until I was tasting her juices in my mouth and until I felt like she was wet enough.

"Open wide and let daddy back inside," I said as I bit down on my bottom lip and rubbed the head of my dick against her clit teasingly. When she was finally done with the teasing, Aris' slowly lifted her hips up and pushed them forward making the head slid in. Because she was so tight, it took me a minute for my dick to finally slide inside of her, but once I was able to get past that barrier it was on and popping. After I got the head in I gave her a few more inches of that long stroke and then slid out slapping the head of my dick against her clit a few times before sliding back inside of my heaven on earth. I had to keep sliding out after a pushing a few more inches inside of her and slapping her clit with my dick because I felt myself about to cum too soon. Her shit was so fucking tight, hot and moist that I just couldn't see myself lasting more than five minutes. I went to slid out one more time, but Aris' hands grasping my hips and pulling me back inside of her stopped me from doing so. We both started moaning simultaneously as her pussy contracted around my dick and sucking me in until I was balls deep inside of her. For a minute I just sat still just readjusting to the feeling of how tight she was and letting her get used to my size again. My dick was pulsating inside of her like it had its own heartbeat. As bad as I wanted to hold out and last I just couldn't take it anymore. I was about to give Aris the best five minutes of her life.

I held the both of her ankles in the air and pushed her legs back until she was doing a split and began giving her those slow yet deep strokes.

"Shhhhhiiiiittt! Ari! Why is yo' pussy so tight?" I groaned lustfully as I continued to slow stroke her pussy.

"Mmm…. Oh my God Roman!" she yelled out as she tossed her head back in complete bliss.

I went from slow stroking her pussy to gradually picking up speed, hitting nothing but guts. Aris' mouth dropped opened forming a perfect "O" shape as her eyes popped open. I felt her hand snaking in between our bodies and pushing up against my lower pecks.

"Uh huh. Move your fucking hand," I growled while slapping her hand away. "You about to take all of this dick," I demanded, climbing on top of her body and pinning her down with my weight so that she couldn't move never missing a stroke. I was pulling all the way out and slamming all eleven inches back deep inside of her womb. Leaning down, I wrapped my mouth around her hard right nipple and sucked it into my mouth. I sucked, nibbled and bit all over her areola while tearing her pussy up. It's been six years since the last time I was deep inside of her guts and I was on a mission in trying to make her pussy remember me. "Roooommmmee!" she screamed out as her muscles contracted around my shaft. "Oh my, God baby you in so deeeeep! I can't take it!" she cried out as her legs started shaking. I watched in amusement as she shook her head from side to side and tears filled the corners of her eyes. Dick was so good that I had her ass ready to cry.

"Yes, you can," I growled through clenched teeth as I started to slow down into a mild/slow tempo; thrusting my dick deep inside of her and slowly pulling out of her only to slam back inside of her. Each time I did that shit, she would gasp out loud as if she had lost her breath. Her pussy would clench around me, and her juices would start leaking from out of her. She was so fucking wet that everything from my lower abdomen and the bed sheets was soaked. With my dick deep inside of her womb, I moved my hips in a circular motion and slowly pull out.

"Ahhh… no, I can't Rome. I can't take it! It's too big!" she screamed out in a breathless pant.

"Yes, you can and with me you will," I said in a matter of fact tone. "Ain't this what you were just masturbating to this morning? You've been wanting this dick and now that you got it you tryna run from it. Well, I'm sorry to crush your little hopes, but I got a goal that I need to accomplish, and I'm not stopping until I see that pussy gush for me two more times," I said as I slowly leaned up to reposition her legs. Now with her legs pushed behind her ears, I lifted her ass up off of the bed and commenced to a pounding to her pussy; beating her shit up like I was mad at it.

"Oh my fucking God! Shhhhiiiiitttt! Fuck. Fuck. Fuck. Fuck Rome!"

Aris arched her back and moaned loudly as her pussy started making farting noises. I was showing her G-Spot no fucking mercy and the shit was driving her insane. "Ohhh shit! Goddammit, you ugly yellow muthafucka!" she screamed out as her muscles tightened and her legs began to shake uncontrollably.

"You getting ready to cum baby?" I groaned into her ear.

"Oh... yes baby I'm about to cum!" she screamed.

"Let me see that pink thing shine!" I growled as I continued to slam deep inside of her as I reached in between her legs and vigorously rubbed her clit sending her over the edge.

"Ohhhhhh fuck! I'm cumming! Oh my, God here it comes! Arrgghhhhh!" She screamed out in pure pleasure. Her thighs started shaking violently, and her eyes rolled to the back of her head signaling the next big wave that was sure to come. Aris' arched back against the sheets and seconds later she was creaming and squirting her juices out so hard that she almost pushed me out in the process. She came so hard that she started crying. I felt my balls tightening and my dick pulsating and just knew that my own release was coming and that there was nothing that I could do to stop it. I hurried and laid on my back pulling her weak body on top of mine holding her in place. With my knees bent and my ass lifting up off of the bed I began jack hammering her pussy; my heavy nut sack slapping against her clit as I pushed my forefinger inside of her ass. Aris leaned up and sunk her teeth into my shoulder biting me to muffle her screams. I growled and pounded against her cervix a few times to get her to let go making her scream in return.

"OhmyfuckinggodRoman!" she cried out as more tears fell. "I'm about to cum again!"

"Fuck me too!" I announced as my dick began to throb. Clenching tightly onto her waist I held her still, giving her pussy several more hard thrusts before I roared and shot my load deep inside of her womb. Me emptying my babies inside of her had her body shaking and her cumming one more time. Once her orgasm subsided, she collapsed right on top of my chest panting heavy. I ain't even gonna lie; a nigga was drained, and sleep was starting to get to my ass.

I wrapped my arms around her waist and held her body against mine while softly planting a kiss on her sweaty forehead. "I love you, ma," I said to her when I finally got my breath back. When she didn't say it back, I looked down only to see her already passed the fuck out. With my semi-hard dick still deep inside of her womb, I ran my fingers through her hair and waited until my breathing started slowing down and for sleep to finally get me. It didn't take shit, but a few seconds before I found myself knocked out. Damn, I really missed this shit.

## Chapter Nineteen

**ARIS**

The next morning when I had woke up after Roman and I had first had sex I was on cloud nine, I couldn't believe it. At first, I thought it was all just a wet dream, but after waking up and seeing Rome lying naked in my bed sleeping like a big baby I just knew it went down the night before. That and how sore I was between my legs was all the conviction that I needed. That happened two weeks ago and since then a bitch has been dancing on cloud nine. I even moved my things to Rome's bedroom and just used my old one as my closet. It was like everything had suddenly gone back to the way I liked it. Since no one really has a clue as to who was behind the shootout at Secrets; everyone has been staying in the house lying low key. Rome would only leave the house if my brother needed him to do something any other time he's in the house with me, cuddling in the middle of the bed watching chick flicks. That and fucking all day long.

Ever since Rome laid that pipe in me; my hormones have been raging all over the place. Lately, all I've wanted to do is fuck him all over the house while Ebony still has Jay. I was always horny and just couldn't keep my hands off of him. You know it's bad when he has to makeup excuses as to why he couldn't perform that night. Let him tell it his dick is still sore from me riding it the night before. After being cooped up in the house for two weeks straight, Rome and I were finally going out today and planned a day full of family fun. We had plans to go pick up Jay from Ebony's house and spend most of our day at Grapeland Water Park. Just a little something to do to get out of the house. I was so excited that I woke up Rome up with some toe curling action and a five-course breakfast in bed. I made a well-seasoned steak, my famous spicy potatoes, cheesy eggs, bacon, hash brown and homemade cinnamon rolls to go with his cup of orange juice and a bowl of cut up fruit. While he was eating, I was getting ready.

Being cooped up in the house will take a toll out on you especially if you're not used to it. Just thinking about all of the fun that we were going to have today had me super excited. I felt like a little kid again. Since we were going to a water park I decided to dress in a gray tank top that crossed in the back, a pair of blue cotton shorts and white fresh out of the box Air Max with my black two-piece bikini underneath it. I was in my full-length body mirror brushing my short hair into a ponytail when Rome entered my old room with a deep frown etched on his face.

That look alone was enough to tell me that something bad had just happened and our fun day at Grapeland would have to be put on hold. "What's wrong bae?" I asked him

Rome slid his phone into his back pocket as he was making his way up towards me. Wrapping his arms around my waist, he pulled my back into his strong chest. "Nothing. I just got a text from Cairo saying that there was trouble at the spot."

Letting out an irritated breath I rolled my eyes as I finished combing out my hair and putting it into a ponytail. "Oh my God!" I sighed in heavy frustration and aggravation. Out of all times, somebody chooses right now to call when a bitch had plans. I just knew somebody was going to piss on my parade.

Rome chuckled as his grip around my waist tightened up. "Don't do that ma."

I couldn't stop my bottom lip from poking out in a childish pout. I felt like crying. "I can't help it. Here I was, looking forward to getting out the house and spending the day with you and Jay as a family and somebody just had to piss on my parade," I said with an apparent attitude.

Rome laughed as he turned me around to face him. I wrapped my arms around his neck just as he filled his hands up with both of my ass cheeks and gave it a slap. "Drop the attitude ma. I'm just going to run up to the spot to see what the fuck is going on and when I get back we can still have our family fun day."

I kissed my teeth and started rolling my eyes at that knowing damn well that wouldn't be the case. "You know that's going to take all day! By the time you get back the water park is going to be closed, Rome!"

"No, it won't. I'm just going to be gone for two hours' tops. By the time I get back we will have enough time to go pick Jay up and still have our fun at the waterpark."

I folded my arms across my chest and further poke my bottom lip out. I heard everything that Rome was saying, but I didn't want to wait in the house by myself for two more hours. I felt like these walls were about to cave in on me. Rome gently grabbed me by the chin and forced me to look up at him.

In a reassuring tone, he said to me, "I promise that I won't take long. I'm just going to go over there to see wassup, and I'm coming right back."

"You promise?" I asked in a childlike voice.

Rome chuckled. "Yea man."

I cocked my head to the side and batted my long eyelashes at him. "Pinky promise?"

Rome laughed. "Man, go on somewhere with that spoiled shit. Didn't I say yeah?"

I started laughing too. "Ok. Ok. I believe you. But before you go gimme a kiss," I said poking my lips out and leaning in for a kiss. Rome laughed and playfully mushed the side of my forehead. "Man, I'm not about to kiss you. For what? So that you could get me to let my guard down and rape me?" Rome said laughing, before playfully pushing me back like I was contaminated, making me roll my eyes.

"Would you quit playing and give me a kiss so that you could get out of here and be back in two hours like you said," I suddenly spat instantly catching another attitude.

I didn't have to repeat myself to get Rome to stop playing and kiss me like I asked. He cuffed my face with both of his hands, tilted my head back while his was tilted to the side and kissed me with so much passion that it took my breath away. Moaning softly, I positioned my hands at his waist and kissed him back matching the same passion he was giving me. We took turns wrestling with each other's tongues and biting at each other's lips. I knew that I had to stop soon because Miss Kitty started purring and I had the urge to rip his clothes off and rape his ass. Being the first to break our intense kiss, I pressed my forehead in the center of Rome's chest and tried to catch my breath.

"I love you ma," Rome said to me as he planted a soft kiss on my forehead.

"I love you too daddy."

"Yo, chill with that word or else we won't be making it nowhere today," he said with a laugh.

I giggled while forcing myself to unwrap my arms from around him. Truth be told I didn't want him to leave me yet. Yeah, I'm spoiled but don't blame that shit on me. Blame that shit on the men in my life.

"Lock up the house and don't go nowhere until I get back. We still don't know who is after us, and I can't stand the thought of anybody getting near you and harming you again."

"Don't worry. I'm not going anywhere if you're not with me."

Rome looked down at me with skepticism before finally caving in and believing me. Rome planted one more gentle kiss onto my lips before grabbing his cell phone and car keys to leave. I stood on the porch and watched him as he backed up out of the driveway and put his car into drive. Waving goodbye, I turned around and stepped back inside of the house locking the door as promised.

## Chapter Twenty

**ROME**

I was sitting parked at a red light looking down at my phone reading a text message from Ebony when all of a sudden the glass from my back windshield was shattered. I knew right then and there somebody was trying to off me in the broad daylight. Before I even had the chance to reach in between my seats for my nine to return fire, a black Expedition pulled up on the side of me, and a barrage of gunfire exploded making my car rock. I felt a few of those bullets hit me and my body jerk from left to right. After what seemed like forever the gunfire came to a cease and the truck pulled off leaving me there coughing up globs of blood. My chest was burning, and my breathing had gotten heavier. I was slowly fading in and out of consciousness. With my mind on Aris I struggled to keep my eyes open, but with every second that was passing my eyes grew even heavier. I felt the life slipping out of me. As I laid there feeling the life slip from out of me, my whole life flashed before my eyes. The last thing I saw was Aris' smiling face. "Ari…" I struggled to get out. I had just gotten the love of my life back to me and now just like that, I was slipping away. I didn't want to leave my baby. I still wanted to fill her stomach up with my seeds, make her my wife and grow gray with her. Determined to get there with her one of these days I began searching for my phone. With the little strength that I had left, I had managed to grab my phone and call Kamron. The phone rang twice before Kamron's deep voice came booming through the speaker.

"Yo, wassup. Talk to yo' boy."

I opened my mouth to say something but instead of words coming out I had blood spilling out the sides of my mouth. "Yo, Rome. What's wrong nigga? Why you sounding like that?" Kamron asked now fully alerted.

"Shot me… I'm hit…they sh…shot…me," I struggled to say. After that, everything instantly went black.

## Chapter Twenty-One

**ARIS**

I was sitting in the living room curled up on the couch patiently waiting for Rome to get back and watching reruns of Love and Hip Hop: New York when all of a sudden I had gotten a text on my phone from Kelly said that she was on her way over to my house and from FedEx about my package being left in the mailbox. Just knowing that it was my new Kindle Fire coming had me jumping out of my spot on the couch and running outside to the mailbox. I know that Roman said not to leave out of the house for anything, but I was only running to the mailbox and back. I hurried down the driveway and opened the mailbox. When I looked inside; there was nothing.

"What the fuck? Now I know I had just a text message saying that my package was here," I mumbled to myself in confusion as I bent over to inspect the empty mailbox for my mail. Now even more confused than ever, I slowly stood back up and was about to head back inside of the house when my feet froze, and fear took over me. You know how you get that feeling when somebody is watching you…

Slowly, I turned around to see an all-black Expedition with Asanti rims and tinted windows parked across the street in front of my house. I know for a fact that that car wasn't t there when I came down the driveway for my mail. My throat tightened and soon it was becoming difficult to breathe. My body violently shook as goosebumps formed on my skin. There was someone in my head screaming and begging for me to run back into the house, but for some reason, my feet were heavy like cement was weighing me down. Something had me scared and so shook that I couldn't move my feet if I wanted to. The window slowly rose down, and the person behind it had me shaking so bad that I ended up pissing on myself. There he sat sitting in the passenger seat with lifeless black eyes and a humorless smirk on his face; looking like the devil himself.

My eyes widened in shock as fear really began to set in. No! Why is he here?!

"Hey, baby. Did you miss me? I told you I was going to come back for you now didn't I?" he asked me; his voice sounding like nails to a chalkboard.

I felt my heart stop beating and pain in my chest. I was too terrified to move. Fear had my whole body paralyzed. I was just standing there looking like a silly duck just stuck as my brain tried to process which rock did he crawl out of and how in the hell did he find me. By the time my brain had registered the situation at hand, he was already climbing out of the truck with his gun in his hand. Run!

I hurried and turned around making a mad dash to the house. Just as my hand was on the doorknob to the front door, the sound of a bullet leaving its chamber froze me once more.

POP!

"Ahhh!!!" I screamed out in agony as a bullet entered the back of my calf muscle and exit out of the side. The pain sat my whole leg on fire. I was in so much pain that I couldn't stop the wet tears from rolling down my face. Hearing his heavy footsteps coming up from behind me snapped me out of the pain I was feeling. Determined to get away from him, I opened the front door and stumbled inside. I went to close the door, but his foot was stopping it.

"Moooovvve! LEAVE ME ALONE!" I screamed as I focused all of my weight on my good leg and tried to pushed the door close.

"You didn't honestly think that I was just going to let you live your happily ever after with that fuck ass nigga now did you," he said sinisterly. "Just like I told you a year ago… if I can't have you, then no one will!" he barked in an evil tone as he used his shoulder to slam my shoulder into the door. With all of my might, I withstood his brute force.

"Bitch! Open this door right fucking now!" he screamed at me.

I was determined to keep his ass on the other side of that door. If he wanted me, then he would have to fight me first. Forcing all of my strength down to my feet, I planted them firmly against the carpet floors and pushed. The pain in my leg had only intensified as warm blood flowed down it. "Yo! Antron! Come and help me grab this bitch," his loud voice thundered.

Fear and panic immediately struck me. I had to hurry and do something. I could barely hold his big ass back. Now imagine with the two of them together. Looking to the right of me, there was a glass bowl that we sat our keys inside just a few yards away from me. Spinning around, I put my back against the door to push. I desperately began to reach for it while at the same time struggling to keep the door closed. I leaned over and just as my fingers were grazing the thick glass the front door came open at the same time I was grabbing the bowl. I quickly spun around and brought the glass clean over his shit.

"Arrrgggghhhh! Fuck!" he screamed out in agony.

I took that as an opening and slammed the door shut locking the door. My chest was rising and falling heavily as I slowly backed away from the door.

"Damn nigga is you alright?" I heard another voice ask.

"Yeah. I'm straight."

"You sure? You bleeding."

"Instead of worrying about me help me get this bitch," he spat heatedly.

Shaking my head, I turned around and tried to run up the stairs as fast as I could. But that was kind of hard to do with only one leg. All of a sudden I was hit with a wave of pain that made me collapse right at the top of the stairs. I looked down, and there was blood everywhere. It was bleeding horribly and if I didn't do anything to stop the bleeding I was going to end up dying. I cursed underneath my breath while holding tightly onto my leg trying to calm the bleeding even it only helps for a little while. Forcing myself to get up I limped all the way to the bedroom that Rome and I shared and climbed underneath the bed. Don't ask me why I did such a thing but I did. At the moment that was the safest place for me to hide. As I laid there in complete fear I thought back on my life where all shit had gone wrong for me. I shook my head as the tears fell harder down my cheeks. Just when I was happy and content with my life shit like this happens. Why does shit always keep happening me? I haven't done anything wrong to no fucking body. Why is a man that I once love and gave my all to trying to kill me and bring so much turmoil in my life? Why did God let this man come into my life? Why. Why. Why?!

The sound of heavy footsteps coming down the hallway had me sucking in a sharp breath of air and my hands clamping over my mouth. I was trying to slow down the erratic beating of my heart. I was completely frozen in fear. I was feeling like I was having a heart attack. My chest was hurt, and my lungs felt raw. My fear intensified with each step they took closer towards my bedroom. I trembled as blood ran down my leg. As bad as I wanted to turn around to see if they were near me fear wouldn't let me do it. Breathing in a sharp breath, I closed my eyes desperately wishing that I was somewhere else. I closed my eyes and prayed that someone would come and save me. I laid there and prayed. Prayed like I have never prayed before. Once I was done, I opened my eyes and everything was all of a suddenly quiet. I laid still while straining my ears for any signs that they were still in my house. When I didn't hear anything, I let out a sigh of relief. Just when I thought it was safe, I felt someone grab one of my ankles and pull me from under the bed.

"Ahhhh," I screamed out right before I felt a hard blow to the back of my head knocking me out. The last thing I saw before blacking out was Quamir and some other dude that I have never seen before standing over my body with a sinister grin on their faces.

TO BE CONTINUED…